"Lon Cohen's really [...] at the *Gazette*," I said. "S[...]d. To Ian MacLaren."

Wolfe looked up and raised his eyebrows. "I sympathize with Mr. Cohen. Without doubt, he would find it difficult, probably intolerable, to work for a newspaper owned by that miscreant. Is there a place nearby that sells out-of-town and foreign papers?"

"Just a few blocks from here," I said. It still amazes me, even after all these years of living under the same roof with him, that someone whose head is crammed with so much knowledge of history, philosophy, anthropology, food, orchids, and most of the other subjects in the *Encyclopaedia Brittanica*, can be so ignorant about the city he lives in. But then, Nero Wolfe hates to leave the brownstone as much as he detests deviating from his daily schedule.

"Find out the names of newspapers owned by Ian MacLaren," he said as he finished the first bottle of beer and stared pensively at doomed number two. "I would like to see as many as are available. Also, when you talk to Mr. Cohen, invite him to join us for dinner tonight. If the notice is too short, perhaps he can come tomorrow."

AND SO BEGINS A NEW MYSTERY FOR REX
STOUT'S NERO WOLFE AND ARCHIE
GOODWIN, WRITTEN WITH ACCLAIMED
AUTHENTICITY BY NERO WOLFE EXPERT
ROBERT GOLDSBOROUGH

Bantam Books offers the finest in classic and modern American murder mysteries.
Ask your bookseller for the books you have missed.

Stuart Palmer
Murder on the Blackboard

Rex Stout
Broken Vase
Death of a Dude
Death Times Three
Fer-de-Lance
The Final Deduction
Gambit
The Rubber Band
Too Many Cooks
The Black Mountain

Max Allan Collins
The Dark City

William Kienzle
The Rosary Murders

Joseph Louis
Madelaine
The Trouble With Stephanie

M. J. Adamson
Not Till a Hot February
A February Face
Remember March
April When They Woo

Conrad Haynes
Bishop's Gambit, Declined
Perpetual Check

Barbara Paul
First Gravedigger
But He Was Already Dead When
  I Got There

P. M. Carlson
Murder Unrenovated
Rehearsal for Murder

Ross Macdonald
The Goodbye Look
Sleeping Beauty
The Name Is Archer
The Drowning Pool
The Underground Man
The Zebra-Striped Hearse

Margaret Maron
The Right Jack
Baby Doll Games
Coming Soon: One Coffee With

William Murray
When the Fat Man Sings

Robert Goldsborough
Murder in E Minor
Death on Deadline
The Bloodied Ivy

Sue Grafton
"A" Is for Alibi
"B" Is for Burglar
"C" Is for Corpse
"D" Is for Deadbeat

R. D. Brown
Hazzard
Villa Head

Joseph Telushkin
The Unorthodox Murder of
  Rabbi Wahl
The Final Analysis of Doctor Stark

Richard Hilary
Snake in the Grasses
Pieces of Cream
Pillow of the Community

Carolyn G. Hart
Design for Murder
Death on Demand
Something Wicked

Lia Matera
Where Lawyers Fear to Tread
A Radical Departure
The Smart Money

Robert Crais
The Monkey's Raincoat

Keith Peterson
The Trapdoor
Coming Soon: There Fell a Shadow

Jim Stinson
Double Exposure

Carolyn Wheat
Where Nobody Dies

A NERO WOLFE MYSTERY

DEATH
ON DEADLINE

Robert Goldsborough

BANTAM BOOKS
TORONTO · NEW YORK · LONDON · SYDNEY · AUCKLAND

The author wishes to thank the estate of the late Rex Stout for its cooperation and encouragement.

DEATH ON DEADLINE
A Bantam Book
Bantam hardcover edition / May 1987
Bantam paperback edition / August 1988

Library of Congress Cataloging-in-Publication Data

Goldsborough, Robert.
   Death on deadline.

   I. Title.
PS3557.03849D4 1987   813'.54   86-47885
ISBN 0-553-27024-9

Published simultaneously in the United States and Canada

*Bantam Books are published by Bantam Books, a division of Bantam
Doubleday Dell Publishing Group, Inc. Its trademark, consisting of the
words "Bantam Books" and the portrayal of a rooster, is registered in U.S.
Patent and Trademark Office and in other countries. Marca Registrada.
Bantam Books, 666 Fifth Avenue, New York, New York 10103.*

PRINTED IN THE UNITED STATES OF AMERICA

O   0 9 8 7 6 5 4 3 2 1

*To Janet, without whom
I am incomplete*

In Rex Stout's *The Father Hunt* (1968) Archie Goodwin reflected, "Before long the day will come, maybe in a year or two, possibly as many as five, when I won't be able to write any more of these reports for publication." That valedictory note did not occur in the saga again till the final volume in the series, *A Family Affair* (1975), when Inspector Cramer, surveying Nero Wolfe's office, observed, "This is the best working room I know. The best-looking. I mention it now because I may never see it again." Perhaps Cramer merely was referring to his threat to have Wolfe's license revoked, but Rex Stout was then eighty-eight, so there was ample cause to assign to Cramer's words an ominous meaning.

Though certainly neither of the foregoing passages suggests that Rex Stout expected the Nero Wolfe series to be extended into the future by another hand once he himself had ceased to write, he did not see the series as concluded when he completed *A Family Affair*. In August 1975 he told me that, if he felt equal to it, he would begin a new Wolfe novel "along about November." That was not to be. Death came suddenly on October 27, 1975. Had Rex lived another five weeks, he would have entered his ninetieth year. Even so, as he saw it, he had not rung down the curtain on the household at West Thirty-fifth Street. More adventures awaited Wolfe and Archie. That did not surprise me. In 1974, when *Triple Zeck* was published, I asked Rex if he had ever considered letting Wolfe perish in his final struggle with Arnold Zeck, even as Sherlock Holmes was portrayed as perishing in his final struggle with Professor Moriarty. "What then, for next year?" he snorted. "Open the tomb and drag him out?" Could he, I persisted, end the series as the Baroness Orczy had her *Old Man in the Corner* series, by letting Wolfe himself commit murder? "I would think it was silly," he said.

Early in our acquaintance, plagued by ill health, Rex put aside unfinished the manuscript of *Death of a Dude*. I tried to jolly him into better spirits by telling him I was writing a Nero Wolfe novel myself. "Let me see a chapter," he said. So I sat down and sweated out a dozen pages which found Archie at Harvard investigating the death of the president of Swaziland, fatally stricken when, at a midday luncheon for honorary degree recipients, someone nudged a poisoned melon ball into his fruitcup. Rex commended my effort, as politeness demanded, but, much to my relief, did not commission me to complete the novel he had left undone. "How would you feel," I asked him later, when, restored to health, he was writing again, "if someone wanted to continue the Wolfe series after you . . . eh, laid aside your pen?" "I don't know whether vampirism or cannibalism is the better term for it," he answered. "Not nice. They should roll their own." "Do you have any plans for rounding out the series yourself?" I asked. "For . . . killing off Wolfe, as Christie does with Poirot?" "Certainly not," he said, with palpable indignation. "I hope he lives forever."

Only on a single other occasion did the question of a series continuator come up between us and that was in another connection. I told him of a letter I had received from a suspect reader who insisted that Rex Stout had a resourceful secretary who now wrote all his books for him. "The name is Jane Austen," he replied, "but I haven't the address." Rex was paying himself the ultimate compliment. Of Austen he had told me earlier, "Jane Austen had an incredible, instinctive awareness of how to use words, which words to use, how to organize them, how to organize her material, how many pages, how much weight to give to this incident and to that one. She was astonishing. No finer novelist than she has ever lived." He said he once dreamed that Jane Austen had come back to life and started writing detective stories. He awoke, he said, in a state of panic. Jane Austen his continuator, indeed. Some bill to fill!

As a matter of record, Rex never accepted story ideas from anyone, though readers often submitted them. New York City's celebrated Parks Commissioner, Robert Moses, once sent him, for his consideration, an entire chapter of a Nero Wolfe novel he had projected. "It was awful," Rex said. In fact, he found none of the material sent him usable. He even refused to listen to the Nero Wolfe radio dramas, based on his characters but scripted by others. "Unbearable," he told me. On one occasion, when he outlined a plot to his friend Alan Green, Green said to him, "Why, Rex, that's the plot of Christopher Bush's *The Perfect Murder*." "Indeed?" Rex said, and never spoke of it again. He was unwilling to accept story ideas even from his editors, who, encountering just once Neronian wrath, never dared to offer them again.

From the early days of the genre, readers have been reluctant to accept an author's decision to terminate a detective series or nature's decision to terminate it for him by terminating him. Reader demand forced Arthur Conan Doyle to resurrect Holmes. In 1928, while Doyle still lived, August Derleth, dismayed at Doyle's diminishing output, inaugurated his own series, Solar Pons being, as Robert Briney noted, "an ectoplasmic emanation of his great prototype," and the seventy stories in which he eventually appeared, "a pastiche . . . of the Holmesian canon as a whole." Later, in collaboration, Adrian Conan Doyle, Doyle's youngest son, and John Dickson Carr sought to add to the canon. Even the collaborators themselves were displeased with the results and abandoned further efforts to keep Holmes on the active list. As for the avalanche of Holmesian pastiches that has followed, with the exception of Rick Boyer's *Giant Rat of Sumatra*, the results have been so flawed that many readers can sympathize with Nicolas Freeling, who effectively closed out his Inspector Van der Valk series by shooting Van der Valk through the heart. In the 1940s Gerald Fairlie continued H. C. McNeile's Bulldog Drummond series, but, since the original stories themselves were never more than thrillers, this was a feat of no great consequence. Following the death of Margery Allingham, her husband, Youngman Carter, completed her last novel, *Cargo of Eagles*. H.R.F. Keating calls it her most forgettable story.

"There should be," says Jacques Barzun, "a collection of watchdogs—watchwolves—to keep guard over the fair fame and right significance of Nero and Archie." Surely he spoke for legions when he protested a TV series which portrayed Wolfe "looking and talking like a stingy landlord, Archie like an ivy-league junior executive," and Cramer making "willowy movements with his torso." Yet, there are those fierce guardians of the sacred scroll who would look with contempt on a Nero Wolfe continuation even if an affidavit from the Archangel Gabriel vouched for its authenticity. Does Lily Rowan really have "deep blue eyes"? Is it his left eyebrow that Archie raises? Count the steps of the brownstone again. Did Rex say seven? And, what's this? Lionel T. Cramer! Fergus, once. A slip. Never Lionel! How dare he! There's nothing to be done with liturgical nuts, of course. They are beyond pleasing. Even when a bona fide Stout manuscript turns up (as indeed one did), they are torn apart, wondering whether to admit it to the corpus.

Rex Stout hoped that Nero Wolfe would "live forever." Did he provide for that possibility? Yes, he did. First, he created, in the brownstone, routines which are immune to time. Second, unlike Doyle, who confined Holmes's activities to the gaslight era and wrote about the era with increasing vagueness as the gap separating him from that era widened, Rex's tales always were contemporaneous with his actual life while writing them. Finally, unlike Christie, whose aging Poirot solved his last case from a wheelchair (by then he was a centenarian!), he decreed, with canny foresight, that Wolfe should ever be fifty-six and Archie thirty-four. Such arable soil invites another planting.

Now we must ask, since it can be done, should it be done? The decade of mourning that followed Stout's death is concluded. The demands of decency have been met. No continuator need feel reproach for curtailing the period of bereavement. To add to the corpus cannot diminish respect for the seventy-three tales Rex Stout wrote. Indeed, since a misbegotten television series actually rallied thousands of new readers to the corpus, why should we suppose the work of an able continuator would not bring about the same desideratum? Let us bear in mind, too, that several commentators, Julian Symons among them, now either speak of Wolfe in the past tense or suggest that the brownstone has been bulldozed and that Wolfe, in retirement, is living in Cairo, Egypt, raising guppies. For readers who are certain that life in the brownstone continues much as usual, this is intolerable. Reassurances from a continuator that Wolfe and Archie remain at West Thirty-fifth Street come as a great consolation to all loyalists.

That it can be done, and that there are adequate reasons for doing it, does not mean that it need not be done with a prudence that, at all times, respects the integrity of the corpus as it has come down to us from Rex Stout. Since 1975 I have been asked to appraise the manuscripts of a score of would-be continuators. More often than not, they were sincere admirers of the corpus. More often than not, though all unwittingly, they had, by their efforts, made a farce of what Rex had achieved. There were manuscripts purporting to have been written by Fritz, Lily, Saul, and even Theodore Horstmann. There was the suggestion that Archie move a live-in girlfriend into the brownstone, to spice things up. And can you conceive of a Nero Wolfe hurtling along a Bermuda road on a motorbike? Wind surfing at Cancún? Hotdogging at Aspen? Or eating Chicken McNuggets at McDonald's? Now here we have, out in the open, one of the major difficulties a continuator must face. Archie and Wolfe must always comport themselves in ways consistent with the expectations Rex Stout raised. That does not mean they cannot surprise us on occasion. Didn't Wolfe once tend bar at a Christmas party, got up as Santa Claus? Didn't he climb mountains in Montenegro? Visit a dude ranch in Montana? Didn't he once shed half his body weight to infiltrate the organization of a master criminal? Didn't he even take up darts for exercise? No, the continuator must not see himself as tightly shackled to the preexistent world of Nero Wolfe. He must, however, with exquisite discretion, contrive exceptions that never give offense. How easy it is to say that. How difficult to carry it off.

Bob Goldsborough, the designated continuator of the Nero Wolfe saga, emerges as winner from a pack of aspirants not because he has had crass ambitions to hitch his wagon to the Stoutian star. He came into the picture with the wholesomest of motives, and it well may be this wholesomeness that has enabled him to succeed where others failed. A midwesterner, even as Stout and Archie had been midwesterners (a factor by no means to be discounted—picture an Archie with a Southern drawl or the clipped accents of a native New Yorker), Goldsborough was introduced to Wolfe and Archie by his mother, when he was a teenager. In 1977, stricken by what was to prove her final illness, Mrs. Goldsborough one day told Bob she wished she had another Nero Wolfe novel to read. Since she had read them all, Bob, at that time an editor of the *Chicago Tribune*, did what any dutiful, gifted son (who had a mother who loved Wolfe and Archie) would do. He sat down and wrote *Murder in E Minor*. With this splendid motivation, he made his story as authentic as possible—no buffoonery, no flippancies, no absurd departures, but a story as close to the spirit of the originals as he could contrive. Maybe he did not have, as Ian Fleming said Rex had, "one of the most civilized minds ever to turn to detective fiction." Maybe he didn't have, as Rex did, an IQ of 185. Maybe he was not a collateral descendant of Benjamin Franklin and Daniel Defoe, as was Rex. Maybe he could not say, as Rex could, that Archie was his spontaneous self and Wolfe his achieved self (though he was not lacking Neronian astuteness and Goodwinian panache), but love covers a multitude of shortcomings (if shortcomings these be), and the end result was a novel that not only pleased his mother but everyone else who read it (including Rex's daughters), save the most surly of watchwolves.

To the mere reader, the task Bob Goldsborough faced—meeting scrupulously the demands Rex Stout's meticulous formulation of Nero Wolfe's world imposes—perhaps seems no great challenge. After all, with Wolfe's routines and habits so clearly indicated, wouldn't it be like traveling on a well-marked-out highway? Yes, as simple as writing a perfect Petrarchean sonnet, painstakingly adhering to the guidelines that govern that verse form. Simple? Try it sometime. Yet, Rex did it over and over again, never repeating himself, always carrying it off successfully. Infinite variations always attentive to the established framework of life within the brownstone. Now that is genius.

A Wolfe continuation that was only a patchwork of preexistent moments in the saga would be tiresome. Still, as in all the stories, enough familiar touches must be given to assure us that this Nero and this Archie are the real thing, not changelings. Fortunately, in forty years' time (*Fer-de-Lance,* the first Nero Wolfe mystery, was published in 1934), Nero Wolfe was able to pile on a lot of habits and idiosyncrasies, so Goldsborough could partake freely of them in *Murder in E Minor* and its sequel, *Death on Deadline,* without the risk of repeating himself or taxing the patience of his readers.

Proper notice is given to Wolfe's telltale nonverbal gestures—he nods the proper one-eighth of an inch to acknowledge a visitor; he raises his shoulder a quarter of an inch and lets it drop to register a significant reaction; he sucks in a bushel of air; he buries his face in a book; he glowers or scowls (*Death on Deadline* is a major scowling case); he traces circles on the arm of his chair with his right index finger; the folds of his cheeks occasionally betray a covert smile; and, when the essential moment arises, he engages in his ratiocinative lip drill. Not surprisingly, Wolfe is an astute judge of, as well as practitioner of, body language. In *Death on Deadline* he tells Archie: "All those things you refer to as body language . . . are integral to the interrogation process.

Remove the opportunity to witness those reactions and you become a sailor without compass, stars, or sextant."

Goldsborough does not ignore the Neronian verbal resources—the splendid rolling Johnsonian periodic phrases, the old familiar words, *witling, flummox, flummery*, and a new one, *bavardage*. Neronian epigrams, e.g. "Intuition is the partner of introspection," and his splendid put-downs, e.g. "Archie . . . outrage is among your more churlish emotions," assure us that Wolfe has lost none of his edge. And there is his scorn for those similes so dear to the *Black Mask* school. As narrator, Archie shoulders his burden fully—droll, witty, caustic when occasion requires it, amiably self-deprecating, simultaneously scornful (once again Wolfe has to be goaded when stalemated), and admiring in his relations with Wolfe, and ready, at appropriate moments, with apt remarks that show off his knowledge of baseball and poker. On at least one occasion he trades off a Mets game with Lily as a reward for sitting through an evening of culture.

The plant room schedule is adhered to, and the meal schedule. The meals are gourmet feasts. On one occasion Archie taxis home so as not to be denied oyster pie; on another, when he must be elsewhere at lunch time, he has Fritz reserve his portion of sweetbreads. Delectable new dishes are concocted, though why Archie, dining with Lily at Rusterman's, settles for something as pedestrian as veal marsala is hard to fathom. Despite events of huge urgency, as usual business is not discussed at lunch time. In *Murder in E Minor*, Wolfe's fee from one client is a year's supply of his favorite beer. The gold bookmark is periodically seen. And, mystery of mysteries, clients and visitors, as usual, always find a place to park in front of the brownstone. All the regulars are in place—Lily, Fritz, Theodore, Saul, Fred, Cramer, Stebbins, Rowcliff, and even Geoffrey Hitchcock. In *Death on Deadline* Bill Gore is briefly acknowledged, though Rex dropped him because "apparently he bored me." Goldsborough drops him, too. For the same reason, one supposes. But we may need him, now that Orrie is gone.

In addition to the necessary touches, there are some pleasantly surprising ones, quite acceptable though post–Stoutian. On one occasion Wolfe, with evident approval, quotes Dorothy Sayers. He watches *The History of the Jewish People* on Public Television. He reads some excellent new books, Zdzislaw Najder's *Joseph Conrad: A Chronicle* and J. Bernard Cohen's *Revolution in Science*, but shudders at a mention of *People* magazine. He shudders also when he hears that an evangelical minister wants to add the *Gazette* to his Christian network. At one point he flabbergasts us when he declares: "The monumental misadventures of my life, and I'm chagrined to say there have been a number, all have centered on women." For amplification we must await further books in the series. Similarly we are left to wonder whether Wolfe ruminates on cases when he is in the plant rooms. He says he doesn't. Archie thinks otherwise. We do learn, at a mealtime conversation, that he thinks Tocqueville's *Democracy in America* the greatest book ever written on America by a foreigner, and that he favors abolishing the constitutional amendment limiting the President to two terms, thus, by merest chance, taking sides with Ronald Reagan, surely something that does not happen too often.

In *Death on Deadline* Saul Panzer is given plenty to do and performs up to standard. Lon Cohen also has a strong role, as well he might, since the *Gazette* itself provides the story line, a powerful plot that surely would have appealed to Rex Stout. Goldsborough's use of a rare Archie Goodwin "Foreword" to underscore the esteem in which Wolfe holds both Cohen and the *Gazette* is well justified. As a professional journalist, Goldsborough knows how to handle this material for maximum impact. Certainly, in using it he has played an ace. If readers don't take to the resumed saga after reading *Death on Deadline*, the fault is not his. It couldn't be done better. BG, we might say, follows AG as naturally as the night the day, and he gives us a night resplendent with shooting stars.

Timidity never has been a hallmark of the Nero Wolfe novels. Each, in its own way, broke new ground.

Even as he entertained us, Rex Stout attacked a wide spectrum of social evils. And so it is here, Wolfe's target being a celebrated czar of the tabloids. Goldsborough spices this challenge with several characteristic Stoutian surprises. Cramer, in an episode reminiscent of the milk carton scene in *The Doorbell Rang*, visits the plant room to deliver to Wolfe a vital bit of information. Wolfe is nonplussed when the newspaper overlord tries to buy him off with an offer to put him on the payroll as a columnist syndicated worldwide. Wolfe places a sensational, full-page advertisement in *The New York Times* and threatens to submit a second one. Fritz gets to announce one of the major developments in the case. Archie is observed wearing a digital watch!

A few things in *Death on Deadline* might have been handled differently. For example, in both Goldsborough novels an attractive ex-wife shows up midway through the book. Should it happen in the next book, I for one shall want an explanation for this hangup. Goldsborough's villain, Ian MacLaren, is namesake of the amiable author of the inoffensive *Beside the Bonnie Briar Bush*. Was this intentional irony or did Goldsborough simply forget? Rex Stout loathed the word *grimace*, used three times here. But how was Bob Goldsborough to know that? I know it only because Rex once chided me for using it. On one occasion Archie said he had never seen Cramer light a cigar. He did see him light one, in *The Rubber Band*. In the opening stages of his interview with Harriet Haverhill, the *Gazette's* principal stockholder, Wolfe seems a touch too deferential. But then, Harriet is a true Southern lady, so probably she merits this unusual notice. There's a scene, too, in which Archie, in the line of duty, gets roughed up. Wolfe could have shown more solicitude on that occasion than he does. I see nothing else to complain about.

One can fondle the same phrases and mannerisms just so many times. Bob Goldsborough realizes that. He confronts honestly and openly the limitations and protocols which Rex Stout set for Nero Wolfe's world, yet he sees to it that Wolfe and Archie achieve freedom and self-expression within those limitations. We hope that he will continue to be circumspectly innovative. The knowl-edge he shows of Rex Stout's intentions and methods would, in an earlier era, have caused him to be burned as a warlock. Yet we are confident that he will continue to enlighten us. Surely we want to know what Wolfe thinks of Maggie Thatcher, Bishop Tutu, and the Liberty Weekend. And maybe Archie's opinion of Roger Clemens. As it is, his handling of his commitment thus far revives an interest in metempsychosis which I haven't acknowledged since I left India forty years ago. As curator of Rex Stout's papers I thought I had been through them thoroughly. If it weren't for references that clearly relate to the present day, I would suspect that *Death on Deadline* was an overlooked Stout manu-script. Goldsborough is about the age now that Rex Stout was when he created Wolfe and Archie. Rex wrote about them for the next forty years. I wish Bob the same period of tenure. I have only one reservation. What if Bob is recruited into the evangelical movement? Or joins the Hare Krishnas? Or accepts an offer from Rupert Murdoch to do a daily column syndicated worldwide? Would he try to enlist Wolfe and Archie to serve these new masters? I'm not really worried. Neither Wolfe nor Archie lends himself to easy manipulation. They would tell Bob where to get off.

John J. McAleer
Mount Independence
7 August 1986

Nero Wolfe doesn't have a lot of friends—by choice. But he's plenty loyal to the ones he has. And one of those friends is not an individual but an institution—the New York *Gazette*, which, usually in the person of Lon Cohen, has helped us a lot through the years, as you may know. Not that the relationship has been one-sided, mind you: Wolfe has done more than a few favors for the paper, too. But the point is, he cares deeply about the *Gazette* and its well-being. This may help to explain why he was willing to take the following case without either a client or a fee (although he eventually got both). I mention this because I don't want to make him seem more eccentric than he is.

—ARCHIE GOODWIN

I've done my share of grousing over the years about Nero Wolfe's obsession with routine: his insistence on lunch promptly at one-fifteen and dinner at seven-fifteen, not to mention the sacred hours of nine to eleven in the mornings and four to six in the afternoons in the plant rooms up on the roof playing with his orchids. Almost nothing will get him to vary that schedule, although one day a few years back, when I was needling him about it, he put down his book, glowered at me, and sucked in a bushel of air, letting it out slowly.

"All right, Archie," he said. "Today is Thursday; I will show my flexibility by forgoing my appointment in the plant rooms if in turn you will call Saul and inform him you are unable to play poker tonight."

He had me, of course, and I backed off. For more years than I'm going to admit to here, I have played in a poker game every Thursday night at Saul Panzer's apartment on East Thirty-eighth near Lexington with Saul, Lon Cohen, Fred Durkin, and one or two others— the cast varies. I think I've missed once in the last five years, and that was because of a virus that knocked me so low that Lily Rowan, so she said later, was going to send over a priest to administer last rites.

Saul Panzer, in case you're new to these precincts, is a free-lance operative Wolfe uses frequently, but just saying that doesn't do him justice. Saul isn't much to look at, what with the stooped shoulders and the permanently wrinkled suits and the usually unshaven face that's about two-thirds nose. But don't be fooled by that or by his size, which makes him look like an aging and only slightly overweight jockey. When you buy Saul Panzer's time—and he doesn't come cheap—you're buying the best eyes and legs in Manhattan and probably in the country. He could tail a cheetah from the Battery to the Bronx during the evening rush hour without losing sight of it, or he could worm his way into the vault at that bank down in Atlanta and get back out again with the secret formula for Coca-Cola. And I mean the old—make that *classic*—formula.

You're probably wondering why I'm going on about Saul and his Thursday-night poker game. I could say it's because this is one of the best parts of my week, which is true, although the real reason is that this story had its beginnings there. But I'm getting ahead of myself.

It was a Thursday in early May, one of New York's first bona fide spring days. Five of us sat around the big table in Saul's dining room. On my left was Lon Cohen, who has an office next door to the publisher of the *Gazette* and doesn't have a title I'm aware of, but who knows more about what makes New York tick than the city council and the police department combined. Next to him was Fred Durkin, thick and balding and a little slow, but A-one when it comes to toughness and loyalty, another free-lance operative Wolfe has used regularly through the years. On Fred's left was Saul, and between Saul and me was Bill Gore, yet another free-lance we use on occasions.

The game had been going for about an hour and a half. As usual, Saul had the biggest stack of chips, and I was up a little, with Fred and Bill more or less even. Lon, consistently the best player after Saul, hadn't won a hand, and it was easy to see why. He'd folded at least three times with what I'm sure were the winning cards, and once he stayed in the game with a pair of jacks against Fred's obvious straight. He was off his game and playing badly, and when we cashed in a little after midnight he was the only loser. "Tough night, Lon," Fred said as he slipped his profits into his wallet and left humming. For him, it was probably the first winning night in months.

Because Nero Wolfe's brownstone on West Thirty-fifth over near the Hudson is more or less on the way home for Lon, we usually share a taxi after poker. "Not your night," I told him, after we'd flagged a taxi on Lexington. "Seemed like you were a million miles away."

"Oh, hell," Lon said, leaning back against the seat and rubbing his palms over his eyes. "I've had a lot on my mind the last few days. I guess it shows."

"Care to talk about it?"

Lon sighed and passed a hand over his dark, slicked-back hair. "Archie, things are up for grabs at the *Gazette*. Nothing has gotten out about this yet, so what I'm telling you is confidential." He lowered his voice to almost a whisper, even though a plastic panel separated us from the cabbie. "It looks like Ian MacLaren may get control of the paper."

"The Scotsman?"

"The same, damn his sleazy, scandal-mongering hide."

"But how? I thought the *Gazette* was family-owned."

"It is, basically. Various Haverhills control most of the stock. But the way this bastard from Edinburgh is throwing dollars around, some of them are getting ready to take the money and run. The weasel's always wanted a New York paper, and now he's just about got himself one."

"How can he be so close to a deal without any publicity? There hasn't been a thing in the papers or on TV, unless I missed it."

Lon was so upset he ignored a very flashy hooker who yelled to us when we stopped for a light on Fifth. "Everybody on both sides seems to be keeping quiet, really quiet. And that even includes the ones who don't want to sell. MacLaren apparently does most of his wheeling and dealing long-distance, from London or Scotland or Canada or wherever he happens to be at the time. I don't think he's even set foot in the *Gazette* building yet. But the day he comes in as owner is the day I walk out, Archie. For good."

"You've got to be kidding. That paper's your whole life."

"Nothing's ever your whole life, Archie," he said,

leaning forward as the cab pulled up in front of the brownstone. "If I was lucky to end up in heaven and MacLaren bought it, I'd request an immediate transfer downstairs. If he gets hold of the *Gazette*, it won't be the same place it is now, nowhere near. And it sure won't be a place where I'd want to work. I almost feel like I'm done there already, and so do some others who know what's going on. What the hell, my profit-sharing and pension will take care of my wife and me just fine for the rest of our lives."

Since I couldn't come up with anything intelligent to say to that, I just left it at good night, handed Lon my share of the meter, and climbed out. As the cab pulled away, I saw him leaning back again, eyes closed and hands laced behind his head.

The next morning, I was at my desk in the office typing a letter from Wolfe to a Phalaenopsis grower in Illinois when he came down from the plant rooms at eleven. "Good morning, Archie," he said, going around behind his desk and lowering himself into the only chair in New York constructed to properly support his seventh of a ton. "How did the poker game go last night?" It was his standard Friday-morning question.

"Not bad," I said, swiveling to face him. "I came out a few bills on the sunny side. It was a grim night for Lon, though. He's really knocked out by what's going on at the *Gazette*."

"Oh?" Wolfe said, without looking up as he riffled through the mail, which as usual I had stacked neatly on his blotter.

"Yeah. Seems the paper is about to be sold. To Ian MacLaren."

Wolfe looked up and raised his eyebrows. Now he was interested. "I've seen no report of this in the *Gazette* or anywhere else."

"I said the same thing when Lon told me about it last night. He says negotiations have been kept hush-hush by both sides."

Wolfe scowled. "I sympathize with Mr. Cohen. Without doubt, he would find it difficult, probably intolerable, to work for a newspaper owned by that miscreant."

"That's about what he said last night. I told him I couldn't believe he'd walk away after all these years, but he seems pretty well resolved to do just that."

"Archie, what do you know about Ian MacLaren?"

Wolfe's expression surprised me. It's the one he usually puts on when he's about to take a case—call it a pout of resignation, accompanied by a sigh that would register on the Richter Scale. But of course we didn't have a case, let alone a client.

"Not a lot," I answered. "He's Scotch. Has newspapers in a bunch of cities around the world. London's one, although don't ask me where else. And I think maybe he's in two or three U.S. towns, too. Lon calls him a sleazy scandalmonger."

"He puts it well," Wolfe said, ringing for beer. "Mr. MacLaren is an opportunist who indulges in sensationalist and irresponsible journalism and runs his papers solely for profit."

Wolfe paused as Fritz Brenner, whom you'll hear more about later, walked in carrying a tray with two chilled bottles of beer and a glass. This occurrence, which takes place up to six times a day, is as much a part of Wolfe's routine as the plant room visits. After Fritz left, Wolfe opened one beer, poured, and flipped the bottle cap into his center desk drawer. About once a week he takes them out and counts them to see if he's gone over his limit, although I've never figured out what that limit is.

"Ever seen any of MacLaren's papers?" I asked.

"No, I only know him by reputation and by what I have read," Wolfe said, dabbing his lips with a handkerchief. "But the point you're trying to make is well taken. Is there a place nearby that sells out-of-town and foreign papers?"

"Just a few blocks from here," I said. It still amazes me, even after all the years of living under the same roof with him, that someone whose head is crammed with so much knowledge of history, philosophy, anthropology, food, orchids, and most of the other subjects in the *Encyclopædia Britannica,* can be so ignorant about the city he lives in. But then, Nero Wolfe hates to leave the brownstone as much as he detests deviating from his daily schedule. For him, getting into a car, even with me at the wheel, is an act of downright recklessness. And when on rare occasions he is forced to venture forth into

deepest Manhattan or beyond, he balances his fundament on the edge of the back seat of the Heron sedan he
owns and grips the strap as if it were a parachute.

This is not to suggest that he was planning to go out
now. No, I was to be the intrepid adventurer. "Find out
from Mr. Cohen the names of newspapers owned by Ian
MacLaren," he said as he finished the first bottle of beer
and stared pensively at doomed number two. "I would
like to see as many as are available."

"Quite a change of pace in your reading habits," I
said.

Wolfe grunted. "Maybe I'll be pleasantly surprised,
although I doubt it. Also, when you talk to Mr. Cohen,
invite him to join us for dinner tonight. If the notice is
too short, perhaps he can come tomorrow. Or early next
week."

When Wolfe invites Lon Cohen to dinner, it's usually
because he wants information. Lon knows this, of
course, but doesn't mind because through the years he's
gotten as good from us as he's given in the form of
scoops involving Wolfe's cases. Also, Lon fully ap-
preciates Fritz Brenner's genius as a chef, not to mention
the Remisier brandy that gets hauled out whenever he
sits at our table.

But why Wolfe wanted to see him puzzled me. This
time we weren't working on anything big, unless you
count the business with Gershmann—not his real
name—a wholesale diamond merchant who had an
exceedingly sticky-fingered employee. But Wolfe, with
some not-so-incidental help from Saul and me, had
already pieced that one together and had delegated me
to meet with Gershmann the next day to tell him who on
his payroll had deep pockets.

So why was Lon getting an invite? I figured it must
have something to do with MacLaren, since Wolfe
wanted to look at some of the bozo's newspapers. But I
was damned if I was going to ask him. Besides, he was
now hiding behind a book, *The Good War* by Studs
Terkel, so I swung back to my typewriter and the letter
to the Illinois orchid grower.

After finishing it, I dialed Lon's number. "Feeling any better this morning?" I asked when he answered.

"So-so. I'm just trying to get through one day at a time," he replied. His voice lacked his usual *joie de vivre.*

"Glad you're so peppy. Anyway, I have two items of business. First, Mr. Wolfe wants to know if you can make it for dinner tonight—or if not, tomorrow."

"Best offer I've had in weeks," Lon said, perking up. "Tonight would be fine. What's the occasion?"

"Beats me. But don't look cross-eyed at a gift horse. Before I ask you the second question, I have to confess that I told the man who signs my paychecks about a certain Scottish party and his interest in the *Gazette.* I felt he could be trusted." I watched Wolfe for a reaction. There was no movement from behind the book.

"No big thing," Lon said sourly. "The whole town will know all about this soon enough. The other question?"

"Can you give me a list of newspapers MacLaren owns—both U.S. and foreign? Mr. Wolfe wishes to peruse a few."

"I'll be damned," Lon clucked. "I don't know why he'd waste his time, but that's his problem—or maybe it's yours. Anyway, sure, I can name a bunch of the rags for you. Just make sure he takes something for his digestion first."

Lon ticked off the titles of papers in England, Scotland, Canada, Australia, and New Zealand, plus one each in Detroit, Denver, and L.A. I thanked him and said we looked forward to seeing him.

"Okay, I've got the list of MacLaren's papers," I said to the cover of the book that was between me and Wolfe. "I'm off on a safari to hunt them down. Lon says you should be prepared for a grim experience. Are you up to it?"

I got no answer, nor did I expect one, so I went to the kitchen, where Fritz was preparing salmon mousse and a mushroom-and-celery omelet for lunch. I told him I'd be back in plenty of time to eat, then walked east to Seventh Avenue in the late-morning sunshine and headed north to Forty-second Street just east of Times Square, where the newsstand is. They had copies of two of MacLaren's American dailies, the Los Angeles *Globe-American* and the Detroit *Star*, and they also carried his London *Herald* and Toronto *Banner*. The guy behind the counter said he could special-order the others, but I figured what I had would give Wolfe all he could stomach.

Except for Toronto, they were tabloids, and their front pages made the *Daily News* and even the *Post* look tame. I won't bore you with details, but here are a few samples: The headline on the L.A. paper, which swallowed most of the front sheet, was "KILLER RAPIST SPOTTED IN LONG BEACH, COPS SAY." The only other thing on the page was a diagonal red stripe in the upper-right-hand corner with the words "WINNING SWEEPSTAKES NUMBERS—P.5!" The Detroit front page screeched in two-inch capitals: "DO SOVIETS PLAN SECRET AFGHAN NUKE ATTACK?" and under the headline was a photograph of an incredibly buxom blonde in a sweater with a caption revealing that she had courageously run out on the field during a game at Tiger Stadium to kiss the first baseman. And the headline on the London paper, which blanketed page one, read "LET'S TOSS MAGGIE OUT, 10 LABOR MP'S SHOUT!"

It was a little before one when I got home. Wolfe was still parked at his desk, with the book in front of his face. He probably hadn't moved since I'd left, except to ring for beer.

"Home is the hunter," I announced, dropping five pounds of newsprint on his blotter in a stack, with Detroit on top, figuring the overendowed blonde would be a nice way to introduce him to MacLaren-style journalism.

He set his book down and glowered at the papers without touching them. "After lunch," he said, and I had to agree. Anyone with a proper appreciation for food knows enough to avoid unpleasantness just before a meal.

THREE

There is a rule in the brownstone that business is not to be discussed during meals. I was interested that day, as we consumed the salmon mousse and then the omelet, as to whether Wolfe would consider Ian Mac-Laren some form of business or simply a topic of curiosity. Twice I brought up his name, and each time I got the answer clearly—MacLaren fell into the business category; Wolfe refused to talk about him, preferring instead to hold forth on contemporary architecture, in particular the trend away from the "less-is-more" school, in favor of more ornamentation on buildings. He clearly favored the latter.

After we made the omelet disappear and went to the office for coffee, Wolfe started in on the stack on his blotter. I watched his face as he paged each of the four; it was a series of grimaces, pursed lips, slight shakes of the head, and in one case, an outright shudder. "More wretched than I had imagined," he pronounced, ringing for beer. When Fritz came in with the tray, Wolfe thrust the papers at him. "Take these and destroy them immediately," he barked.

"I wish you wouldn't hold things in," I said. "Say what you feel."

"Pfui. I assume you looked at them?"

"Yeah, I skimmed a couple as I walked back from the newsstand. Pretty grim."

"'Grim' hardly covers it. They are abysmal caricatures of journalism. The depth of news coverage is farcical, the editorials simplistic and Neanderthal, the graphics grotesque." He thumped the blotter with his finger, an unusual show of energy.

"At a quick glance, I thought the L.A. paper's sports section was pretty good," I ventured. "Lots of statistics."

"Fodder for the gamblers, no doubt," Wolfe grumbled.

"It's so cheerful here that I'd like nothing more than to while away the afternoon talking about Ian Mac-Laren's contributions to the Fourth Estate, but as you may recall, I have a three-thirty appointment with our client the diamond merchant. That should result in a fat check, made out to you, so it would be nice if I showed up on time."

"I have noted your unswerving devotion to duty," Wolfe said, "and I hope you will manage to be home on time for Mr. Cohen's arrival." I had an answer ready, but before I could unload it, he was back behind his book.

I figured the morning walk to Times Square was enough exercise for one day, so I felt no guilt whatever in flagging a cab to midtown for my meeting with Gershmann. He didn't want me to come to his office on Forty-seventh Street in the diamond market, suggesting instead a back booth in a deli about a block away.

He was waiting when I got there at exactly three-thirty. It took me about a half-hour to lay the whole thing out, including all the evidence needed to convince him that an employee was taking home a lot more than his salary every week.

After I finished, Gershmann pumped my hand, thanked me more than he needed to, and pulled out his checkbook. If he was chagrined that he had to go outside the close-knit diamond community for help, he didn't show it. "Just out of curiosity," I said, "and although it's none of my business, how do you plan to deal with the situation?"

"There are very definite procedures for this kind of thing," Gershmann said in a voice that dropped thirty degrees. I didn't press the matter further. As we shook hands again, he handed over the check in an amount hefty enough to keep the brownstone running for several weeks. And that's saying plenty, because not only does Wolfe need to ante up for such incidentals as the four cases of beer he consumes every week, he also has to pay me, his confidential assistant, man of action, and all-round gofer, to say nothing of Fritz, the finest chef in the universe, and Theodore Horstmann, who fusses over the ten thousand orchids in the plant rooms up on the fourth floor.

And then there are the grocery bills and the books, of course, but you get the idea. Simply put, the place takes a lot of cash to keep it going. And that cash only comes in if Wolfe feels like working, which is seldom before the bank balance slips to five figures. Right now, that balance was well above the danger level, and would be even higher tomorrow with the addition of Mr. Gershmann's generous draft. We were in for a leisurely spell.

I got back to Thirty-fifth Street a few minutes after five, which meant Wolfe was still up playing with his orchids. I unlocked the safe and tucked our latest check in, then wandered out to the kitchen, where Fritz was in high gear for dinner, and poured myself a glass of milk. "What's the program?" I asked.

"Breast of chicken in cream with foie gras on noodles," he said. "I remember how much Mr. Cohen liked the chicken breast another time when he was here."

"Nice choice," I said, and meant it. Fritz is a magician with chicken. But then, he also is a magician with beef, lamb, pork, veal, and any fish you can name. If there's a Cooperstown for chefs somewhere, he ought to have a spot there, with his puss and his name in capital letters on a brass plaque along with the words "He keeps Nero Wolfe happy—which alone is reason enough to be in the Hall of Fame."

Not that Wolfe and Fritz didn't have their differences over food—and some of their bouts had been dandies. Like the time Fritz used tarragon and saffron to season a platter of starlings and Wolfe went into a pout and refused to eat it because he wanted sage instead. Despite their occasional tussles, Wolfe knows Fritz's batting

average is well over .950, so he picks his fights cau-
tiously—and rarely.

My stomach already was pondering the chicken
breast as I went back to the office and typed a letter to an
orchid grower in Pennsylvania who wanted a peek at the
plant rooms on a trip he was making to New York next
month. Permission granted. Wolfe almost never denies a
serious request to see his precious orchids. I call it
vanity; he says it's the sharing of information, although
visitors always learn far more than they could ever teach
either Wolfe or Theodore.

After finishing the letter and putting it on Wolfe's
blotter for his signature, I started in on the germination
records but was interrupted by the phone.

"Archie, it's Lon. I'll be hung up at the office for a
while yet. I'll tell you why when I get there. It'll probably
be pushing seven."

I told him not to worry, that we might even postpone
the start of dinner by as much as three minutes if he was
late. As I turned again to the germination cards that
Theodore brings down daily, I heard the whine of the
elevator. My watch said six-oh-two, which meant Wolfe
was on his way down from the plant rooms.

"Lon called—he'll be a little late. Trouble of some
kind at the paper," I said as Wolfe came in and headed
for his desk. "I'll lay nine to five it has something to do
with MacLaren."

"Very likely," Wolfe said, reaching for the Terkel
book. "We can delay dinner if necessary." His tone told
me he found the idea extremely distasteful. But he also
felt—he's said so many times—that "a guest is a jewel,
resting on a cushion of hospitality."

As it turned out, we were able to stay on schedule.
Lon rang the doorbell at six-fifty-seven, which meant he
had plenty of time for Scotch on the rocks in the office
while I worked on bourbon and Wolfe downed his
second beer.

"Sorry I'm late," Lon told Wolfe, settling into the red
leather chair with his drink. He looked beat. "Things are
jumping at our place. Turns out the *Times* is breaking a
story in tomorrow's editions that MacLaren has made a

bid for the *Gazette*. I don't know how they caught wind of it, but they called our chairman, Harriet Haverhill, and asked her to respond to MacLaren's statement that he was making an offer for *Gazette* stock. She gave them a 'no comment,' then called the city desk to alert them, and we really had to scramble to get something into tonight's Final."

"Indeed?" Wolfe said. "Mr. Cohen, with your sufferance, I would like to defer the subject of Ian MacLaren until after dinner. I assure you I'm most interested in hearing about him, but—"

"Say no more," Lon cut in, laughing and holding up a hand. "I agree completely. I've been looking forward to this meal, and the best way to enjoy it is with conversation on more pleasant topics."

So twice in one day MacLaren got scrubbed as a mealtime subject. And knowing how both Wolfe and Lon felt about him, I was beginning to be anxious to meet the guy to see whether he had horns, fangs, or maybe a third eye in the middle of his forehead.

Still, events at the *Gazette* hadn't noticeably damaged Lon's appetite. He managed three helpings of the chicken and went for seconds on the tart. As we ate, Wolfe held forth on why he thought the constitutional amendment limiting a President to two terms should be repealed, while Lon—bless his heart!—took the opposite view. I scored Wolfe the winner, but just barely.

We left the table strewn with polished plates for Fritz to clear and crossed the hall to the office. Lon settled back in the red leather chair, with a snifter of the long-awaited Remisier at his elbow. It looked so good I treated myself to some, too, instead of Scotch. Wolfe, of course, had beer.

"Mr. Cohen, you know from Archie that I've become very curious about Ian MacLaren," he began, switching to business.

"So I gathered when he phoned and said you wanted to see some of his papers. Naturally I'm curious as to why you're curious. By the way, did you read any of the rags?"

"Enough to confirm my opinion of the man's journalistic standards. I have several questions about him, sir, but you proceed, please. You said earlier that his bid for the *Gazette* is now public knowledge?"

"Well, not quite yet," Lon replied, looking at his watch. "We learned that the *Times* will break a piece in tomorrow's editions, so our management finally got up off their collective duffs and decided to run something, if just to keep from getting scooped on our own story. But it'll only make the Late City Edition, which is less than ten percent of our circulation. It will be on the street in about half an hour."

"How serious is MacLaren's bid?"

"Damn serious," Lon said. "The *Gazette* is very closely held. Private ownership. And that ownership is in the hands of a small number of people, most of them members of the Haverhill family. All MacLaren has to do is win a few of them over."

"I want to get to the family later," Wolfe said. "First, what is your own opinion of Mr. MacLaren?"

Lon savored the Remisier. He might have been too beat to notice all this curiosity on Wolfe's part was out of the ordinary, but I wasn't. Something unusual was afoot, so I paid close attention. "As far as I'm concerned, MacLaren is the worst thing that's happened to journalism in decades. You've seen his papers. He's in the business for the cash. Rather, I should say the cash and the power."

"Has he ever started a newspaper?"

"Nope, in every case he grabbed an existing one by throwing money around. He's made a profit on just about all of them, so you can't knock his business success. But what he does when he gets a paper . . ." Lon scowled. "He gives it his stamp—if you want to call it that. He usually turns them into tabloids, fills the front page with shrill headlines, slices stories in half, throws in girlie pictures, and cuts loose with an editorial policy that's about twenty degrees to the right of Jesse Helms. As far as I'm concerned, he combines the worst of the original William Randolph Hearst and Rupert Murdoch."

"How long has he owned his papers, at least the ones in this country?"

"I happen to know the answer to that one," Lon said, "if only because I've been reading up on the guy. He bought the L.A. paper in '74, that was his first one. Then he swallowed Detroit in '75 and Denver a year later. You might be interested to know that in all those years, none of the three papers has ever endorsed any Democrat for President, the Senate, or the House. They've always backed the Republican candidate."

Wolfe shuddered. "What does he want with the Gazette?"

"One of his goals—he's been quoted on this several times—is to control a paper in the largest city in every English-speaking country. He's already done that in Canada, Australia, England, Scotland, Ireland, New Zealand, even South Africa. That leaves only the U.S.— New York. The Gazette just happens to be the only possible target here. The other dailies in town all are held by big media companies that aren't about to sell." Lon drained his snifter and I gave him a refill.

"And the owners of the Gazette are prepared to sell?"

"That's a question," Lon said, turning to salute me for keeping the Remisier flowing. "A few apparently are, from the talk I hear around the building, but whether or not MacLaren can finagle a majority of the stock remains to be seen."

"How many owners does the Gazette have?" Wolfe demanded. "And how hard would it be for this man to buy them out?"

"Okay, here's the picture. First, there's Harriet Haverhill, whom I mentioned. She's chairman of the board, the widow of Wilkins Haverhill, who bought it back in the thirties. It wasn't much then—sort of a pseudo-populist tabloid with pretensions to compete with the Times and the Herald Trib. Haverhill made it into a broadsheet, beefed up the metropolitan coverage, and built a strong home-delivery network. And his editorials got tough with city government—so much so that La Guardia nicknamed him 'the Bulldog,' not to mention a few other unprintable names. All in all, he built the

Gazette into a first-rate paper. He died in the early sixties, and she's been in charge ever since. One hell of a woman. She's over seventy now, and is the largest single stockholder, with a little more than one-third of all the shares. The figure I've heard most often is thirty-five percent."

"Is she likely to sell?"

"Definitely not, and that's one of the most encouraging things right now," Lon answered. "From the start, MacLaren is frozen out of the biggest chunk. Which means he's really targeting the others."

"And they are . . . ?"

"The next two largest holders are Harriet's step-children, David and Donna—Donna Palmer—who have about seventeen-plus percent each. David's president of the company, but that's pretty much a figurehead job. He has wanted more for years, but for my money, the guy's a loser. He's erratic, has a hot temper, plus a real fondness for the bottle. His wife, Carolyn, has far more brains and savvy than he does. Harriet would never let him run the company if she could prevent it.

"Donna, the stepdaughter, is pretty much out of the picture." Lon held the snifter to the light and squinted. "She's divorced, lives up in Boston, where she runs a public-relations firm. I don't think she's much interested in the paper, or in New York, for that matter."

"Is that all the family members who share in the ownership?"

"No, there's also Scott Haverhill, Harriet's nephew, with about ten percent. He's the general manager, and he wants the top spot about as badly as David does. He's an oily bastard, always trying to ingratiate himself with his aunt and maneuvering behind the scenes to weasel more power. She'd probably choose Scott over David to run the whole show, but only just barely. Lesser of two evils."

"You've accounted for about eighty percent of the ownership," Wolfe said, ringing for more beer. "The rest?"

"It's in smaller pieces," Lon said. "My boss, Carl Bishop, the publisher, has five percent, and he'd hold out against MacLaren till the finish. Elliot Dean, the family lawyer, who's been around for a hundred years, has about two or three percent, I think. He was a confidant of Wilkins Haverhill, and he's been Harriet's adviser since the old man died. A magazine publishing company, Arlen, has a piece, and so does a guy named Demarest, whose family sold the *Gazette* to Wilkins Haverhill."

Wolfe leaned back and practiced lacing his fingers over his middle mound. "Which holdings do you see as being completely safe from Mr. MacLaren?"

"Harriet's, of course, and Bishop's. And I can't imagine Dean selling out on her," Lon said. "The kids I wouldn't be sure of for a minute—any of them. Same with Arlen and Demarest. They'd both go where they could get the biggest—and quickest—profit, and right now, that looks like MacLaren. The *Gazette*'s a profitable operation, but neither one of them may ever get another chance like this, and they've got no loyalty to the paper."

"So the anti-MacLaren forces, to call them that, control only about forty-three percent of the shares?"

Lon nodded. "Our story in the late edition doesn't go into any detail on this, of course. Just a few graphs quoting MacLaren and a comment from Mrs. Haverhill saying only that the *Gazette* was interested in learning more about the offer."

Wolfe asked more questions about MacLaren, the *Gazette*, and the family, but you've already gotten the flavor. It was nearly eleven when Lon yawned, stretched, and lapped up the last of his fourth snifter of Remisier.

"I still don't know why you're so interested in that miserable Scotsman. But if anything I've said tonight gives you an inspiration about how to stop him, it will bring me more satisfaction than this meal has, which is saying a lot. Don't bother getting up, Archie, I'll see myself out."

I walked him to the front door anyway, partly because a guest in the brownstone is a jewel resting on a cushion of hospitality and partly because I feel better when I do the final bolting of the front door for the night myself. It's force of habit, spurred by the knowledge that there are at least ten people loose in Manhattan who would be more than happy to help arrange Nero Wolfe's funeral, not to mention a few who'd chip in to buy me a tombstone too.

When I walked back into the office, Wolfe was sitting upright, staring straight ahead, with his palms down on the desk.

"Archie, what does a full-page advertisement in the *Times* cost?"

"Beats me," I answered, raising one eyebrow and easing into my desk chair. "Well up in the thousands, I suppose. You planning a spectacular new way to solicit clients? A little showy, isn't it?"

He glared but said nothing, then closed his eyes. Because I have a thing about time, I checked my wrist and waited. After seven minutes, he woke up and blinked. "Instructions," he said.

"Yes, sir." I flipped open my notebook.

"Call the *Times* tomorrow morning and determine the cost of a full page. Let me know the price, although it will make little difference. Then go to their office and place the advertisement that—"

"What advertisement?"

"Don't interrupt! The advertisement that I'm about to give you. First, the headline, in forty-eight-point type . . ."

With that, he began dictating one of the most unusual messages a reader of the *Times* is ever likely to see. It took almost forty minutes, and he stopped occasionally to check a fact in his *World Almanac*. When he was done, I read my shorthand back to him, and he made a few minor changes.

"They won't print this," I ventured.

"I disagree. Through the years, the *Times* has run thousands of open letters and advocacy advertisements from individuals and organizations. It's part of their tradition. You like wagers, Archie; I'll be happy to give you odds they will accept it."

I grinned. "You're too confident; I pass."

"Make sure to keep a carbon when you type it," he said, getting up to go to bed. That was totally uncalled for. I always make carbons.

FOUR

At a few minutes before eight the next morning, Saturday, I was where I preferred to be at that time of day: sitting at the small table in the kitchen with grapefruit juice, Canadian bacon, eggs, pancakes, toast, black coffee, and the *Times* propped up on the rack in front of me.

"Well, there it is," I said to no one in particular as I scanned the front page.

"There is what, Archie?" Fritz asked. He was fussing with a tray to take up to Wolfe in his bedroom, where he always has breakfast.

"A man named MacLaren is trying to scoop up the *Gazette*," I said. "The story's on page one of the *Times.*"

"Mr. Cohen's paper? Bought by that rogue?"

Whenever I think I've got Fritz completely pegged, he does something to throw me off. Because he spends so much time creating world-class meals, I tend to forget how well-read he is. He sees a copy of the *Times* every day, although he doesn't usually get to read it until evening. And then there are all those European magazines he subscribes to. I guess what really bothered me was that I seemed to be the only one around who hadn't known much about the Scots Citizen Kane until the last day or so.

The *Times* story, under a two-column headline in the lower-right-hand corner of the page, added nothing to what Lon had told us last night. In essence, it reported that MacLaren had issued a statement saying he was offering forty dollars a share for *Gazette* stock, and that he already had a "sizable percentage" in his control.

According to the story, he refused to be specific about how much he held.

There also was a comment from a securities analyst on Wall Street who specializes in media companies. He said his firm currently valued *Gazette* stock at about thirty-two dollars, and was quoted as saying MacLaren's offer was "unrealistically high, based on the company's estimated profits over the last year."

The *Times* reporter had reached Harriet Haverhill, but all she gave him was a "no comment" to anonymous reports that various members of the family had already sold their holdings to MacLaren.

I clipped the *Times* article and slid it into my top-right desk drawer for later reference, then turned to the *Gazette*, whose own story was briefer than the one in the *Times* and was back on page five. It reported MacLaren's statement about offering forty bucks a share, but didn't use his "sizable-percentage" comment. Harriet Haverhill was quoted as saying she would "carefully study Mr. MacLaren's offer." There wasn't much else, other than a short biography of MacLaren and a listing of the newspapers and other properties he owned.

After clipping the *Gazette* article and adding it to my collection, I called the *Times*, but found that the advertising department was closed until Monday. I debated ringing Wolfe in the plant rooms, but decided to wait till eleven, when he came down. He handles bad news better when he's behind his desk with beer and book.

As it turned out, he seemed unconcerned that we couldn't make any progress on the advertisement (he hates the word "ad") until Monday, and seemed equally unfazed when I reminded him that I would be spending the rest of Saturday and all of Sunday with Lily Rowan at the country place she'd just bought up in Dutchess County. Lily liked to call it a cottage, which I thought was a quaint way to refer to a layout including a four-bedroom, three-bathroom house with a sauna and two fireplaces and an in-ground pool and tennis court on a ten-acre spread overlooking a stretch of the Hudson which looks like the setting for a travel poster.

I won't bore you with details of my weekend, except

to say it was relaxing. I kept in touch with the outside world just enough to know that the MacLaren Organisation offer for the *Gazette* rated thirty seconds on a national TV news show Saturday night, and that the Sunday *Times* carried an extensive piece on MacLaren's meteoric rise to fame and fortune in the business section.

Monday morning after breakfast, I called the *Times*, and after being passed around to a half-dozen voices, I got a syrupy-sounding woman who told me that the "open, one-time rate" for the type of advertisement I had in mind would be $32,932 on a weekday, $39,699 on a Sunday. I then buzzed Wolfe in the plant rooms, per his instructions, and gave him the two figures. "If you still want to go through with this, I assume we do it on a weekday?"

"Yes!" he snarled, banging down the receiver. One thing he hates even more than being interrupted when he's playing with his plants is spending money on anything other than food, beer, books, and orchids.

The rest of my morning was taken up trying to get the advertisement into the *Times*. My first stop was the local branch of the Metropolitan Trust Company, where I had a cashier's check drawn for almost thirty-three grand. Then it was off to the *Times*. They liked my check, all right, but one very polite, very attractive, very redheaded young woman patiently explained in a voice like bells that because of what she called the "controversial nature of the copy," it would have to be approved.

"How long will that take?" I flashed my most sincere smile.

"We might be able to get back to you today," she answered with a sincere grin of her own. "It depends on how busy Mr. Warner is. He's the one who decides if it's acceptable, and he may want to make some changes. Or he may not want to run it at all."

"If we do get this worked out today, when can the ad run?"

"Probably Wednesday's editions." Another sincere smile. We were on the same wavelength.

"Not tomorrow?" I asked, smiling again and raising

one eyebrow, which Lily once told me is my most appealing expression.

"No, not tomorrow," she said, raising an eyebrow of her own. Bright girl. "We'll make sure you get a call right away, Mr. Goodwin, when a decision has been made."

After a few more feeble attempts to speed things up, which got nowhere, I wound up by giving the redhead our phone number, and she expertly filled out an impressive array of paperwork on the order. I was revising my opinion of redheads.

It was after eleven when I got back to the brownstone. Wolfe was at his desk going through seed catalogs when I sat at my own desk and turned to him.

"Well, the check's been cut and the ad—advertisement—is in the hands of the *Times*, but it may not pass their censors."

"Indeed?" he said, looking up from the catalog. "On what grounds?"

"They didn't tell me. They just said that because of its controversial nature, it would have to go through some sort of approval process."

"Pah!" Wolfe spat. "They won't alter a syllable."

"I don't care how confident you are," I shot back. "A sawbuck says they make some changes. Even money."

"Archie, your ten dollars is lost," Wolfe said smugly, turning back to the seed catalog.

I actually hoped he was right, but I felt my money would be doubled. What bothered me just then was that the *Times* might not call back, for whatever reason, and the whole damn thing would be delayed several more days. Then I'd have to wait longer to find out what Wolfe had in mind. I worried needlessly, though; just after lunch, the phone rang.

"Nero Wolfe's office, Archie Goodwin speaking."

"Yes. Mr. Goodwin, this is *The New York Times*. May I please speak to Mr. Wolfe?" A clipped male voice.

I mouthed the name of the paper silently to Wolfe and he picked up his receiver while I stayed on the line.

"This is Nero Wolfe."

"Ah, yes, Mr. Wolfe, my name is Bob Warner, of the

Times. I'm phoning to tell you that your ad copy is acceptable as written. We can have it ready to run in Wednesday's editions. If you have no specific instructions other than the forty-eight-point headline, we'll set it up in one of our standard body type sizes. Is that agreeable?"

"Yes, it is, Mr. Warner," Wolfe answered.

"Also, we can have a proof to show you tomorrow morning."

"Mr. Goodwin will come to look it over. Thank you."

After we hung up, I shook my head. "All right, gloat all you want to. I'm told it's healthy."

"Archie, I do not gloat," he said, but the folds in his cheeks deepened, which gave him away. That's his version of a smile.

I reached for my wallet, pulled out a ten, and walked over to his desk, laying it on the blotter with a flourish.

"Nuts, I still call it a gloat," I said as he folded the bill neatly and slipped it into his vest pocket.

Every morning, three copies of the *Times* are delivered to the brownstone, one each for Wolfe, Fritz, and me. But I was so antsy on Tuesday night to see how our page came out that at ten-thirty I left Wolfe reading in the office and walked out into the balmy night, heading east to Ninth Avenue, where I hailed a cab to the Times Building, the one place I knew for sure I could get the next day's edition at that hour.

The cabbie waited while I went into the lobby and got a paper from the box. As we headed back south, I riffled through the first section, toward the back. There it was. Not that I worried about how it read, mind you. I had been to the *Times* that morning for a look at a page proof, which seemed fine to me except for a couple of typos their proofreaders already had caught.

I just had to see how the finished thing looked, though. I couldn't read it in the cab—the light was too dim. When I got back to the office after an absence of twenty minutes, Wolfe didn't even look up from his book, and I could study the text uninterrupted. So you can keep up, here it is:

AN OPEN LETTER TO EVERYONE WHO LOVES NEWS-PAPERS

As most of you know from reading this newspaper and others and from watching television news programs, the New York *Gazette* currently is the acquisition target of Mr. Ian MacLaren of Edinburgh, Scotland, who owns numerous other newspapers around the world.

Many of you read the *Gazette* as well as the *Times*. Others do not. For those not familiar with the *Gazette*, a few facts:

1. According to the most recent figures from the Audit Bureau of Circulations, it has the sixth-largest daily circulation of any American newspaper and the eighth-largest Sunday circulation.

2. It was named—along with the *Times*—as one of the ten best American papers last year in a poll of college journalism professors. It also finished in the top ten in a similar poll three years earlier.

3. In the last fifteen years, the *Gazette* has won eight Pulitzer prizes, four of them for local reporting. Only three other newspapers, one being the *Times*, have won more Pulitzers during the same period.

Whatever significance you may attach to any or all of the above items, one point is inarguable: the New York *Gazette* is an excellent newspaper, flawed to be sure, but with a balanced and independent editorial voice, a commitment to local coverage, and a genuine concern for this city and its environs. The *Gazette* is a precious asset to New York and its residents, more than 900,000 of whom pay thirty cents a day to read it.

Now a few facts about Ian MacLaren:

1. He controls newspapers in England, Scotland, Ireland, Australia, New Zealand, Canada, South Africa, and the United States.

2. His three American papers have not won a single Pulitzer prize in the years he has owned them—more than a decade in each case. Yet his Los Angeles paper won Pulitzers in three of the last five years before he purchased it in 1974.

3. His American papers speak with a single editorial voice—Mr. MacLaren's. For instance, in each of the last three presidential campaigns, all three of his newspapers supported the Republican candidate. And in every campaign for the Senate or House of Representatives in that period, his papers have endorsed the Republican.

Again, each of you will attach your own degree of significance to the above information, which can be documented. But I suggest that you buy a copy of any of his publications at an out-of-town newspaper stand. His United States papers are the Los Angeles *Globe-American*, Detroit *Star*, and Denver *Times-Arrow*. His Canadian paper, the Toronto *Banner*, also may be available. You will find them interesting reading, and I invite comparison between each of these newspapers and the *Gazette*.

My bias is of course apparent, and it is the reason I purchased this advertisement. Although my work as a private investigator has enabled me to live in relative comfort, I am by no means a rich man, and the cost of this page has made a substantial impact on my balance sheet.

However, I feel strongly that the *Gazette* should remain free of Mr. MacLaren's control, and I offer my services as a catalyst to bring together individuals or groups interested in the future of the *Gazette*.

I stress that I have no financial holding in the *Gazette*. I have never met Mr. MacLaren or any of the current owners of the paper. I have not the capital, nor the inclination, to become one of its principals. I represent no individual or syndicate— indeed, I am not aware if any potential buyers exist, other than Mr. MacLaren. My concern is solely as a newspaper reader and a resident of the city of New York.

In both of these roles, I will be the poorer if the *Gazette* becomes the property of Mr. MacLaren. I bear him no ill will, but I will do whatever I can, given my limited resources, to prevent him from gaining control of the newspaper.

If you have a serious interest in pursuing an ownership role in the *Gazette*, I will be happy to meet with you, although it must be with the understanding that I have no credentials and am in no way an agent for the current owners of the newspaper. My telephone number and address are printed below.

—NERO WOLFE

"The fat's in the fire now," I said, walking over to Wolfe's desk and slapping the page down in front of him. "Do you have any idea how many calls we're going to get tomorrow?" I asked as he looked up peevishly from his book. "We ought to put in some extra lines and hire a battery of operators. Come to think of it, right after breakfast I may go over to Lily Rowan's and help her mop the kitchen floor. She was toying with firing her maid, and I can't stand the thought of her facing a task that menial alone."

"Archie, shut up!" Wolfe barked as he picked up the paper and scanned it.

"Yes, sir."

"Most of the calls can be disposed of easily, certainly the ones from the media, and they'll undoubtedly comprise the majority. As to the others, your notebook. Instructions."

For the next ten minutes, I took down notes on how he wanted the callers handled. After he finished, I yawned, stretched, and announced that I was turning in. "Tomorrow's going to be a bear, whatever you think. I need every minute of sleep I can get. And what's really fun about this deal is all the money it's bringing in for us. Remember what you said in the *Times*—you are by no means a rich man."

I figured that might at least get a small rise, but he ignored me. He was poring over his prose in the *Times* between sips of beer, and the expression he wore—I call it his smug look—drove me from the room.

And he claims he doesn't gloat.

FIVE

I did have the satisfaction, for what it was worth, of being right: all hell did break loose Wednesday morning. I got up an hour earlier than usual and had my standard breakfast while reading the home-delivered edition of the *Times*. I showed Wolfe's advertisement to Fritz, which probably was a mistake, although he almost surely would have spotted it later in the day anyway.

"What did it cost, Archie?" he asked in a tone that almost quavered. Whenever Wolfe isn't working, poor Fritz frets that we're on our way to the poorhouse and that the brownstone will be sold out from under us to pay off the debts. "Relax," I said as I polished off my breakfast. "It's only money, and you know how easily he can earn it when he's in the mood."

Fritz was muttering to himself in French as I walked down the hall to the office with my third cup of coffee. I checked my wrist; seven-fifty-four, and still no calls. Less than three minutes after I'd settled in at the desk, though, the phone woke up. The early bird was an Associated Press reporter, demanding to know more about what was going on. I explained to her that the advertisement spoke for itself—Nero Wolfe had nothing more to say at present. She was persistent, but I can be pretty damn persistent myself, and I got rid of her in under four minutes.

For the next three hours, that receiver was glued to my left ear. I kept a log of the calls—there were thirty-two in all, most of them predictable: the three wire services, including Reuters, four TV stations, seven radio stations, the *Times*, *Post*, *Daily News*, *Newsday*, *Village*

Voice, Washington Post, Boston *Globe, Time, Newsweek,* and several other assorted publications, including three of MacLaren's own papers. Crews from two TV stations also arrived at the stoop, sniffing footage of Wolfe in action, but Fritz barred the door, so they had to satisfy themselves with outside shots of the brownstone.

All the media calls basically followed the same pattern. Here's a representative sample, from memory. I'm picking up the dialogue after I assured the caller that I was authorized to speak for Nero Wolfe, who, I insisted, wasn't available:

Reporter: What's Wolfe up to? Does he want to find buyers for the *Gazette,* or does he want to run it himself?

AG: You read the advertisement. It spells out precisely what his motives are.

R: Have any prospective buyers contacted him yet?

AG: How could they? Our line has been tied up with calls from people like you.

R: Has Ian MacLaren phoned?

AG: We've only had calls from the media, electronic and print.

R: How much did that ad cost?

AG: No comment.

R: Is there anyone special Wolfe would like to see buy the *Gazette?*

AG: No.

R: What's his beef with MacLaren?

AG: You're supposed to have read the ad. He doesn't have an argument with Mr. MacLaren—he doesn't even know him. Mr. Wolfe simply doesn't like the kind of papers he publishes.

R: What doesn't he like about them?

AG: Oh, come on, you're wasting my time and yours. Mr. Wolfe made it very clear in the *Times.* Go back and read it.

Of course there was some variation in the conversation, but that one, which happened to be with a local TV reporter, was typical. Some people don't seem to like doing their homework.

There were other, more interesting calls. One came

from Lon Cohen. "Archie, what in God's name is Wolfe up to? Why didn't you let me know about this? Why—"

"Whoa, whoa, one question at a time. As to what my boss is up to, your guess is as good as mine, but it looks to me like he's trying to prevent something you don't want to see, namely Ian MacLaren gobbling up your newspaper. As to why I didn't let you know about it, I have orders, and I'd better follow them if I want to keep getting paychecks. You know how that is."

Lon calmed down when I promised to keep him posted as much as possible, given my instructions from Wolfe. But he got nothing more for the *Gazette* story on the Wolfe advertisement than anyone else. Orders.

The other intriguing calls, all of which came after the initial flood from the press, included one from Harriet Haverhill's office, requesting that Wolfe come to see her, and one from a man named Carlton with a British accent worthy of *Masterpiece Theatre*; in a chilly voice he announced he was calling for Ian MacLaren, who also desired an audience. I told them both we would be back to them later in the day. As to prospective buyers, the list was short: the publisher of a chain of small upstate papers and a guy who said he owned a wholesale hardware business in New Jersey but had always wanted to be a newspaper owner. I told them both they would be hearing from us, but neglected to say when.

The morning was so hectic that I was caught by surprise when I heard the elevator coming down from the plant rooms. Wolfe walked into the office with a raceme of *Odontoglossum pulchellum*, which he put in the vase on his desk before easing into his chair. "Good morning, Archie, did you sleep well?"

"My sleep ended so long ago I can't remember it. The last three hours have been a circus. While you've been eating in your room and playing with your posies, Fritz and I have held off the Fourth Estate. It was even worse than I expected."

Wolfe didn't answer, giving all his attention to his morning mail, most of which was wastebasket fodder. "Okay, ignore me if you want to," I snapped. "But just so you know, since eight o'clock there have been more than thirty calls, plus TV crews battering away at the door yelling for an interview with you. By the way, the last call that came was from *Sixty Minutes*. They want to do a segment on the great Wolfe. I said we'd think it over. Let's face it, you're hot. I mean really *hot*. A media darling. The next thing will be the ultimate—a cover story in *People*."

Wolfe shuddered. "Confound it, report."

"Here's the rundown," I said, listing the calls and my responses to them.

His eyes stayed closed until I finished. "We'll see Mrs. Haverhill first, preferably this afternoon," he said, frowning. "Then Mr. MacLaren, assuming he's in New York. Ask if he can come tonight; if not, tomorrow."

"You were right that they'd both call—you said so last night. What made you so sure?"

Wolfe turned a hand over. "How could they not? Regardless of whether Mrs. Haverhill wants to see the *Gazette* sold, she has no choice but to talk to me. As chief executive officer of the company, she would be remiss if she didn't find out what I'm up to. As for Mr. MacLaren, I've gotten in his way, and he is not the type who takes interference of any kind lightly. He is obliged to meet me, size me up, and determine how to try to deal with me. He thrives on challenges, and I have provided one. You should have no trouble getting either of them to come here."

For a while, I was close to proving Wolfe wrong on that last statement. I returned the call to Harriet Haverhill's office, and the same woman who had called me before—presumably Mrs. Haverhill's personal secretary—didn't like it when I told her that Wolfe never leaves home on business. "I'm sorry, but Mrs. Haverhill has an extremely busy afternoon, and she really can't spare the time away from the building."

"I'm sorry too," I said. "Mrs. Haverhill requested this meeting, and if she wants to see Mr. Wolfe, it will have to be on his turf. Otherwise, no meeting. Mr. Wolfe is free from two-thirty to four."

The secretary put me on hold. "All right," she said

frigidly when she came back on. "Mrs. Haverhill says she can come at three o'clock. Please confirm the address."

She had lost face, something executive secretaries dread, and she was trying to regain some of her honor with the address ploy. I repeated it to her politely and thanked her very much, but she didn't thaw.

Getting MacLaren to show was no trouble at all. A bored female at his New York number put me through to the same brisk British voice I'd talked to earlier. Mr. Carlton said Mr. MacLaren would be pleased to visit us that evening. I hung up and turned to Wolfe, who was behind his book. "Okay, we've got Haverhill at three, MacLaren for nine. That's two out of two. I assume now that you want me to call *Sixty Minutes* back and set up a time for their film crew to come."

I got exactly what I expected: silence.

Wolfe and I were in the office after lunch, a lobster salad with avocado followed by blueberry pie. At two minutes past three, the doorbell rang. I went to the front hall and peered through the one-way glass panel in the door, then returned to the office.

"She's brought company," I told Wolfe. "A white-haired guy with a cute little mustache. Should I bring them both in?"

He closed his book slowly, marking the place with a thin strip of gold that had been given to him years ago by a pleased client. "Very well," he said, scowling. He's rarely happy when women are in the house, and now he was getting an uninvited second guest as well.

I opened the door. "Hello, I'm Archie Goodwin," I said to the woman.

"I'm Harriet Haverhill," she answered, offering a hand, which I took. "This is Elliot Dean, my attorney and friend."

I sized her up first, as they crossed the sill. Harriet Beaufort Haverhill was a well-preserved seventy-plus, slender, about five-five, with neatly coiffed white hair, light blue eyes, and a nicely arranged face that was almost wrinkle-free. She wore a gray tailored suit that probably set her back at least half a grand, along with a white blouse and a string of pearls that cost at least twice what the suit did.

Dean, who was in the neighborhood of seventy himself, was maybe three inches taller, had his own head of white hair, and a little white mustache about the size of a kiddie toothbrush. He also had one of those pinched "I'd-rather-be-almost-anywhere-else" expressions, the kind that made you wish he was. He wore a double-breasted blue pinstripe that probably also had a price tag in the half-grand range and his alma mater's tie. Yale, of course. I offered a hand and he took it without enthusiasm.

As we walked into the office, I made the introductions while ushering Mrs. Haverhill to the red leather chair, while Dean steered himself to one of the yellow ones. She seemed to know instinctively that Wolfe wasn't a hand-shaker, so no offer was made. He did, however, stand, which was something of a tribute, although she probably didn't realize it. He also never rises for anyone, particularly a woman.

"Mr. Wolfe," she began in a clear, pleasant tone that had a slight Southern flavor, "thank you for seeing us. Elliot—Mr. Dean—asked to come, and I agreed, as long as he understands this is a confidential conversation."

Dean leaned forward in his chair, looking pained. "Harriet," he said, wheezing, "I want to remind you that I advised against this, and I—"

"Elliot, please." Harriet Haverhill's voice was quiet, but it crackled. Dean clammed up, but frowned at the hunk of carved ebony on Wolfe's desk which a man named Mortimer had used as a murder weapon.

"Mr. Wolfe," she continued with a slight smile, "there are several things I'd like to say before we get to why I'm here. First, and I should have written you about this years ago, I appreciate the consideration you always have shown the *Gazette*. Mr. Cohen and Mr. Bishop have often told me how you have given us exclusive stories. You've been a good friend to the paper."

"Madam," Wolfe said, adjusting his bulk, "we've gotten as good as we've given. Mr. Cohen has been of immeasurable help to us as well. On balance, I like to think the accounts are square."

Harriet Haverhill nodded. "Nevertheless, your friendship is appreciated. And that includes the nice things you said about us in the *Times* advertisement."

"I say what I mean," Wolfe replied. "You don't need me to point out the *Gazette*'s strong points."

"It's still nice to hear," she said. This was quickly turning into a mutual-admiration society, and I began worrying about Wolfe. I get concerned on those rare occasions when he goes mellow in the presence of a woman.

"You know," Harriet went on, "when Wilkins died, there were people all over the company waiting for me to fall on my face—*hoping* I would fall on my face. I'll admit I was terrified for the first few months, but I was also determined that the *Gazette* stay in the family and continue to be the kind of paper my husband had wanted it to be."

"Did the others wish to take it in different directions?"

"Oh, I don't mean to suggest that I was the paper's only salvation," she replied. "Lord, that sounded pretty pompous, didn't it? And I suppose what I'm going to say next will sound slightly paranoid. But the fact is that I've always been resented by the other members of the family. I married Wilkins less than a year after his first wife died, and both of his children, David and Donna—they were in their teens at the time—made no attempt to hide their feelings. They treated me like an outsider."

"Did that attitude moderate as they got older?"

"If anything, it increased. Oh, our relations have been outwardly civil. And in Wilkins' presence, both of them always were polite, even deferential, to me. But it was a facade. That facade fell away totally when Wilkins died and they found that he had willed most of his holding in the *Gazette* to me. Their resentment was really out in the open then—especially with David. But I knew Wilkins had wanted me to run the paper, and I—"

"You made the *Gazette* greater than Wilkins ever dreamed," Dean cut in, reaching over and putting a hand on Harriet's arm. If a man can utter a sympathetic wheeze, I guess you can say that's what Dean did.

"Elliot, it would have been every bit as good, and better, if he had lived." She might have been scolding a six-year-old. "Anyway, Mr. Wolfe, through the years I've worked hard—maybe sometimes too hard—to prove myself. I've been pushy sometimes, and probably seem hard-bitten to plenty of people inside the *Gazette* and out. I'm not unaware that my employees call me 'The Iron Maiden' and 'Harriet the Heartless.' "

"Stop talking that way!" Dean snapped, increasing the pressure on her arm.

"It's true," she said, gently pulling away from him. "I know what's said of me, and in a funny way, I'm proud of it. Maybe that's because I didn't have any kind of management background. In the small Southern town where I grew up, young ladies didn't dirty their hands on such things as commercial ventures. And my first husband, who was financially very successful, never wanted me to have anything to do with his business dealings, so I went into middle age almost totally ignorant of that world. My days, both in Georgia and later when we moved up North, were spent on what my people called 'good works'—charities of all kinds."

"Moving on to your second marriage," Wolfe said, soaking all this up without comment, "did Mr. Haverhill take it upon himself to give you a business education?"

Harriet wrinkled a brow and cocked her head. "I suppose that's one way to put it, although it was hardly a formal sort of thing. But the paper was all-consuming to him and he enjoyed talking about it with me, all the facets—advertising, circulation, the newsroom operation, even the management of the building itself. When he found I was interested, he naturally began sharing more and more of the details with me, and before too many months went by, he was even occasionally asking my advice."

"His children undoubtedly resented this."

"Yes, especially David. It actually made poor David furious. I've always suspected he used his father's dependence on me as an excuse for his drinking. I didn't mean to get off on a tangent, Mr. Wolfe. The real reason for my wanting to see you, of course, is that page of yours in the *Times*."

"Of course." Wolfe nodded.

She's one cool customer, I thought as I watched her in profile. An intriguing mix of toughness, honesty, and femininity. I began to appreciate why she'd been so successful, and I knew Wolfe did too. I can always tell when he approves of a woman, which isn't very often. Probably no one else would notice it, but he unbends just a little.

"Mr. Wolfe," she said, smoothing her tailored skirt with a manicured hand, "I won't beat around the bush. I'm terribly worried about the *Gazette*, and I—"

"Harriet, should you be talking like this to a stranger?" Dean piped up. He was wearing his loyal retainer look again.

"Elliot, I know what I'm doing." Again, that crackle. She turned back to Wolfe. "I started to say, I'm worried about the paper, and I'd like to know why you *really* bought the page in the *Times*." Me, too, I thought.

"My motive, or at least part of it, should have been clear from the text. I don't want to see that man in control of the *Gazette*, and I'm offering my services, which are admittedly limited, to help prevent that occurrence.

"However, as you no doubt have concluded, I did have another motive, closely tied to the first, for expending over thirty thousand dollars. I wanted to meet both you and Mr. MacLaren, and I felt the advertisement was the quickest way to effect these meetings."

Harriet raised an eyebrow. "Well, you've certainly succeeded, at least with me, although I must say that's an expensive way to arrange an introduction. But I'm here, and you've got my attention, Mr. Wolfe. As a matter of curiosity, have you heard from MacLaren?"

Wolfe nodded. "He's coming tonight. After dinner."

"This man's a mountebank!" Dean squawked, shooting halfway out of his chair. His face turned an interesting shade of purple. "Harriet, he intends to pump you for information so he can turn around and peddle it to that goddamn swindling Scot! Let's get out of here."

Harriet waved him off patiently, keeping her blue eyes on Wolfe. "As I said, Mr. Wolfe, you've got my attention."

"Thank you. I'm going to have beer. Will either of you join me for that or something else?"

They declined again, and Wolfe stretched his arms out, palms down on the desk. He thinks he's exercising when he does that. "If newspaper and television reports are accurate, Mr. MacLaren is mounting a serious campaign to gain control of the *Gazette*. Does he have a chance to succeed?"

Harriet looked at the ample sapphire on her finger and then back at Wolfe. "I think he does," she said, pausing as Fritz walked in bearing a tray. After he left, she went on. "I own, personally, about thirty-four and a fraction percent of the company's stock. What is the fraction, Elliot?"

"As your adviser, I warn you I don't think you should be discussing these matters with this man," Dean muttered testily. "Let's leave, before we regret it."

She turned to him, giving me the back of her head. "You asked to come along," she snapped. "It was your idea, not mine, but I had a notion you might provide moral support. I know what I want to say, Elliot. If it bothers you, I suggest you go out and wait in the car."

"I'm just thinking about you and the paper," Dean sputtered, but we all knew he'd lost.

"I know you are, but let me go on—this is important." Harriet's voice had risen an octave, and her facade of coolness for the first time showed some cracks. Her hand was shaking as she flicked invisible lint from her skirt.

"Anyway," she said, returning to Wolfe, "I own something over thirty-four percent of the stock, substantially more than any other shareholder. And I can assure you, I have no intention of selling to MacLaren—ever."

"That leaves almost two-thirds of the shares."

"Not really. Elliot here has three percent and Carl Bishop, our publisher, holds almost five, and I'm certain they're safe," she said, looking at Dean for confirmation. He gave a grim nod.

"All right," Wolfe conceded. "Fifty-eight percent

remains for which Mr. MacLaren presumably can forage. How comfortable are you about that?"

"Not very. It's unclear how much of the remainder I can count on. My stepson and stepdaughter each control seventeen-and-a-half percent, left to them by their father, and with the price MacLaren claims he's willing to pay, it wouldn't surprise me if they'd sell to him."

"Might they not also sell in part to spite you?"

Harriet had regained her composure and gracefully tilted her head to one side. It was probably a mannerism she had learned as a Southern belle. It still was effective. "I don't think so, Mr. Wolfe. Despite what I said before, I don't want you to get the idea that our family is feuding and plotting like a bunch of Borgias, like something out of *Dynasty*. It's hardly that intriguing, I assure you. But Donna—my stepdaughter, Donna Palmer—has no desire whatever to become involved in the *Gazette*. She runs a very successful business in Boston, and she'd like to expand into an advertising agency as well. If she sold her stock, or even some of it, the capital would give her the opportunity to grow."

Wolfe drank beer and set the glass down. "Do you know if she's met with MacLaren?"

"She's been on vacation in Europe for the last two weeks; she gets home tomorrow, and I was planning to phone her then. Unless she saw him over there, I doubt if they've talked, but I don't know for sure."

"And your stepson?"

"David—David is . . ." She paused, searching for the right words. "He is not chairman-of-the-board material, despite the fact that he now holds the title of president. I don't mean to sound cruel, but . . . well, it's no secret that David isn't a strong leader. He could never handle ultimate control of the *Gazette*."

"And he wants that control?"

"Yes, no question. He's had ambitions, but I'm afraid he hasn't shown overly good judgment in critical situations. When we had that printers' strike four years ago, you may remember that he called the head of the union a 'cheap thug' during a televised press conference."

Wolfe nodded. "There was talk of a lawsuit."

"Yes, but fortunately it blew over after the strike got settled. That's just one example of how David handles himself under pressure."

"He knows your feelings about his abilities?"

"He most certainly does. He also knows he'll never get any of my holding in the *Gazette*. On my death, my shares will go into a trust to be administered by Elliot here, plus Carl Bishop and a man named Fitzpatrick from the Consolidated Bank and Trust Company. That fact is not widely known, and I would appreciate your discretion."

"You have it," Wolfe said as Dean squirmed in his chair. His face was turning fuchsia, he wanted to cut in so badly. He made a few more noises, but confined himself to groping for his mustache. I was beginning to feel sorry for the guy.

"It has always been my hope that I would eventually get David and Donna to sell their shares to the trust. And my nephew Scott, too. He has a ten-percent holding. But until this MacLaren business came up, there didn't seem to be that much of a hurry."

"How do your stepchildren feel about the trust?"

Harriet studied Wolfe coolly for a second, then decided to be candid.

"Donna seemed pretty neutral when I first told her about it six months ago. Of course she didn't know then that she'd have a chance to make a lot more money—the kind MacLaren apparently is offering."

"In either case, she'd stand to make a great deal, wouldn't she?"

"Donna may not care about the *Gazette*, but she does care about money, Mr. Wolfe. She's a shrewd businesswoman, and if I were betting, I'd give odds that she'll sell to him rather than to the trust. I don't like to hear myself saying it, but there you are." She took a deep breath as Wolfe resettled himself. Maybe it was my imagination, but I was beginning to see stress lines on her regal face.

"What about your stepson? Will he sell? Indeed, has he already?"

"It wouldn't surprise me in the least. For the last

several days, I've been pressing him to find out what, if anything, he's done, and he keeps avoiding me. He's barely been in the office at all. But I'm bringing things to a head on Friday. I've called a special board meeting for that morning—it's one of the reasons I have to reach Donna tomorrow. I'm going to make a plea that everyone hold onto their shares, at least for now. Although I honestly don't know what good it will do. In some cases, it may already be too late. And I've asked MacLaren to come and see me that afternoon as well."

Dean couldn't hold back any longer. "Harriet, you didn't tell me about MacLaren!" he rasped. "How can I function as your adviser when I don't even know what's going on half the time?"

"I'm sorry, I was going to tell you on the way over here, but I forgot," Harriet said, showing no regret. "I only made the appointment this morning."

Elliot resumed both his slump and his pout.

"You mentioned your nephew," Wolfe said. "What part does he play?"

"Scott is the son of my husband's younger brother, Lucas. When Lucas died, Scott inherited his holding, which is almost exactly ten percent. He's general manager of the company now. He wants more than that, but like David, he has his limitations."

"Such as?"

"He's extremely ambitious, which in itself is all well and good. But Scott hasn't got the . . . well, the vision, to run a large newspaper. I know that must sound arrogant, because it's tantamount to saying that I *do* have the vision."

"As you do," Dean cut in. I resisted the urge to pick him up by the collar and deposit him on the stoop. Harriet Haverhill was some lady, but a body can take just so much grovelling.

"The fact is, except for Wilkins, the Haverhill men just haven't been strong," Harriet said, ignoring him. "I'd personally take Scott over David, but both their wives would make better executives than they are, particularly Carolyn—David's wife. Now, there's a dynamo.

I sometimes wish she were my daughter instead of my daughter-in-law."

"Does she have an active role at the *Gazette*?"

"No. She's all wound up in charitable activities around town. She's made quite a name for herself in fund-raisers, and I think David is jealous of her popularity, which I'm sure is why he's always kept her away from any kind of role at the paper. As a stepmother, I shouldn't be saying this, but I often wonder why she married him in the first place."

"Back to your nephew," Wolfe said. "Is he likely to sell to MacLaren?"

"I honestly don't know. When I first told Scott about my plan to establish a trust, he didn't like it at all—I believe he had always held out the hope that someday he'd get to be chairman. I think he sensed I put more faith in him than in David. And I'm sure he was hurt that I didn't name him one of the three trustees."

"He's got enough equity so that if he stayed in your camp, along with Mr. Dean and Mr. Bishop, you could maintain control of the newspaper," Wolfe observed.

"Don't think that hasn't been on my mind. Together, the four of us hold fifty-two percent. By Friday I hope to know exactly where Scott stands—where *everybody* stands. Mr. Wolfe, you've asked most of the questions, you're exceedingly good at that. Now I've got one: What kind of reaction have you gotten from your letter in the *Times*?"

"You've been most candid," Wolfe began, taking a deep breath. "I'll return that candor, although as you'll see, it isn't a sacrifice; I have little to lay before you. Mr. Goodwin spent much of the morning answering the telephone. We've had many inquiries from newspaper and television reporters, but only two calls from potential purchasers, if indeed they can be so termed. Neither of them is a likely candidate.

"It is possible, however, that more calls have come in the last hour," he continued. "Both instruments in this room are turned off so we wouldn't be interrupted, and Mr. Brenner will have fielded any messages. Archie, call Fritz."

I switched on the phone, buzzed the kitchen, and got a quick fill-in. "Three," I said, looking first at Wolfe and then at Harriet. "All from the media."

"I have another engagement," Wolfe said, glancing at the wall clock, which read three minutes to four. "Mr. Goodwin will keep you abreast of any major developments." He hefted his bulk upright and dipped his chin a full half-inch. For him, that's a flourish.

In one of those fluid motions I would have expected from a woman forty years younger, Harriet Haverhill rose, and Elliot Dean scrambled to his feet, clearing his throat and tugging on his school tie. "Thank you very much for your time," she said to Wolfe. "I would appreciate knowing what Mr. MacLaren has to say tonight."

"It's very possible he will tell you himself when you meet with him on Friday," Wolfe said, dipping his chin a second time. Score another point for etiquette. Sometimes I wish I had a video camera, to record such momentous occasions. As I ushered our guests to the hall, Wolfe boarded the elevator to the plant rooms.

Harriet gave me a smile that rated close to ten on the sincerity scale, and I got a whiff of a nice scent, although I couldn't name it. Dean harrumphed all the way down the stairs. He was still in a snit as they climbed into the dark blue Lincoln limo at the curb. I waved from the stoop as it pulled away, but I can't report whether they returned it because the windows were tinted. I'll just assume they did.

SEVEN

I went back to the empty office and dropped into my desk chair. What are we doing? I asked out loud. There's no case, and the bank balance is down over thirty big ones because of that silly ad. The owner of the *Gazette* comes to see us, and she doesn't seem to know what the hell is going on with her own crazy family. Wolfe talks to her for an hour and comes away with nothing, zero. But then, what was he after in the first place? Okay, so he's a genius and I usually can't keep up with him. This time, though, there seemed to be nothing to keep up with. I decided he was showboating, but then I vetoed that because I couldn't see where it was getting him.

I finally concluded that all those years up in the subtropical plant rooms, four hours a day, six days a week, had baked his brain. Having established that, I turned to the germination records Theodore had left for me and began entering them on file cards, vowing to nag Wolfe again for a personal computer so we could cut down on all the paperwork orchid growing entails. During the next hour, four more calls trickled in, two from reporters with suburban newspaper chains, one from a Connecticut daily, and a fourth from a television evangelist down in Delaware who announced in rolling syllables that he felt he was "being called to own a newspaper." I handled the three reporters using the basic formula I'd worked up over the past few hours and assured the reverend that he'd be hearing from us, and to be patient.

"God works in many ways," I told him.

"Amen, brother," was his answer.

Someday I'll learn.

When Wolfe came down from the orchids at six, I filled him in on the calls, leaving the preacher till last so I could enjoy his expression. And he didn't let me down, breaking into one of his better scowls, accompanied by a low growl. He hates evangelists.

"What's the program for tonight with MacLaren?" I asked.

Another scowl. "Archie, patience has never been one of your virtues," he said, picking up his book and ringing for beer. "The program, as you refer to it, will be dictated in large measure by Mr. MacLaren's demeanor, and by his reactions to my first few questions." Getting the hint that the discussion was over, I ambled into the kitchen to see if I could give Fritz a hand with dinner. All I got for my effort, though, was a bunch of questions as to whether we had a new case. I ducked them, and also Fritz's query about how much the page in the *Times* had cost. I was afraid that if I gave him the figure, he'd pass out on the spot, which might delay dinner.

Over lamb kidneys with green pepper and dumplings, Wolfe held forth on corporate social responsibilities in a capitalist society, and I have to admit that my contributions to the discussion were slim to none. Maybe I'd been around Fritz too much, because, despite my faith in Wolfe, I found myself starting to worry about why we were spending all this time on a non-case.

Back in the office with coffee, Wolfe retreated behind *The Good War*, leaving me to watch the clock and wonder whether the Scotsman was really going to show up.

At five minutes after nine, the doorbell rang. I went to the hall, and through the one-way glass I saw MacLaren on the stoop—I recognized him from his photographs—along with a guy about a head taller who looked like he'd have no problem qualifying for the Jets' defensive line. The latter was wearing a raincoat and a scowl.

I walked back to the office doorway. "They're coming

in pairs today," I said to Wolfe. "MacLaren's here, and
he's got a hulk with him. Undoubtedly a bodyguard.
Instructions?"

"I'm only interested in seeing Mr. MacLaren," he
answered, never taking his eyes off the book.

"As you wish, sir," I said, in what I thought was a
pretty good imitation of Sir John Gielgud. I opened the
door with the chain lock on. "Yes?" I inquired mildly,
through the crack.

"I'm Ian MacLaren; I'm here to see Nero Wolfe." His
voice had a healthy dose of Scottish burr and he spoke
with an economy of language I found ominously nasty.

"We're expecting you. Who's your friend?"

"George? He goes everywhere with me."

"Not in this house, he doesn't. Have him wait in the
car," I said, pointing through the crack in the door at the
second stretch Lincoln that had graced our curb that
day. I swung the door open for MacLaren, but blocked
the hulk. Okay, so opening the door was a mistake, but I
really felt George would head for the limo.

Instead, he grabbed my shoulder with a beefy hand
and started to bull his way in. I blocked him again, and
he clipped my cheek with a right hand that knocked me
back against the doorjamb. Like a lot of big guys,
though, he thought one punch would be enough, and
he let down his guard. Bracing my right foot, I caught
him with a left to the stomach that staggered him. I
didn't give him time to recover and laid a right to the
same spot, which was flabbier than I would have thought
from eyeballing him. The second one buckled his knees
and the third, another left, doubled him over. Both
hands went to his stomach and he let out a soft little sigh.

"Stop that!" MacLaren snapped, shooting his cuffs.
"George, wait in the car," he said disgustedly. "Come to
the door if I'm not out in an hour."

George managed a groan and stumbled down the
stairs as we went in. I think I damaged his ego. "Was that
necessary?" MacLaren demanded as I closed the front
door behind us.

"I don't like anyone thinking I'm a pushover just

because I happen to be six inches shorter than they are," I shot back. "Tell George he needs to work on blocking lefts."

We stopped in the doorway to the office. I performed the social niceties. "Ian MacLaren, this is Nero Wolfe." Wolfe looked up, but at me, not our visitor.

"What happened to you?" he snapped.

I realized then that George's punch had scored some points. My hand went to my left cheek and I winced from the tenderness, coming away with blood on my fingers. "Mr. MacLaren's . . . uh . . . driver and I had a debate on the stoop as to who would be sitting in on this conversation. I outtalked him."

Wolfe snorted as MacLaren eased into the red leather chair. "I assume Mr. MacLaren's driver remained outside."

"In the car," I said, dabbing my cheek with a handkerchief.

Wolfe turned his attention to our visitor while I settled in at my desk. The press baron, whom I had in left profile, seemed to be all angles—long straight nose, pointed chin, deeply lined cheeks, a flat head covered with well-groomed dark hair flecked with white. Somehow the pieces fit together pretty well, though; I was forced to admit he wasn't at all bad-looking, hardly an ogre. And his gray suit, while maybe not as expensive as Dean's, was a nice fit. He studied Wolfe with a democratic smile as he crossed his legs.

"Is *he* going to stay?" he asked, motioning to me.

"Mr. Goodwin is always present at discussions in this room," Wolfe said. "Anything you have to say to me you can say to him. If you have something too confidential for his ears, I cannot be bothered with it."

MacLaren's dark eyes swept the room. "Is it bugged?" he asked quietly.

"No, sir," Wolfe replied. "You have my word of honor on that. We do not have tape recorders in this house, although Mr. Goodwin takes notes in shorthand. And if you were to insist that he not do so, it wouldn't matter; he can reconstruct verbatim conversations several hours in length." MacLaren shot a piercing glance at me and then concentrated on Wolfe.

"All right," he said. "That ad you bought in today's *Times*—I could sue you."

"That would be futile. There's not an actionable word in the text, and you know it."

"I'm not so sure." MacLaren's smile was disarming. "Anyway, that's not why I've come. I demand to know what you're up to."

"I should be asking that question," Wolfe purred.

"I think it's pretty obvious. You read the papers and watch TV. And you talked about it in your ad. I want the New York *Gazette*. No secret there."

"How close are you to getting it?"

"I'm not prepared to discuss that right now." MacLaren grinned coolly at Wolfe. "The record shows that I usually get what I want, though. Don't bet against me."

"Indeed I won't," Wolfe said. "Assuming your success—which I'm not yet prepared to do—how do you plan to change the paper?"

"I don't have to answer that, but I will; the *Gazette* will remain the same as it is now."

"Flummery!" Wolfe spat.

I expected a violent reaction from MacLaren, but got another smile instead. "Actually, I can see one change," he said, massaging his chin. "It just occurred to me. How would you like to be a *Gazette* columnist—three times a week?"

"More flummery," Wolfe grunted.

"Not at all," MacLaren said. "You could write on anything you felt like. You'd be syndicated nationally, of course. And here in New York, we'd promote you like crazy," he went on, sweeping his arm in an arc. "TV commercials, radio spots, billboards saying 'Nero Wolfe—only in the *Gazette*!' Millions would read you daily. And—"

"Enough!" Wolfe showed him a palm. "You wouldn't want me on your payroll for long, sir. My first column would be devoted to castigating you and the caliber of your newspapers."

"So much the better!" MacLaren countered heartily. This was beginning to get interesting. "Great publicity for me. For you. For the *Gazette*. Name your salary."

Wolfe sat rigid in his chair. "Sir, enough of this bavardage. We're wasting each other's time."

"Why don't you like my papers?" MacLaren demanded, leaning forward in the chair with his hands on the arms.

"Come now, sir. You know the answer. They're execrable examples of journalism."

"Readers in eight countries don't agree," MacLaren said, still smiling but sticking out his long chin. "Together, the MacLaren Organisation papers sell more than seven million copies a day. There's not another newspaper group in the world that can claim a circulation total even close to that, and many of them have far more papers than we do. I know what the public wants, and our circulation proves it."

"What it proves is that the public, or at least part of it, likes pictures of nubile women in states of undress and page-three stories about the peccadilloes of movie and television performers," Wolfe remarked dryly.

MacLaren ignored the comments and charged on. "As for your statement in the *Times* about our not winning Pulitzers, you should be aware that those things are handed out to the same papers every year. It doesn't matter what their entries are."

"Could it be that those papers consistently do the best work?" Wolfe queried softly.

"Ah," MacLaren sighed, doing another arc-sweep with his hand. "The fact is, I'm not part of the old-boy network of editors and publishers who give these awards to each other. We haven't won any Pulitzers because of that and for an even more basic reason: we never send any entries in. I have no respect whatever for these prizes, and I've said so publicly often enough."

Wolfe's eyes narrowed. "Mr. MacLaren, you don't yet have control of the *Gazette* or you wouldn't be here. I doubt that you're even close to acquiring the paper."

MacLaren did some squinting of his own, then broke

into another grin. "You don't know that, you can't. You're fishing. It's a ploy, a very transparent one at that, to get me to tell you exactly how many shares are committed to me. No doubt she put you up to it."

"She?"

"Really, Wolfe. Ingenuousness doesn't become you. I know that Harriet Haverhill was here earlier today, never mind how. I'm damned if I'm going to become naked before mine enemies."

"Henry the Eighth," Wolfe said.

"You're up on your Shakespeare," MacLaren said approvingly. "End of Act Three. Poor stupid Cardinal Wolsey to his servant Cromwell. I'm not about to make Wolsey's mistake. I bid you good night, sir," he said as he got up to go. "And I do wish you'd reconsider being our columnist. It would be a brilliant coup—for both of us." Wolfe looked grumpily at MacLaren but said nothing as we walked out of the office. I followed him to the hall and held the door as he strode out and down the steps to the Lincoln, where George presumably was still licking his wounds.

"The legend grows," I said when I returned to the office. "First, *Sixty Minutes* calls, and now a nationally syndicated newspaper column. All you need is a guest spot with Johnny Carson, and there'll be no other mountains to climb. Move over, Iacocca."

"Do something about your face!" he snarled. "You look like an alley brawler."

I'd forgotten my cheek, and I turned to go upstairs to clean it up.

"Archie!"

"Yes, sir."

"You fought outside earlier."

"Yes, sir."

"Well?"

"I guess I was just a little quicker," I said, trying to sound modest but not too modest. "It comes from eating right, sleeping well, and thinking pure thoughts."

He tried to scowl, but gave himself away when the folds in his cheeks deepened. I thought he was going to say "satisfactory," but he checked himself and reached for his book.

"Good night," I said, and went upstairs. When I saw myself in the mirror, I realized I was no bargain to look at. I cleaned the cut, slapped a bandage on it, and fell into bed. I don't remember hitting the pillow.

EIGHT

For the next two days, I was jumpy, although weeks later, when I told Wolfe about my uneasiness, he shrugged. "It's only in retrospect that you think you sensed tragedy," he said. "You are much too impulsive and spontaneous to possess anything that could be termed prescience. Intuition is the partner of introspection, and you certainly are not blessed with the latter."

I considered arguing with him, but I would then and there have had to look up a couple of the words he used, which would have shot my timing, so I let it drop.

Whether he believes it or not, I did have bad vibes all of Thursday and Friday. I couldn't blame it on anything going on in the brownstone. The operation was normal, unless you count the pitcher of orange juice that slipped out of Fritz's hand and smashed on the kitchen floor. With Wolfe, it was the usual routine—baby-sitting the orchids, reading, and beer, sandwiched around his meals. A few more phone calls about the ad rolled in, but they weren't worth mentioning.

Our Thursday-night poker game did get canceled, however. Saul was working on a case over in New Jersey, and figured he'd be tied up well into the night. I went out anyway; my cheek looked almost normal, and Lily let me drag her to the Mets game at Shea, where they got pounded by the Cubs. The best part was that the game was over early enough for us to do some dancing at the Churchill. Friday, I spent most of the morning typing Wolfe's correspondence, including the monthly check he sends to a cousin in Montenegro, and balancing the books, and the most exciting thing about the afternoon was getting a haircut while listening to Charley the barber filibuster on why private cars should be barred from Manhattan.

Friday night, Lily and I went to dinner at Rusterman's, which was my payback for getting her to go to the game the night before. I didn't mind a bit, though—we had veal marsala, and it was superb as usual, almost up to Fritz's standards. I thought I was doing a good job of covering up my jitters, but I should have known better.

"You've got something on your mind, lover," Lily said, reaching across the table to squeeze my hand as those dark blue eyes went right through me. "Want to tell kindly old Dr. Rowan about it?"

"I would, but there's really nothing to tell," I said with a grin. "I've just got this feeling, this . . . premonition about the *Gazette*." With that, I filled her in on the events of the last few days, including the *Times* ad, which she had seen.

After I finished, she made a contribution, giving me a rundown on Carolyn Haverhill, whom she knew from several charities the two had worked on. "Really a take-charge type," Lily said approvingly. "Whenever we've served on boards together, she's ended up being chairman. Seems to thrive on the responsibility. I've wondered a few times whether Carolyn might end up running the *Gazette* someday—especially after meeting her husband."

"I think her mother-in-law wonders the same thing," I said, "or at least wishes for it."

After dessert, Lily suggested more dancing at the Churchill, but I begged off. "I can't believe it, Escamillo," she said, using the nickname she'd tagged me with years ago after I'd outsmarted her from a slightly irate bull in a pasture. "Don't you know it's the woman who's supposed to use the headache excuse? I can't remember the last time you turned down a chance to go dancing—at least with me. Shocking."

I apologized and set things right by agreeing to a firm, no-excuses-allowed date for dancing the next

Friday. I saw Lily as far as the lobby of her building while the cab waited, and I was back at the brownstone before eleven-thirty.

Wolfe was parked in the office with a half-full glass of beer and the London *Sunday Times* crossword puzzle.

"Any calls?" I asked, easing into my desk chair.

"No." He looked up and then turned back to his puzzle.

"Sorry to interrupt you. I know how important your little diversions are."

He glared and started to say something, when he looked toward the doorway. I turned and saw Fritz standing there.

"Pardon me," he said, "but something has happened. You would want to know about it."

"Yes?" Wolfe said.

"I was down in my room, listening to the news on the radio. One of those newspaper people who was here the other day is dead."

"My God, somebody got MacLaren," I said.

"No, Archie." Fritz looked pale. "It was the lady, Mrs. Haverhill. She killed herself. With a gun."

"What?" Wolfe bellowed.

"A suicide," Fritz answered. "So they said on the news. In her office at the paper."

"Impossible." Wolfe set his jaw and shook his head, totally dismissing the idea.

"What do you mean?" I snapped. "I know you don't always believe the media, but are you saying the station made this up?"

"I mean it's inconceivable that that woman killed herself. She was murdered—you know it and I know it."

"Please explain to me how I know it."

"Archie, I suggest you do a little reflecting, challenging as that may be." He tossed the puzzle aside, levering himself to his feet, and headed for the door.

"You mean that's it? You're going to bed? No further comment, nothing?"

He stopped his one-seventh of a ton in the doorway. "What would you suggest? The woman is dead. Tomorrow is soon enough to discuss it. Good night."

"I'm sure glad you're not letting this get to you," I said to his back. "If there's anything I can't stand, it's hysterics. Thank heaven . . ." I let it trail off, because I'd lost my audience. The elevator door shut, and the motor groaned as it carried its passenger to the second floor.

NINE

The next morning, Saturday, my alarm clock's wail interrupted an interlude with a chestnut-haired nymph under a tree on a grassy hillside. She was about to murmur something in my ear when the siren went off, and I cursed as I punched it into silence. It wasn't until I'd gotten my feet planted on the floor that I remembered Fritz's bulletin the night before, and then I swore again.

I was still exercising my vocabulary when I got down to the kitchen, where the hot griddle cakes, link sausages, English muffins, orange juice, and a pot of coffee were waiting. I nodded to Fritz and sat at my small table, where as usual he had the *Times* propped up on a rack. Harriet Haverhill's suicide was on the front page, of course, although the article was fairly short—probably because her death was discovered too close to deadline time to permit more.

I read through the piece three times, and committed the following basic information to memory: (1) Harriet Haverhill, age 72, was found dead in her office at the *Gazette* at seven-forty by a security guard making his customary rounds; (2) she had a single bullet wound in her right temple; (3) a .32-caliber automatic was clutched in her right hand; (4) no suicide note had been found; (5) she had spent most of the day in individual meetings with other principal owners of the *Gazette* and with newspaper magnate Ian MacLaren; (6) these meetings were presumably to discuss MacLaren's desire to add the paper to his collection; and (7) "sources close to

Mrs. Haverhill" said she had seemed in good spirits throughout the day.

As I reread the article and finished my breakfast, I could feel Fritz's eyes boring in on me. "Well?" I said, turning to face him.

He blushed and looked apologetic. "Archie, he wants to see you up in his room, as soon as possible."

I started to ask why he hadn't told me that when I came down, but checked myself. Among the many things Wolfe and Fritz agree on is that a meal should never be interrupted or delayed for business, and I appreciate that line of thinking, at least where it concerns my breakfast. I took a last swig of coffee, went up one flight, knocked, and was commanded to enter.

Wolfe sat at the table by the window, barefoot and looking even larger than he usually does in the office, probably because the yellow dressing gown and the yellow silk pajamas under it seem to magnify his size, and that's a lot to magnify. He finished a blueberry muffin and set to polishing off the shirred eggs. "You've seen the *Times*?" he said between bites, gesturing toward his own copy that lay folded on the corner of the table.

"Yes, sir."

He made a face. "A skeletal report. Call Mr. Cohen. Get him to show you the office where she was murdered. I want a complete description. Also, I must see Mrs. Haverhill's stepchildren, as well as the nephew and Mr. Bishop."

"Separately or together?"

"I prefer them separately, and—"

"And how am I supposed to lure them here?" I cut in. "Run another ad in the *Times*?"

He raised his eyebrows. "Actually, your sarcasm is not far off the mark. I was about to suggest that if any one of them balks, say I'm considering an advertisement that would promise a reward for information about Mrs. Haverhill's murder."

"At this rate, you'll become one of the *Times*'s top ten advertisers, right up there with Bloomingdale's and Saks."

Wolfe took a sip of chocolate. "I'm not going to place such an advertisement, but the threat alone will be sufficient to get each one of them here."

"In that case, it should be a snap. When do you want them?"

"You know my schedule as well as I do," he said airily, reaching for the *Times*. "Let that alone govern you."

There had to be a good comeback to that, but I was damned if I could think of one, so I closed the door hard behind me, not quite a slam, and went down to the office. I got Lon on the second ring.

"Archie, this place is an asylum. I can't talk. What's on your mind?" Behind him, the *Gazette* sounded like the Tower of Babel. When I told him I wanted to see Mrs. Haverhill's office, he said the police were still climbing all over it but probably would clear out by noon. "How does this request of yours tie in with Wolfe's ad?" he said in a voice that was now almost a shout.

"Look, I'll fill you in as much as I can when I get there," I said, raising my own voice so he could hear me above the journalistic din. "Give me a time."

He said twelve, and I said I'd be there at the stroke of the hour. I then set to figuring out how I was going to get the various younger Haverhills plus Carl Bishop to appear as ordered at Thirty-fifth Street. After fifteen minutes of seeking inspiration from the globe, the bookshelves, the sofa, the safe, and almost every other object in the room, I snapped my fingers. I had the answer. And it could be done, I bet myself, without a single telephone call.

In the kitchen, Fritz was working on lunch—sweetbreads amandine in patty shells. "Save some for me for later," I told him as I refilled my coffee cup from the pot on the stove. "I'm going to be out at mealtime, but I don't want to be robbed of my fair share."

Fritz smiled as he always does when his cooking gets a compliment, but then a frown took over. "Archie, are you going out because of . . . Mrs. Haverhill?"

"What you're really asking is: 'Are we working on a case?' The answer is yes and no. Yes, Mr. Wolfe is interested in her death. No, we don't have a client, and therefore, we don't have any prospects of a fee."

Fritz's gloom deepened. "The papers say she killed herself."

"Mr. Wolfe doesn't believe that."

"What do you think, Archie?"

"Look, I'm not paid to think, and according to Mr. Wolfe, if I were, I'd be getting my checks from the state unemployment office. I'm paid to run errands, chase down clues, and haul everyone from Jimmy the Greek to Queen Elizabeth back here so His Lordship can grill them in the ease and comfort of his own home."

That little speech made me feel good, although it didn't do much for Fritz, who turned back to his work with a mopey mug. I carried my coffee to the office, where I cleaned up some paperwork, changed the typewriter ribbon, and otherwise tried finding innovative ways of keeping busy. By ten-thirty I decided I needed air. I wasn't anxious to be around when Wolfe came down from the plant rooms; the next time I saw him, I wanted to report some kind of progress.

The sky was gray but the breeze was warm as I headed east at what exercise books probably call a healthy pace. I turned north on Sixth Avenue, catching a glimpse of that spire that tops off the Empire State. I'd have to remember to ask Wolfe if that's the kind of architectural ornamentation he likes. It suits me well enough, although my personal favorite is the shiny silver spike on the Chrysler Building.

Up near Times Square, I stopped for a glass of milk at a lunch counter, then worked my way north and east until I was in the upper Forties close to First Avenue. My watch read seven minutes to twelve when I turned into the *Gazette* Building's block. Two squad cars and mobile units from three TV stations were packed in as close to the front entrance as they could get, and knots of gapers stood on the sidewalks on both sides of the street gawking up at the building, as if anticipating jumpers.

The circus goes on, I thought as I spun through the revolving door and into the two-story Gothic lobby with its neon *Gazette* logo sending down a glow from high on the marble wall. There were two baby-faced uniformed cops, neither of whom I recognized, among the dozen or so people standing around buzzing. I went to the reception desk, where I signed in while a security guard called Lon's office. "He's expecting you," the guard mouthed through a ham-and-Swiss sandwich, giving me a laminated pass that I clipped to my breast pocket. "Twentieth floor" was his next mumble.

I knew it was the twentieth floor—I'd been in Lon's office more times than I could remember. I caught a nonstop elevator and swung his door open at one minute to noon.

"Don't you knock?" he growled, looking up from a littered desk in his 9×12 office.

"Smiley down in the lobby said you were expecting me." I grinned, dropping into a straight-backed chair. "Things calming down a bit?"

"This is the first time in more than two hours that there haven't been at least three other people in here," he rasped. "I haven't even had time to get down to the city room. And now you . . ." He turned his palms up and rolled his eyes.

"Sounds to me like your day's improving steadily," I said, crossing my legs.

Lon yanked at his tie and leaned on his elbows. "Archie, what's this all about? I can understand—and agree with—Wolfe's concern about MacLaren's gobbling up the paper, but how on earth does that tie in with Mrs. Haverhill's suicide?"

"He doesn't think it was suicide."

Lon groaned. "Oh, come on, Archie! You're not going to tell me that—"

"That's exactly what I'm going to tell you. He claims it's murder."

"How the hell can he think that?" Lon said, cupping his chin in one hand and shaking his head. He eyed the cold coffee in his mug and rejected it.

"You've got me. He hasn't shared his thought processes, but if Nero Wolfe says it's murder, I'll buy it."

"What choice have you got—you're working for him."

"Hey," I said, leaning forward, "has Wolfe ever gulled you?"

"No," Lon admitted. "You've both kept a few things from us at times, though."

"Only during a case. Afterward, you always get the story first—and complete."

"Okay, all right," he said, throwing up his hands. "You don't have to call in your markers. You came to see her office, right?"

I nodded and we went down the hall to a set of mahogany double doors at the end that had no name or number on them.

"The police are through in there now—they decided not to seal it. That," he said pointedly, "is how cut-and-dried they think the suicide is. But we may still have some company," Lon said over his shoulder as he turned one of the French-door handles and pushed. The suite was large, lush, and crowded. A local television crew—young blond reporter, soundman, and lightman—were packing their gear under the indifferent gaze of another security guard.

"It's okay, Eddie," Lon told the guard. "The gentleman's with me. We'll close up after we're through."

"Yessir, Mr. Cohen," Eddie said, tipping his hat as he ushered the TV crew out. I sidestepped to keep from being trampled.

"Quite a layout," I whistled, admiring the high-ceilinged room, which was bigger than Wolfe's office and a damn sight fancier. Or maybe "fussier" was a better word. I felt like I'd just opened *Architectural Digest*, which is one of Lily's favorite magazines. Everything was lacquer or velvet. Not surprisingly, it occupied corner space, so there were sweeping windows on two sides. We had entered at one end, and the desk, an elegant white number the size of a pool table with delicate curvy legs, was on our right. Three heavily draperied windows and a credenza with a computer terminal were behind it. At the far end of the room, some thirty-five feet away, was a light blue sofa, centered under two windows and flanked by end tables with tall lamps on them. Several light blue chairs of a style similar to the sofa were scattered around the room. On the walls hung French impressionist oils that fit in perfectly.

The left wall was dominated by built-in bookcases and a large TV screen. On either side of the bookcases were dark wood doors.

"Where do they lead?" I asked Lon.

"The nearest goes to a powder room. And that far one connects with a bedroom-bathroom-kitchen suite. This is actually an apartment, and it's where she lived most of the time. She liked being on the premises—she almost never spent the night at her place up on Park. That was more for entertaining, big parties for local muckety-mucks or visiting publishers, things like that."

"The body was found at the desk?"

Lon nodded. "The gun was still in her hand."

We both snuck a look at the desk blotter. If there had ever been any blood there, it was gone now.

"Whose gun?"

"Her own. She kept it in her right-hand drawer ever since that editor got kidnapped down South some years back."

"Did a lot of people know it was there?"

"I doubt it." Lon frowned thoughtfully. "I didn't, until today. Carl Bishop's the one who told me about it. But I suppose we'd be amazed to learn how many executives keep handguns in their offices."

"No argument there," I said. "Did anyone hear the shot?"

"Apparently not, although that's no surprise, considering how thick the walls are—and the fact that it happened after working hours."

"I thought a newspaper never closed."

"It doesn't, Archie—the newsroom, that is. But all the advertising, circulation, and executive offices on the upper floors are usually empty by six or so. Those of us who are still around at that hour normally head downstairs where the action is."

"Who found Mrs. Haverhill? And when?"

"A guard on his rounds noticed the door to her office ajar at seven-forty and stuck his head in to see if everything was all right. The medical examiner estimated she'd been dead at least one hour."

"The *Times* story said there was no suicide note. Is that true, or did somebody cover it up?"

"I was one of the first ones here after she was found, and there wasn't any note then. The only others ahead of me were the guard who found her, his supervising captain, and Carl."

"So even though it was long past six, you and Bishop were still both on the executive floor, and not in the newsroom?"

Lon shot a hard glance at me. "Be careful, Archie; you're beginning to sound like Cramer. The reason we were both still in our offices was that we were waiting—that is, Carl was—for a call from Harriet, to find out how the meeting with MacLaren had gone. Satisfied?"

"Hey, don't get testy. I'm just trying to find out what happened. Doesn't it seem odd to you that there wasn't a note?"

Lon shrugged. "Not really; lots of people end it without an explanation. What does strike me as strange is *why* she did it. I always figured she'd fight MacLaren to the finish." He stared at her desk.

"But you're convinced it's suicide?"

Another shrug. "My guess is that after all the meetings yesterday, she must have realized MacLaren had enough commitments from the other family members to control the paper. She'd have lost everything she'd worked years to build. Must have been more than she could handle."

"Doesn't that seem out of character?"

"Archie, who's to say what's out of character when a personal crisis comes up?"

I could have posed a dozen more questions, but I figured that was Wolfe's province. I did, however, ask Lon to describe the position of the body when they found it, and then I spent a few more minutes looking around and poking my head into the powder room and bedroom of what had been Harriet Haverhill's sanctuary.

"I've got one more favor to ask," I told Lon after he'd locked the double doors and we were heading down the hall to his office.

"Only one?"

"For now, anyway. I'd like to talk to Bishop."

"He's been swamped all morning. Police, interviews with reporters from TV and the other papers, and God knows how many meetings."

"Try."

Lon heaved a sigh. "This time, Archie, you're going to end up owing me. Today is worth at least two more of Fritz's meals."

"We're booked through June, but I'll pencil you in for a Wednesday in mid-July, and another in August."

Back in his office, Lon phoned Bishop. "You're lucky," he said, hanging up. "He's just finishing a meeting with some of the editors. Let's go in."

We went one door farther down the hall, and it swung open as a half-dozen shirtsleeved men and two women with sober expressions trooped out, most of them nodding to Lon. Then Elliot Dean popped out of the next office, spotted me and tried to shrivel me with his beady little eyes. When that failed, he stalked past. We walked in to find Carlton Bishop, publisher of the *Gazette*, himself in shirtsleeves, standing behind his own billiard-table-size desk, hands jammed into his pants pockets. There were sweat stains under his arms. I'd met him once several years before, and he hadn't changed all that much, except his white hair was a little thinner and he understandably looked haggard.

"Carl, you remember Archie Goodwin," Lon said.

Bishop nodded grimly. "What brings you by?" he asked in the gravelly voice I recalled from our other meeting. "Don't tell me some paper has hired you to cover this?"

"No," I said. "I work for Nero Wolfe, as you know. He believes Mrs. Haverhill was murdered."

"Wha-a-a-t?" Bishop mouthed the word, although almost no sound came out. He dropped heavily into his chair and stared out the window while Lon and I also took seats.

"Carl, I've already told him this is crazy," Lon said.

Bishop swung around in his chair, letting me know his patience was running thin. "Goodwin, first of all, the police seem convinced she killed herself, and so am I. Second, I know your boss has no use for MacLaren—I read his letter in the *Times* and I agree with almost everything in that letter. But to accuse the man of murder—"

"Mr. Wolfe hasn't fingered anybody specific yet."

"Who's his client?"

"He hasn't got one, at least as far as I know."

"You mean he's trying to drum one up?"

"I haven't said that," I answered. "All I know is that Nero Wolfe is positive this was a murder."

"Well, what the hell do you want from me?"

"I was coming to that. Mr. Wolfe would like to talk to you in his office. And also, individually, to David Haverhill, Donna Palmer, and Scott Haverhill."

"Oh, he would, would he? How does he think he's going to get us to his office?"

"Mrs. Haverhill didn't mind coming there," I said quietly. "Earlier this week."

Bishop kneaded the arms of his chair. He looked like hell. "I know," he whispered. "She told me."

"I'll ask you the same question I asked Lon," I said, pressing my advantage. "Has Nero Wolfe ever gulled you?"

Bishop shook his head.

So far, so good. I pushed on. "He's been a good friend to the *Gazette*, and he still is. To use a favorite phrase of Lon's, this time I'm calling in our markers. Will you come—and get the others to come?"

Bishop ran a hand through his white hair and surrendered. "Yeah, I can go and see Wolfe—why not? I can't guarantee the others, but I'll talk to them. I'll let you know, probably through Lon."

"Fair enough," I said, rising to go. "He'd like to see you all before the weekend's over." I thought about shaking hands, but figured Bishop wasn't in much of a mood to be friendly with anyone. I didn't blame him.

TEN

It was just after two when I got back to the brownstone, which meant Wolfe was still in the dining room attacking his lunch. I went straight to the kitchen, where Fritz warmed the plate of sweetbreads he had set aside for me. I knew he was dying to ask how my mission went, but he didn't, and I wasn't about to volunteer anything. I needed some quiet time to chew on the events of the last few hours before I got debriefed by Wolfe.

I polished off the sweetbreads and chased them with a generous wedge of peach pie and a glass of milk. When I finished, Fritz handed me a stack of phone messages. One was from yet another would-be purchaser of the *Gazette;* the other four were reporters, all of whom probably wanted Wolfe's comments on Harriet Haverhill's death and whether it was somehow connected with his letter in the *Times.*

I took the messages and a cup of coffee to the office, where Wolfe was already planted in his favorite chair with a fresh book, *Joseph Conrad, a Chronicle*, by Zdzislaw Najder, and two fresh bottles of beer. At my desk, I drank coffee and contemplated the mirror on the wall. After several minutes, Wolfe set his book down and broke the silence. "Well?" he demanded sourly.

"I didn't want to disturb you," I said innocently. "I never know when you're in the middle of a particularly riveting passage, and I realize how irritating it can be when someone starts talking just at the time—"

"Stop blathering! Report."

"Yes, sir," I said, turning toward him. First came a

thorough description of the death scene, and I didn't leave anything out. He leaned back with his eyes closed, and if he was listening as carefully as I thought, he got a complete picture of the big office, from the color and thickness of the carpet to the size of the desk and the way Harriet Haverhill—according to Lon—was slumped over the desk when they found her. It took me about fifteen minutes, and after I finished, he remained motionless, his eyes still closed.

"I also saw Bishop, if you're interested," I said. He opened his eyes to slits and nodded.

"First off, you should know that they'll all be trooping over to see you—Bishop and the three heirs. I haven't worked out specific times yet, but I was able to do it without resorting to that silly suggestion of yours about another ad in the *Times*." That didn't get a rise, so I went ahead with a verbatim report on the short conversation with Bishop, which was easy. After I finished, he heaved himself upright and tried to pour beer from an empty bottle.

"Bah. You say you got these people to come here. All you really got was Mr. Bishop. You're relying on him to pull in the others—there's no guarantee he can do that. And to get him, you traded on the goodwill we've built up with the newspaper."

"I'd like to win my sawbuck back," I told him. "I've got ten that says they'll all be here before the weekend's over. And as for goodwill—hell, you're still so far ahead of the *Gazette* on points, regardless of what you tell Lon when he comes for dinner, that they could do you favors for decades without balancing the books."

Wolfe sniffed. "No bet," he said.

I grinned. "Okay, let's assume they'll all be here by tomorrow. Maybe one of them will turn out to be a client—as in money. We'll need a slug of it just to break even on this project."

"I'm not interested in securing a client," Wolfe said stiffly. "Get Inspector Cramer."

That one threw me, but who am I to argue with genius? I dialed the Homicide number, which I knew from memory, while Wolfe picked up his receiver. After going through an underling, I heard the familiar gruff voice; I stayed on the line.

"Cramer here."

"Good afternoon, Inspector, this is Nero Wolfe. If your schedule allows, I'd like to discuss the murder of Harriet Haverhill with you at my office."

A silence of maybe five seconds followed, although it seemed longer. "Suicide, you mean."

"No, sir, I mean murder."

Cramer spat a word, then took a deep breath. "Wolfe, this isn't funny."

"I'm not attempting to be comedic, I assure you. I take murder every bit as seriously as you do. And I think it would be mutually beneficial if you could spare time for a conversation."

"By God, I'll . . . All right, dammit, but this better be good," he wheezed, slamming down his phone.

I looked at Wolfe. "I agree that it better be good. I can hardly wait."

"Archie, shouldn't you start lining those people up? I didn't take your wager, but it still remains to be seen whether you can deliver them, despite your braggadocio."

It's just like him to change the subject. I spun around and dialed Lon's number at the *Gazette*, figuring he'd still be at work, Saturday or not. "I know, Archie, you're calling to nag me about the visits to your office," he said. "I think Carl's set them up, but he wants to talk to your boss first—I'll transfer you."

I cupped the receiver and signalled Wolfe to get on the line, whispering Bishop's name. "Mr. Bishop? This is Nero Wolfe."

"Yes, Mr. Wolfe. I told Lon I wanted to speak to you before coming over. I've talked to David, Donna, and Scott about seeing you. But everything has its price."

"Indeed?"

"Yes, and here's ours. We want an exclusive for the *Gazette* that you're claiming Harriet was murdered and are conducting an investigation into her death. I've discussed it with all three of the Haverhills, and they agree with this stipulation."

"All right," Wolfe said. I shot a look at him, but his big mug revealed nothing.

"I've also talked to our editor-in-chief, Lloyd Williams, and he concurs with me that Lon Cohen is the man to write the story, because you know each other so well."

"Tell Mr. Cohen he's welcome to call me—immediately, if he wishes."

"Excellent," Bishop said. "I can be at your office anytime today. As for the other three, here's the situation: David and Donna insist on seeing you together—preferably tomorrow afternoon. Scott doesn't mind coming alone, and he says sometime tomorrow is fine; he's not particular."

Wolfe looked at the wall clock. "Can you be here at six? I invite you to stay for dinner, as well. We're having pork tenderloin."

"Six is fine," Bishop said. "I'm sorry I'll have to decline on dinner, though. Lon's told me what marvelous meals you serve, but I have a previous engagement." Wolfe left it to me to handle the Sunday appointments with Bishop, and we worked it out that the brother-sister act would come at two and the nephew at four. Any other day Wolfe would be up with the orchids at the later hour, but Sundays he strays from his schedule.

Moments after I hung up with Bishop, Lon called for his interview, and I listened in at my desk. It was fairly brief, a few basic questions asked by a skillful reporter and answered tersely by Wolfe. "You know what this means, of course?" I said sourly after he'd finished. "We get flooded with media calls all over again tomorrow after they see the *Gazette*. And I'll have to field every damn one of them."

"That's only fitting," Wolfe said, one corner of his mouth turning up slightly, "since you devised the fiendishly clever stratagem of playing on the *Gazette*'s debt to us. With that debt now more than paid, they feel comfortable in extracting favors."

I opened my mouth to really flatten him, but before I could get it out, the doorbell rang. I went to the hall, and flicking aside the curtain, saw the thick figure of

Inspector Cramer, who looked as if he was ready to eat a bear.

"Come in," I said heartily, swinging the door open. "It's nice to see you again." Of course, he steamed by me like I was invisible and made straight for Wolfe's office, where he homed in on the leather chair, slammed his size twelves on the floor and stuck his chin out. Before he could start in, Wolfe asked if he'd join him in a beer.

"You're darned right I will. Now, what's this crap about murder? Can't anyone die in the five boroughs without you trying to butt in and promote a goddamned case out of it?"

"I do not have a client," Wolfe replied coldly.

"Balls!" Cramer roared, jamming an unlit cigar into his mouth. I've never seen him fire one up.

"Whether or not I am being paid should be immaterial to you. Rather, you should want to know why I think Harriet Haverhill was murdered."

"Okay," Cramer shot back, "let's say I'm curious. Oh, thanks, Fritz," he said as a cold bottle of beer and a glass were set on the small table on his right.

"You may be aware that I placed an advertisement in the *Times* earlier this week," Wolfe said, shifting his bulk.

"Yeah, I saw it. I should've known that was the start of trouble."

Wolfe ignored the comment. "As a result of that open letter, Harriet Haverhill came to see me on Wednesday, along with her lawyer, Mr. Dean. Our talk centered on the *Gazette*, specifically on the other share-holders and whether they would be disposed to sell out to Ian MacLaren."

"And?" Cramer said, gulping down half a glass of beer.

"And she seemed to feel there was a strong likelihood that her late husband's children and his nephew might indeed sell their shares."

"There's your reason for suicide," Cramer said triumphantly, waving the stogie. "She was going to lose her paper."

"No, sir, I don't believe it. I saw enough of the woman to know she was not suicidal. She was too self-possessed and had too much pride and character to succumb to that ultimate admission of failure."

"So now we're playing the amateur psychiatrist," Cramer snorted. "Well, let me just fill you in on what the facts show: First, Harriet Haverhill was found dead in her office with her own pistol in her hand. Second, cause of death, a bullet to the brain, from that same gun. It had been the only shot fired. Third, her fingerprints were the only ones on the weapon. Fourth, the lady had had a very rough day. We talked to both of her step-children, and they told my men that they'd informed her of their intention to sell out to the MacLaren Organisation. The nephew—what's his name, Scott?— was apparently waffling, but he too was leaning toward grabbing the money and running. We also interviewed MacLaren, who told us his meeting with Mrs. Haverhill late yesterday afternoon was hardly cordial. He told her that he had commitments for a majority of the *Gazette* stock and even offered to buy hers. She apparently threw him out of her office on his ear at that point."

"What time was that?"

"He says a few minutes after six. They had started talking at five-thirty."

"Who saw Mrs. Haverhill after MacLaren left her?"

Cramer leaned forward in his chair. "Nobody, but what does that prove? Her secretary, who has a small office next door to Mrs. Haverhill's suite, went home at five-thirty, just after she ushered MacLaren in. She always leaves at that time."

"Does it strike you as strange that Mrs. Haverhill left neither a letter nor some kind of message?"

Cramer worked the stogie around in his mouth. "It's a common misconception that everybody who kills him-self scribbles a farewell note. In this city last year, probably half the suicides didn't see fit to explain why they did it. My guess is she was so depressed after MacLaren left that she acted on impulse—reached into her desk drawer where she kept the pistol and . . ." He spread his hands, palms up.

"Nonsense," Wolfe snapped. "Under no circum-stances would this woman have destroyed herself."

"Listen to the expert," Cramer said, his face turning red. "You talked to her for how long—twenty minutes? A half-hour? And now you claim to know just how she'd react in the worst crisis of her life. I never thought you'd stoop to this to get a case," he snarled, getting to his feet, throwing the chewed-over cigar at the wastebasket, and missing by a foot. "A woman is dead, tragically, and you want to twist this to your own advantage. Well, just remember you can only operate if you have a license."

He turned on his heel, and I got up to follow him, but he stomped out the front door and down the steps before I got to the hall. All I saw from the one-way panel was his broad behind as he climbed into the unmarked black sedan waiting at the curb.

"He seemed a touch angry," I said when I was back in the office.

Wolfe looked up from his book. "With reason. He now sees a murder case looming, one he wishes would go away. But it won't, and neither will we."

At six o'clock I was in the office looking over the Saturday *Gazette*'s coverage of Harriet Haverhill. They gave it their banner headline, along with a two-column picture of her, a portrait by that famous Canadian photographer that probably had been taken at least five years ago. The article was a straight reporting job and referred to her death as "an apparent suicide." No mention was made of Ian MacLaren or his visit to the *Gazette* Building. As I read the story a second time, I wondered how they'd play Lon's piece about Wolfe in the Sunday editions.

The elevator rumbled and the doorbell rang at the same moment. I went to the hall, saw through the glass that it was the publisher himself, and let him in, hanging his trench coat on a hook and directing him to the office, where Wolfe had just gotten seated.

"Good evening," Bishop said. "I wish we were meeting under more cheerful circumstances." He apparently knew about Wolfe's handshake phobia and went directly to the red leather chair.

"Sir," Wolfe responded, dipping his head a gracious eighth of an inch. "Would you like a drink? I'm having beer."

"Scotch, thanks, with a splash of water," he replied, unbuttoning the coat of his gray suit. He still looked like he'd had a sleepless night. I went to the serving cart in the corner and mixed a Scotch for him and another for me, while Fritz came in with Wolfe's standard order.

"As you know," Wolfe said, pouring beer and watching the foam settle, "Mrs. Haverhill visited here three days ago."

Bishop nodded. "Yes, she told me about it. Your letter in the *Times* was quite a surprise to her. Let me ask you," he said, taking a sip of his drink, "why is it you're so sure Harriet was murdered?"

"You knew the woman well, sir, I met her but once. Are *you* convinced she took her own life?"

Bishop studied the glass in his right hand, then looked up, meeting Wolfe's steady gaze. "I'm just now, a day later, getting used to the fact that she's gone. We've worked together for more than twenty years. Yes, I believe she did kill herself. I know she didn't seem a candidate for that kind of ending, but this MacLaren business had really been eating her up. It had depressed her terribly. Far more than she let on." He shook his head and took another swallow of Scotch, bigger than the last. He pulled a pipe from his pocket and jammed it into his mouth, but noticing Wolfe's grimace, he didn't light up.

"How do you feel about the possibility of Mr. MacLaren running the *Gazette*?" Wolfe asked.

"*Ruining* the *Gazette* would be more like it, and it's the worst thing that could happen. I've known for weeks that it's a strong possibility, but I'm still not prepared to accept it—any more than Harriet was."

"I gather you would not have sold your shares to him?"

"You gather right, although I'm just small potatoes. I don't think he gives a damn about my holding. Same with Elliot Dean's," he said, chewing on his pipe. Shades of Cramer. "Elliot has an even smaller piece of the company than I do—together we've got a little more than seven percent."

"Still, a tidy amount," Wolfe nodded. "Is Mr. Dean as strongly opposed to a MacLaren takeover as you are?"

"Hell, yes. Elliot was a tiger where Harriet's interests were concerned. He would have walked on hot coals for her."

"The family's younger members obviously lack the same degree of fealty," Wolfe remarked dryly.

Introducing the first and only complete hardcover collection of Agatha Christie's mysteries

Now you can enjoy the
greatest mysteries ever written
in a magnificent
Home Library Edition.

Discover Agatha Christie's world of mystery, adventure and intrigue

Agatha Christie's timeless tales of mystery and suspense offer something for every reader—mystery fan or not—young and old alike. And now, you can build a complete hardcover library of her world-famous mysteries by subscribing to The Agatha Christie Mystery Collection.

This exciting Collection is your passport to a world where mystery reigns supreme. Volume after volume, you and your family will enjoy mystery reading at its very best.

You'll meet Agatha Christie's world-famous detectives like Hercule Poirot, Jane Marple, and the likeable Tommy and Tuppence Beresford.

In your readings, you'll visit Egypt, Paris, England and other exciting destinations where murder is always on the itinerary. And wherever you travel, you'll become deeply involved in some of the most ingenious and diabolical plots ever invented ... "cliff-hangers" that only Dame Agatha could create!

It all adds up to mystery reading that's so good ... it's almost criminal. And it's yours every month with The Agatha Christie Mystery Collection.

Solve the greatest mysteries of all time. The Collection contains all of Agatha Christie's classic works including *Murder on the Orient Express, Death on the Nile, And Then There Were None, The ABC Murders* and her ever-popular whodunit, *The Murder of Roger Ackroyd.*

Each handsome hardcover volume is Smythe sewn and printed on high quality acid-free paper so it can withstand even the most murderous treatment. Bound in Sussex-blue simulated leather with gold titling, The Agatha Christie Mystery Collection will make a tasteful addition to your living room, or den.

Ride the Orient Express for 10 days without obligation. To introduce you to the Collection, we're inviting you to examine the classic mystery, *Murder on the Orient Express*, without risk or obligation. If you're not completely satisfied, just return it within 10 days and owe nothing.

However, if you're like the millions of other readers who love Agatha Christie's thrilling tales of mystery and suspense, keep *Murder on the Orient Express* and pay just $9.95 plus postage and handling.

You will then automatically receive future volumes once a month as they are published on a fully returnable, 10-day free-examination basis. No minimum purchase is required, and you may cancel your subscription at any time.

This unique collection is not sold in stores. It's available only through this special offer. So don't miss out, begin your subscription now. Just mail this card today.

☐ **Yes!** Please send me *Murder on the Orient Express* for a 10-day free-examination and enter my subscription to The Agatha Christie Mystery Collection. If I keep *Murder on the Orient Express*, I will pay just $9.95 plus postage and handling and receive one additional volume each month on a fully returnable 10-day free-examination basis. There is no minimum number of volumes to buy, and I may cancel my subscription at any time.   70110

Name_____

Address_____

City_____ State_____ Zip_____

QB
Send No Money...
But Act Today!

BUSINESS REPLY MAIL

FIRST CLASS   PERMIT NO. 2154   HICKSVILLE, N.Y.

Postage will be paid by addressee:

The Agatha Christie
Mystery Collection
Bantam Books
P.O. Box 956
Hicksville, N.Y. 11802

"Hah, that's for sure," Bishop agreed. "I know I can be candid with you; together, I wouldn't give a subway token for those three—wait, let me modify that. I really can't say that I know Donna all that well. She actually seems to be bright and at least reasonably honest. But as for those two clowns . . . I'd almost rather see Mac-Laren get the paper than have either of them running things."

"My impression is that Mrs. Haverhill held the same opinion of them, particularly the stepson."

"Absolutely. If MacLaren had been just about anybody else, instead of the unprincipled slime that he is, I think she might have sold out without a fight."

"You had great admiration for her."

Bishop smiled ruefully. "A fine newspaperwoman. She ran the paper the way Wilkins would have wanted. Her first concern was always editorial excellence. I don't mean to say she wasn't interested in making a buck—the *Gazette* turned a nice profit every year. But she plowed a lot of money back into the product. I'll give you an example of her priorities: I spent thirty years on the news side—as a reporter, a copy editor, city editor, managing editor, and then eleven years as editor-in-chief. She was publisher at that time, and one day she comes to me and says, 'Carl, I want you to take over as publisher.' I told her I didn't know a damn thing about how to do it, and she answered by saying the publisher ought to come from the editorial side of a paper, to ensure that it never loses sight of its primary mission."

Bishop waved away my offer of a refill. "Do you know that I'm just about the only publisher of a major U.S. daily that didn't come up through the business or advertising ranks? I'm not going to speculate on how good I've been at the job—others will have to make that judgment—but I've always tried to keep in mind that we're a news organ first and an advertising vehicle second. I must say, however, that I've learned to be diplomatic in dealing with our big advertisers, as hard as that sometimes is."

"Would you have been willing to serve as Mr. MacLaren's publisher?"

Bishop made a face. "Definitely not, although it's moot, because he wouldn't want me. He has a history of bringing in his own team at the top whenever he buys a newspaper."

"Then what? Were you prepared to retire?"

"I'm sixty-three, and financially I'm well enough off. I still feel good and I love to work, but yeah, I would have said to hell with it. Our kids are grown and my wife and I bought a great place in the Bahamas where we'd like to spend more time."

Wolfe poured the second bottle of beer into his glass. "You were at the *Gazette* when Mrs. Haverhill's body was found?"

"Yes. I knew she'd been meeting with MacLaren, and I was mainly waiting around to see how it had gone—my office is just down the hall from hers on the twentieth floor. Earlier she said that she'd call me when they were done. The first I knew there was trouble was when Sal Milletti—he's captain of our security force—barged in on me. One of his men, Eddie Reimer, had found her when he was checking the floor on his rounds and called Sal on the radio. They were the only ones who'd been in her suite before I got there."

"Were the others still in the building—the stepchildren and the nephew?"

"Donna was in with David—and David's wife, Carolyn. The three of them were talking in the conference room on the twelfth floor. Scott was alone in his office just a few doors away."

"Why was Carolyn Haverhill there?"

"I guess I should have mentioned her before," Bishop said. "She's a powerhouse. I frankly don't know what the hell she ever saw in David, other than his dough, of course. Although I think she comes from money herself. I could live with her running the *Gazette*, I think—she's bright enough, and knows how to make decisions. The big negative about her is the joker she's married to, though. Anyway, you asked why she was there: she usually is, when there are big corporate decisions to be made."

"Did she come by invitation?"

Bishop nodded. "David likes to have her around when things get tense. He knows she's a damn sight smarter than he is."

"How do she and Donna get along?"

"All right, as far as I know. I think Donna's happy to have her on the scene, too, as a steadying influence on the turkey."

"What is the cousin's attitude toward Carolyn?"

"Scott? Oh, I think he resents her. He detests anything to do with David—guilt by association."

Wolfe pondered the desk blotter for several seconds, then leveled his gaze at Bishop. "I would like to have Carolyn Haverhill come here tomorrow with her husband and his sister. Is it too great an imposition to ask you to arrange that?"

"Not at all. I was going to suggest it myself when we talked on the phone. I'll try to reach her tonight. Actually, David would probably welcome having her along."

"Back to the *Gazette* Building," Wolfe said. "Was Mr. MacLaren still there when the body was discovered?"

"I'm not sure—I think he'd gone. I do know that after he talked to Harriet, he went off looking for Elliot."

"And found him?"

"Uh-huh. Dean has a private law practice, but as Harriet's counsel he also has an office in the building. MacLaren apparently met with him there after he left Harriet."

"May I assume you are familiar with the terms of Mrs. Haverhill's will?"

"Yes. At one time, she was going to divide her *Gazette* holdings among her stepchildren and Scott, with David and Donna each getting forty percent of her stock and the other twenty going to Scott. But in recent months, she decided to will her shares to a trust—are you aware of that?"

"She touched briefly on it when she was here."

Bishop studied the ice in his glass. "The bottom line was that she felt none of the kids was up to running the operation. Rather than turn it over to them when she died, she would sink her holding into a trust, with the trustees being me, Elliot, and a banker."

"Mr. Fitzpatrick," Wolfe put in.

"Right. And all the papers—God, there were a lot of them—got drawn up a couple of months ago. What a lawyer's dream."

"And what were the reactions of the younger Haverhills?"

Bishop decided another Scotch would be okay after all, and I went to the table with his glass. "From what I heard, some of it from Harriet and some second-hand, they didn't like it very damn much—especially David, who went on a two-day binge when he found out. Scott apparently did some whining too, but I'm not sure about Donna, who's more removed from the scene."

"With this action, was Mrs. Haverhill not cutting herself off from possible rescue from a takeover? Either one of her stepchildren's shares, coupled with her own, would ensure absolute control of the newspaper."

"Of course I've thought about that myself—and I came close a couple of times to asking Harriet about it," Bishop said. "For what it's worth, I have two theories: One, at the time the trust instrument was being drawn, there was no hint whatever of a MacLaren takeover. He was rumored to be more interested in a Chicago paper and had pretty much publicly stated the New York newspaper market was too fragmented for him—despite all that publicity about his wanting a paper in the biggest city of every English-speaking country. Second, if the idea of a takeover *did* occur to Harriet, I suspect that she felt somehow she could play on the family angle to convince one of them—probably Donna—to sell to the trust."

"What about the trio trying to take over?" Wolfe posed. "The two stepchildren's shares together would effectively checkmate Mrs. Haverhill. Add the nephew, and you're at forty-five percent."

Bishop shook his head. "David and Scott didn't get along very well—ever. It's hard to visualize them in bed together."

Wolfe winced at the figure of speech. "Are the Arlen Company and Mr. Demarest committed to Mr. Mac-Laren?"

"Oh, you know about them? As far as I know, they are. On several occasions through the years, Harriet tried to buy them both out, but no sale. They each said they liked the idea of owning part of a newspaper, which really means they were waiting for a big-bucks buyer to come along someday. They knew damn well that in a closely held setup like the *Gazette*, their relatively small holdings could turn out to be critical."

"To your knowledge, had Mrs. Haverhill had recent conversations with either party?"

"Not that I was aware of," Bishop said. "I think she'd pretty much given up on them."

"How would you describe her frame of mind yesterday?"

"I didn't really see much of her—just small snatches here and there. I was in her office for a few minutes in the early afternoon, around two-thirty, to talk about a problem we were having with one of our distributors over in Jersey. At the time, she seemed fairly cheerful, although maybe a little distracted."

"Whom had she met with by then?"

Bishop took the unlit pipe out of his mouth and looked at the ceiling. "Let's see . . . I know she and Donna had talked first thing in the morning, and then just before noon she had David up to her office for maybe fifteen or twenty minutes. Then she had to be at the Waldorf for a big benefit luncheon—she was on the executive committee and sat on the dais. I was with her right after she got back, and Scott was due in to see her around three, I think."

"During your visit, did you ask how her earlier meetings had gone?"

"No," Bishop said, running his hand through his hair. "I figured I'd get the whole story from her after she met with MacLaren. I usually stay at the paper until at least seven, sometimes seven-thirty."

"Was Mrs. Haverhill in the habit of confiding in you?"

"I guess you could say that. I wasn't as close to her when it came to purely financial matters, say, as Elliot Dean was, but on almost anything to do with the running of the paper, she asked my advice. We worked very closely and very well together."

"Do you know any of the particulars of her meetings with her family members and Mr. MacLaren?"

"I haven't really had much time to talk to any of them, certainly not to MacLaren—I haven't even seen him. But from what I gather, all three of those kids had pretty much made up their minds to dump the stock. David's the only one I discussed it with, though. I caught him in a sober moment this morning, and he said he and his stepmother really got into it yesterday. Claimed she accused him of being a traitor to the family."

"Does that sound like her?"

"Well . . . yes . . . actually I can picture her saying that," Bishop replied in his gravelly tone. "I don't know how much you saw of her when she came to see you, but Harriet can—could—be one tough cookie when the occasion warranted. She had a temper, an explosive one, although she knew how to use it effectively. I once half-jokingly accused her of turning it on and off like a faucet."

"Have you spoken with Mr. Dean since the murder?"

Bishop gave Wolfe a thin-lipped smile. "You're determined to call it that, aren't you? Well, by God, if you're right—and I don't think you are—you'll get my full cooperation in running her killer down. As to Elliot, yes, I've seen him once, also just for a couple of minutes. We really didn't have much time to talk. As you can appreciate, the *Gazette* has been a madhouse all day."

Wolfe nodded. "I was curious as to why Mr. Mac-Laren chose to visit him after his meeting with Mrs. Haverhill."

"I guess that's one you'll have to ask Elliot yourself; it didn't occur to me to bring it up," Bishop said, glancing at his Rolex. "I really have to be going. As it is, I'm already late for a dinner party, although it's the last thing I feel like doing right now. I know everybody there's going to want to talk about Harriet." He took a deep breath and got to his feet, slipping his pipe back into its pouch.

"Mr. Bishop, you spoke of cooperation a moment ago, and you've already indulged me liberally by persuading the Haverhill family members to see me. Now, if I may prevail further on your good nature, I also would like to meet with Mr. Dean once more. As you may know, he was here with Mrs. Haverhill, and was not the least bit happy about it. I would appreciate your asking him to see me again, preferably Monday, or Tuesday at the latest."

"No problem," the publisher said. "Elliot will grumble, but that's his nature. In the long run, all he cares about is protecting Harriet. I'll call him tomorrow and do a little arm-twisting."

Wolfe thanked Bishop and I escorted him to the hall, helping him on with his raincoat and holding the front door. I went back to the office and found Wolfe's chair empty, which was fine with me. That meant he had gone to the dining room, and I headed in the same direction. For more than an hour, my stomach had been primed for Fritz's pork tenderloin, and I wanted to keep it happy.

TWELVE

With the exception of my out-of-town sojourns with Lily Rowan, I religiously read two newspapers, the *Times* and the *Gazette*, all the way through every day, and I also usually skim the *Daily News* and the *Post*. Maybe it's because I've been around Wolfe for so long, but I've always preferred getting my news from papers rather than television. It's a little like favoring meat and potatoes over crepes.

If anything, my newspaper reading increases when we're on a case, and I guess Harriet Haverhill's death qualified, despite the lack of a fee or a client. That's why I was up earlier than usual Sunday, and that's also why I grabbed the *Gazette* first instead of the *Times*, my usual starter.

The story was on page three, along with the up-to-date photo of Wolfe that I'd given Lon a few months back. The headline read "NERO WOLFE CALLS HAVERHILL DEATH MURDER," and it spread over four columns. I won't bore you with the whole shebang, but in essence it said that "the famous private detective" was convinced that what the police termed a suicide was really homicide. Lon had neatly worked in most of Wolfe's comments from their telephone conversation and also quoted Inspector Cramer, who insisted the police had no reason whatever to suspect foul play. He covered himself, though, by adding that "We, of course, will fully investigate any developments, however unlikely, that might arise." Ungrammatical, but he made his point.

David Haverhill also was quoted, saying that the grieving family, while it appreciated Wolfe's interest, felt that his stepmother's death was indeed a suicide and hoped that the unhappy event wouldn't be turned into a circus.

I read this while sitting at my usual spot in the kitchen with breakfast and coffee. Fritz, who'd been bustling around getting a tray ready to take up to Wolfe, waited until I finished and then cut in. "Archie, they're calling again." He was miserable. "Before you came down, there were three—the *Times*, the *News*, one from television—all wanting to talk to him about that article in the *Gazette*. Also, a Mr. Bishop called to say that someone named Carolyn would be joining the others here this afternoon. The messages are on your desk."

I thanked him and tried to take the worried look off his face by saying that all this publicity was good for business in the long run, but Fritz saw right through me. He knew damn well we didn't have a client—it said so right there in the *Gazette*—and as long as that was the situation, he would go right on moping.

Moping or not, I let him keep fielding calls from the kitchen and said I'd return them later, then took both papers to the office, where I finished reading them at my desk. The piece about Wolfe was only one element in the extensive coverage the *Gazette* gave Harriet Haverhill. There was also an editorial praising her leadership, a long biographical article with a lot of pictures, and a piece describing the funeral service that would be held Tuesday at Riverside Church.

The *Times* ran a long article about her on their obituary page, plus an editorial, even more glowing than the *Gazette*'s, in which they called her a "worthy, honest, honorable competitor who did far more than her share to raise the standards of journalism, both in New York City and across the nation."

After I finished, I dialed Wolfe's bedroom. "I assume you've read the papers," I said.

"Yes," he grumped.

"Cheer up. That's the best picture of you they've ever run. What does it take to satisfy you?"

"The coverage was adequate. What do you want?"

"First, Carolyn will be coming with the others today.

Second, the phones are ringing again—from the *Times* and a bunch of others. Fritz is taking them in the kitchen. Anything special you want me to say?"

"Just reiterate my conviction that this is a murder. If they want specifics, as they surely will, you must say that I have none. As to any other questions they may ask, I trust that your combination of experience, intelligence, and ingenuity will suffice." He hung up before I could react to that last bit, which I think was supposed to be a compliment, but with Wolfe, you're never completely sure.

Fritz came in with seven more messages, and I started on the callbacks, which took me almost an hour. They were all singing the same song, of course: Why did Wolfe contend she was murdered? And they all came away empty-handed, which made them crabby. In fact, a couple were downright rude, particularly a TV reporter, known for his charm and Grecian profile, who, when he found he wasn't getting anywhere with his questions, demanded to know in an enraged shout if this was a slimy publicity stunt on Wolfe's part to generate more business. "Hasn't the fat guy got any shame at all?" were his last words before I slammed down the receiver. Another TV newshound, a woman, announced that she and a crew were coming over immediately to interview Wolfe, and she didn't seem to hear me when I said he wouldn't see them. When she and two guys with their gear actually did show up an hour later, they exercised their thumbs on our bell for ten minutes and finally gave up, settling for some exterior footage of the seven steps that probably would be featured on the eleven-o'clock news.

By the time I'd returned the last call, which was to a paper in New Jersey, I was tired—make that *very* tired—of the members of the press, and I made a mental note to tell Lon that reporters ought to be forced to take lessons in civility.

At ten-forty, Wolfe came down from his room carrying the *Times Magazine* and the "Week in Review" section, both of which he always read in his office before doing the magazine's crossword puzzle. He sat, rang for beer, and started in on the "Week in Review." After five minutes, I swiveled and faced him. "Do you want a fill-in on the morning's calls, or are you totally satisfied that I took care of everything in my usual superb fashion?"

Wolfe sighed and set the paper down. "I suppose I'm going to hear a report whether I care to or not. Very well, get on with it."

I gave him a quick rundown on most of the conversations, but I switched to verbatim when I got to the really obnoxious ones, mainly to enjoy the expressions on his face. He scowled, frowned, and made some acid observations about the state of journalism in America, particularly the TV brand. He was in the middle of a diatribe about photogenic morons when the phone rang.

"Here comes another one," I groaned. "You can listen in and get a firsthand earful." Wolfe grimaced but picked up his receiver.

"Nero Wolfe's office, Archie Goodwin speaking."

"Yes, Mr. Goodwin, my name is Audrey MacLaren. May I speak to Mr. Wolfe, please?" The voice was smooth, cultured, and British.

I looked at Wolfe and he shook his head but stayed on the line. "I'm sorry, he's occupied right now. I'm his confidential assistant, however; can I help you?"

"Well . . . yes, if you would relay a message to him. You may recognize my name—I'm the former wife of Ian MacLaren, and I just read the story in today's *Gazette* about his investigation. He's right, Harriet Haverhill was murdered. I know who did it, and I would like to hire him to prove it."

Wolfe's eyebrows went up, and mine probably did too. I looked at him for instructions and got an almost imperceptible nod. "I will certainly pass your message along," I said. "Assuming Mr. Wolfe finds it of interest, when would you be available to come and see him? Are you in New York?"

"Yes, I live here now—Connecticut, that is. And I could come at any time that is convenient for Mr. Wolfe."

"What about tomorrow, say at"—I paused and Wolfe held up three fingers—"say at three o'clock?"

"That would be fine," she said, and I gave her our address and took her phone number.

Wolfe and I cradled our receivers together. "Well, I'll be damned," I said. "What do you make of that?"

He was frowning. "We need to know more about this woman—before tomorrow."

"Saul?"

"Yes, get him. See if he can come today."

As I said at the beginning of this narrative, Saul Panzer is a free-lance operative, the best in the business. What I didn't mention is that for Wolfe he'd drop anything else he had going. Despite that high regard, however, he might not be able to help us on such short notice, given the demand for his services.

But we were in luck. Saul answered on the second ring, and when I told him Wolfe wanted to know if he was available, he said he'd be right over. Twenty minutes later, I opened the front door, and Saul, in his standard-issue rumpled brown suit and flat cap, stepped over the sill, winked, and strode into the office.

"I appreciate your coming," Wolfe said, reaching across the desk to shake hands, which says a lot about his feelings for Saul.

"No problem," he answered, dropping into the leather chair and nodding at my offer of coffee. "Things have been a little slow the last few days." I didn't believe that, but it sounded good.

"As you surely know," Wolfe said, pressing his palms down on the desk blotter, "I am interested in the death of Harriet Haverhill."

Saul nodded and Wolfe went on. "I am convinced she was murdered, and I'll be happy to elucidate if you wish."

"Not necessary," Saul said.

"Very well. What do you know about a woman named Audrey MacLaren?"

Saul took a sip of coffee and screwed up his already wrinkled face. "First wife of that newspaper guy who's been trying to grab the *Gazette*," he said. "English. Got dumped by MacLaren when he married a society babe from out West—Palm Springs, I think. After the divorce, which was maybe three years ago, she moved here from London. She had a couple of kids by him, never remarried. If I remember right, she lives someplace over around Stamford or Greenwich."

One corner of Wolfe's mouth turned up slightly, which showed amusement but was more than anything else a salute to Saul. As I've mentioned, both Wolfe and I pride ourselves on being thorough newspaper readers who generally keep up pretty well with current events and names in the news, but we're simply not in the same league with Saul Panzer, who always seems to know more than the *World Almanac, People,* and *Who's Who in America* combined.

"Saul, I'm seeing this woman tomorrow at three," Wolfe said. "I realize this is absurdly short notice, and I'll certainly understand if you decline, but I'd like before our meeting to know a number of things about her."

"Fire away." Saul didn't pull out a notebook because he doesn't use one; he keeps everything filed away upstairs, which seems to work just fine.

Wolfe finished his coffee and pushed the cup away. "Mrs. MacLaren is coming here tomorrow because she says she knows who murdered Harriet Haverhill and wants to hire me to unveil him. This reeks of flummery, perhaps a puerile attempt to implicate her former husband, for whom I gather she holds no warm regard. But the woman has piqued my curiosity.

"What I want to learn is something of the circumstances of their divorce. Were the proceedings initiated by her husband, as your comments about the woman from Palm Springs would seem to suggest? What are the custody arrangements? What kind of settlement did she receive? For instance, does she maintain any kind of equity in his publishing empire? And does she have a residual bitterness toward Mr. MacLaren? Now, if you find this kind of investigation as distasteful as I do," he said, making a face, "perhaps you'll want to decline."

Saul shook his head. "I've gotten into lots seamier stuff than this. I could just about give you the answers to some of your questions right now, but they'd be at least partly speculation, and that's not what you want. I should have something by tomorrow at this time. I'll check in with Archie," he said, thanking us for the coffee and rising to go.

I saw him to the door, made a crack about how I bluffed him out of the biggest pot in our last poker game, and went back to the office, which Wolfe had vacated. My watch read eleven-fifty, meaning, this being Sunday, that he had gone to the kitchen to strategize next week's meals with Fritz. That left me to straighten up the office for our afternoon visitors.

THIRTEEN

Compared to Wolfe's rigid schedule during the week, Sunday in the brownstone is downright free-wheeling. Sometimes he goes to the plant rooms to putter, sometimes not. And the meals are pretty much catch-as-catch-can after breakfast. This day, partly because guests were coming at two, Wolfe ate early in the kitchen with Fritz—the two of them boldly experimented by adding pompano and scallops to their New Orleans bouillabaisse recipe and pronounced the operation a success. That was more meal than I felt like, so I made a pastrami-on-rye sandwich that I had with a glass of milk in the office while reading the accounts of Saturday's Mets-Dodgers game at Shea, a sixteen-inning dandy won by the Mets on an inside-the-park home run.

Starting about one-thirty, I caught myself looking at my wrist every three or four minutes, so I went upstairs and got busy with such matters as deciding which suits to take to the cleaners tomorrow. I was back at my desk scrubbing the typewriter keys with a little brush at five after two when the doorbell rang.

Seen through the one-way glass in the front door, they didn't seem like brother and sister. David Haverhill appeared older than his forty-four years. He was tall and lanky, probably an inch over six feet, with hair the color of a grocery sack. It fell on the right side of a long, angular face that looked like it didn't know how to smile. And I'm sure a smile was the farthest thing from his mind right now. He came in pale and stayed pale.

It was easy to pick out Carolyn—David was clutching

her arm possessively. She was tall, too, and blond, her hair just a shade lighter than platinum. She wore it skinned back tightly and tied in a bun—without doubt my least-favorite style—and her well-arranged, blue-eyed, ivory-skinned face had a self-assured look. Ten to one it was her usual expression.

I'm happy to report that Donna Palmer bore no discernible resemblance to her brother. She might have been five-four—in her heels. She probably put "dark brown" on her driver's license, although I would have called her hair black, and she wore it shoulder-length, framing an oval face with green eyes, a slightly turned-up nose, and a mouth that looked like it knew how to smile, even though now wasn't the time. And if Lon hadn't told me she was thirty-nine, I would have pegged her at seven years younger.

"Mr. and Mrs. Haverhill, Mrs. Palmer? Please come in," I said, swinging open the door and standing aside. He scowled, Donna frowned, and Carolyn stayed with her assured look, chin tilted up. But none of them said a word as they walked into the front hall, where I caught a hint of Madame Rochas on Donna. I also got a good look at her figure, which was fuller and more to my liking than Carolyn's. I guided Donna to the red leather chair, motioning the couple to the yellow ones, then went around behind the big desk to push the buzzer. "Mr. Wolfe will be right in. May I get any of you something to drink?"

"Thank you, no," David grunted as if speaking for all of them. I'd bet he'd already had a couple.

I looked at the two women, my face asking the same question. They both shook their heads, Donna giving me an almost-smile and Carolyn keeping it poised and unshakable.

I headed for my desk just as Wolfe entered, detoured around the guests, got behind his own desk, and sat. "Mrs. Palmer, Mr. and Mrs. Haverhill," he began formally, dipping his head a fraction of an inch to each of them. "I appreciate your making the time to see me. Now, if—"

"Well, we don't appreciate being here," David said. His voice was pitched just below a shout. "It's because Carl twisted our arms—that's the only reason we came. Well, maybe not the *only* reason," he corrected himself, with a glance at his wife, who nodded serenely. "We also want to know why you're running around telling the whole world our stepmother was murdered. It's a sad enough time for us without having her memory defiled by all this murder talk!" He was halfway out of his chair during the tirade, and he sank back when he finished, brushing his wispy hair off his forehead and thrusting his jaw forward. When he was mad, his nose twitched.

Wolfe considered him for several seconds, then turned to the women. "Does either of you wish to make a statement before I begin?"

"I agree with David," Donna said in a voice that was both soft and strong as she crossed one nicely formed calf over the other and smoothed the skirt of her blue dress. "It's tragic what happened to Harriet, and to have this murder gossip on top of it . . . I know you're a friend of the *Gazette*, but I just don't understand this."

Wolfe turned to Carolyn, who gave him a shadow of a smile. "I have some thoughts, but I'd prefer to hear what you have to say first," she said in a husky tone. This one is interesting, skinned-back hair and all, I said to myself. I began to see why Harriet and Lily had been impressed with her.

Wolfe leaned back, his eyes going from Donna to her brother and then to Carolyn. "As I'm sure you all are aware, Harriet Haverhill was here last Wednesday, along with Mr. Dean. She—"

"It was because of that stupid ad of yours in the *Times*," David hissed.

"If I may continue." Wolfe narrowed his eyes. "Yes, it was my advertisement that brought her here. And I had sufficient time with her to convince me that this was in no way a suicidal person."

"Oh, great," David said, leaning forward again as if he were getting ready to spring. "Ten minutes with her, and you're the world's greatest expert on Harriet Haver-hill."

"I make no claims to expertise regarding Mrs. Haverhill." Wolfe was getting annoyed. "But I do put to use what powers of observation I possess. Are you completely satisfied that your stepmother killed herself?"

"Completely. And so are the police," David declared flatly.

Wolfe turned to Donna. "I pose the same question to you."

She hesitated, shifting in her chair. "Well, she was awfully upset Friday when we talked. I don't think I've ever seen Harriet so disturbed."

"What were the circumstances of your meeting?"

"She had phoned me the day before—Thursday. I'd just gotten back from a vacation abroad—in fact, I was still unpacking when the call came. She said she needed to talk to me, that it was extremely important, that it involved the future of the *Gazette*. She asked me, really almost begged me, to come down from Boston as fast as I could. I told her I'd take the shuttle Friday morning. I was still jet-lagged, but I was in her office just before nine the next day."

"You knew why she wanted to see you?"

"I—yes, I had a pretty good idea."

"How could you, as you had been in Europe for several weeks?"

Her green eyes flicked toward her brother, then back to Wolfe. "David had called me at my hotel in Florence and told me that Ian MacLaren was making a serious bid for the paper. He thought I ought to know."

"How did you feel about Mr. MacLaren as a prospective proprietor of the *Gazette*?"

Donna lifted her slim shoulders, then let them fall. "Honestly, I didn't have strong feelings one way or the other. This may sound callous, but I don't have any particular loyalty to the paper. I've never really been a part of it. Oh, I know I have a substantial financial interest, but as far as any kind of an *emotional* tie, no. Maybe it's because my father has been dead for so long, or because I've lived away from New York for so many years now."

"And your feelings toward your stepmother?"

Another shrug. "I've never *disliked* Harriet, but I've also never felt terribly close to her. She was . . . someone who happened to marry my father."

"In your estimation, had she done a good job of running the newspaper?"

"Yes-s-s, I suppose so," Donna said, wrinkling her forehead. "The *Gazette* is certainly well-respected, from what I see and hear."

Wolfe drained the beer from his glass and poured the second bottle. "Were you unhappy that she never gave your brother an opportunity to be in charge?"

David started to cut in, but Donna showed him a palm. "Unhappy? Maybe, although I think 'puzzled' would better describe it. Harriet was well into her seventies, and I kept thinking she'd want to step down. But she seemed determined to hold on."

"Had you ever talked to her about retiring?"

"Oh, the subject came up once or twice through the years, but she always insisted that she felt fine and thrived on hard work."

"What about your conversation with her on Friday?"

"A rough one," Donna said, nibbling at her lipstick. "She told me right at the start that MacLaren was making a hard run at the other shareholders and asked if he'd approached me."

"Had he?"

"No, although David had told me I could expect to hear from MacLaren almost immediately on my return from Europe. Anyway, Harriet begged me to sell my shares to her for the trust she was planning. She asked me at the very least *not* to sell to MacLaren. She was known for her temper, but I've never seen her as furious as she was Friday."

"What did you tell her?" Wolfe prodded.

Donna paused for a deep breath. She didn't look at her brother. "I said that if MacLaren really was going to offer me the price per share that David had told me about, I'd sell to him. Mr. Wolfe, I had been thinking for a long time about selling my *Gazette* holding anyway. I'm looking to expand my business in Boston, and frankly, I need the cash."

"Had you considered selling to your brother?" Wolfe asked, gesturing toward David with a hand.

"It never came up," she answered smoothly, "probably because together we own only a little over a third of the stock, and it wasn't likely that he would have been able to get enough of the rest for a majority. In all honesty, I was ready to go where I could get the most money."

"How did Mrs. Haverhill react to your answer?"

"She was furious. She tried to use the family-loyalty angle, but I told her I wasn't buying it. I said that was hypocritical of her, especially considering that she had effectively blocked David's chances of being either publisher or chairman. Then she told me my father would have wanted the paper kept out of MacLaren's hands at all costs. My answer was that it was presumptuous of her to tell me what my father would have wanted. I am quite capable of figuring that out for myself. Basically, that's how our meeting ended."

"Did you see her again?"

Donna shook her head and studied the carpet.

Wolfe tried to pour beer, found the bottle empty, and set it down. "Mrs. Palmer, where were you Friday evening between six and—"

"Hold on!" David Haverhill shrilled. He was out of his chair again. "We said we'd come here, but we didn't say we'd sit for an inquisition, which is what this is beginning to sound like. Donna, you don't have to answer any more questions. This man has overstepped his bounds. He—"

This time it was Carolyn's turn to cut in. "David, it's all right," she said, laying a hand on his arm and talking to him as a mother would to a child. "We don't have anything to hide. After all, we were together almost all of that time."

"Of course we don't have anything to hide," he whined, shaking off her arm, "but it's the idea that we're being treated like suspects when there hasn't even been a *crime*, for God's sake."

"Mrs. Palmer, please continue," Wolfe said coldly, fixing Haverhill with his three-star glare.

"From midafternoon until Harriet was . . . discovered, I was in the small conference room on the twelfth floor."

"Was someone with you all of that time?"

"No. I don't have an office in the *Gazette* Building, of course; I come to New York so infrequently. When I am here, I usually set up shop in any available conference room. I had a lot of paperwork from my business to catch up on, so I brought it with me from Boston. I was alone from, oh . . . about three-fifteen or so until around six-thirty, when David and Carolyn came in to talk. We were still there when the word came . . ."

"And no one saw you for more than three hours, until your brother and your sister-in-law joined you?"

"That's not quite true. I was making a lot of phone calls related to my business—I'm in public relations—but I did leave the conference room at least twice to ask one of the secretaries to photocopy some papers for me."

"What did you talk to these two about?"

"A little about my trip, but mostly about my meeting with Harriet, and David's, too. But I suppose you want to ask him about that yourself."

"I do indeed." Wolfe turned to David, who had been casting increasingly greedy glances at the bottles on the serving cart. "Mr. Haverhill, am I correct that you met with your stepmother shortly before noon that day?"

"Yes." You'd have to pry his mouth open to get more than that. It was obvious he wasn't going to volunteer anything.

"And the essence of your conversation?"

He crossed his arms and tilted his head to one side, probably thinking that pose made him look like a tough customer. "If you're so damn smart, I think you can pretty well guess that, can't you?"

"I'd prefer to hear it from you, sir."

David looked from Donna to Carolyn to me. He wasn't seeing us, he was merely giving his eyes a change from Wolfe. "All right," he sighed. "She asked me, almost before I had a chance to sit down, if I would sell my shares to that damn trust of hers. I told her thanks, but no thanks. She yelled something like 'So you're going to sell out to MacLaren,' and I said that's exactly what I planned to do.

"We went back and forth for a few minutes, and she pulled the same thing on me that she had on Donna—saying I owed it to the family name to make sure the paper stayed out of MacLaren's clutches, or words to that effect. She was vicious, making a lot of uncalled-for remarks about—unnecessary remarks," he concluded lamely. "But I wouldn't budge, and at that point she called me a traitor to the family. That set me off, and from then on it was mainly a shouting match, which ended with me walking out of her office. I don't have to take that kind of talk from her—or anyone." He sank back into his chair as if this second, longer diatribe had exhausted him.

Wolfe made a rumbling noise in his throat, but it could have been because he was out of beer. "Mr. Haverhill, how would you describe your relations with your stepmother?"

"We . . . got along. I wasn't overly fond of her, and she certainly didn't care that much for me. But I like to think we behaved professionally toward each other."

"Is it fair to say you resented her?"

David seemed to deflate at the question. He rested his elbows on bony knees and swallowed a couple of times. "Yes, that's fair," he said as his wife leaned over to touch his shoulder. "Of course I resented her—the stepmother, the oldest child, all of that. Sounds like something out of Grimm's fairy tales, doesn't it? Anyway, I realized years ago that as long as she had anything to say about the operation of the *Gazette*, I'd never get to the top."

"Did you think you might have if you sold your interest to Mr. MacLaren?"

"As a payback, you mean? Oh, no, no," David responded vehemently. "I didn't mean to suggest that. I knew MacLaren would bring his own people in to run the paper—he always does. Either way, there was no hope for me, but at least with MacLaren I would stand to make a substantially larger profit than if I sold my shares to the trust."

"I'll ask the same question I posed to your sister," Wolfe said. "How did you feel about Mr. MacLaren being owner of the *Gazette*?"

"A lot of the things that have been said and written about MacLaren have been exaggerated, and in many cases terribly unfair," David said. Maybe he'd rehearsed this part. "His papers really aren't that bad. He could bring some new liveliness to the New York newspaper scene."

Wolfe flinched. "When did he first approach you about buying your shares?"

"He called me and we had lunch two weeks ago. He asked if I'd be willing to sell, and after I found out what he was prepared to pay, I told him he could count on my shares."

"But you haven't sold them yet?"

"No, it was a verbal agreement, but I was—still am—fully prepared to turn all my stock over to him the minute the papers are signed."

"Did you discuss anything else during lunch?"

"Well, he told me he had negotiated with Arlen Publishing and the Demarest family and their shares were his. Also, he asked me about Donna's and Scott's holdings. I said he'd have to take that up with each of them, that I could not and would not speak for either one."

"Sir, I'll ask you another question I asked Mrs. Palmer: Where were you from six P.M. Friday until you learned of your stepmother's death?"

I expected that to set him off again, but maybe his batteries were running down. "You know where I was for much of the time—with my wife and sister in the twelfth-floor conference room. From well before six till six-thirty, I was working in my office, which is on the same floor."

"Did anyone see you during that time?"

"No," David said defensively. "But that's not surprising; this is the area where the general offices are: accounting, purchasing, general manager, building management. Most of those people go home at five-thirty, six at the very latest. I'm usually the last one on that floor to leave."

"And that night you stayed unusually late?"

"Well, yes," he said, a belligerence building in his voice. "Donna and I were still around because we wanted to find out how Harriet's meeting with MacLaren went."

"How were you going to find out?"

"Oh, I guess neither Donna nor I told you, did we? Harriet had sent a memo around earlier in the day asking for a meeting with all of us after she'd finished talking to MacLaren."

"Indeed?" Wolfe's eyes opened wide. "Who received copies of this memo?"

"I presume all of us in the company who held stock—me, Donna, Scott, Carl, Elliot Dean."

"How was the memo worded?"

David screwed up his face. "Mm, it was just typed on a half-sheet of paper, nothing formal. I think it said 'Dear David: Please stay until after I've talked to I.M. I'll want to meet with you for a few minutes then.' And she signed it."

"I got the same note, same wording," Donna confirmed.

"When were these sent?"

"I got mine about four-thirty," David answered.

"That was probably about the time mine was delivered to me in the conference room," Donna chimed in.

"How did Mrs. Haverhill even know you would still be in the building to receive the memo?" Wolfe asked Donna.

"I'd told her in the morning that I was going to be working in the conference room until at least six."

"I assume neither one of you has your copy of the note?"

They both shook their heads and David spoke. "So many memos float around a paper that if we kept them all, we'd suffocate inside of a week." He sneered at Wolfe, who ignored him.

"But you're sure her signature was genuine?" His eyes moved from one to the other.

"Without doubt," Donna announced crisply. "She had a very distinctive signature. And they were delivered by her secretary, Ann Barwell—at least mine was."

"Mine too," David yapped.

"Very well," Wolfe said, leaning back. "Do you know specifically why she wished to meet with you?"

David shrugged, bored. He had a short attention span. "I assumed it was to announce that MacLaren was going to get control of the paper; what other reason would there be?"

"Madam?" he said, turning to Donna.

"That's what I think, too," she said. "But after her meeting with him, she just couldn't face us—or anything."

"This presumes that your cousin also was selling to him," Wolfe observed.

"I'd say that was a foregone conclusion," David said. "I didn't talk to Scott after he saw Harriet that afternoon, though I know he also had been approached by MacLaren and had decided to sell. But you'll get a chance to ask him yourself; rumor has it he's coming here later today." He took a malicious pleasure in the word "rumor."

"That's correct." Wolfe nodded, turning toward Carolyn. "Madam, I haven't forgotten you. What were the circumstances of your presence in the *Gazette* Building on Friday?"

She opened her mouth to reply, but David was faster. "Carrie was there because I asked her to be—we make all our big decisions jointly. We're a team, and I consider her completely equal on that team." She's a damn sight more than your equal, I thought as my eyes moved to Wolfe for his reaction.

"I'd like to hear what Mrs. Haverhill has to say," he replied testily.

Carolyn liked being the center of attention. She struck a pose that would have warmed the most jaded fashion photographer and cleared her throat. "As Dave said, we're a team on matters affecting either of us. Several times in the past, he's asked me to sit in on family conferences involving the *Gazette*. It looked like this would be an important occasion, and of course he wanted me there."

"When did you arrive?"

"In the building? Let's see, it was about six-fifteen, wasn't it, dear?" she asked David. Her smile was stingy and studied.

He looked at her adoringly and she went on. "I came right up to Dave's office—he was just finishing up a small meeting—and we talked for maybe five or ten minutes before going down the hall to where Donna was working. I hadn't seen her since she'd gotten back and was anxious to hear about her trip."

"Mrs. Haverhill, how did you feel about what was happening at the *Gazette*?"

"You mean the sale to the MacLaren Organisation? Oh, I was sorry to see the paper passing out of the family's hands. But you know, as impressive and decisive as Harriet could be, she also was rigid. And I think that rigidity was what ultimately would have cost her paper."

"By rigidity, I assume you mean her unwillingness to delegate authority to others, specifically members of the immediate family?"

Carolyn's smile was glacial. "Of course, that and her dictatorial ways in general. Whenever either Dave or Scott came up with an idea on how to improve some aspect of the operation, she invariably belittled or dismissed it. She just couldn't bear the idea of letting go."

"How did you and she get along?"

Carolyn struck another pose that would have looked swell in *Vogue*. "We respected each other," she said, running a well-maintained hand along her slender neck.

"Harriet had many fine qualities, I don't mean to suggest otherwise, and I always enjoyed her company in social situations. She adored the *Gazette*, she was witty and well-informed, always interesting to be around. And I think she enjoyed seeing me; she always seemed to."

Wolfe shifted uncomfortably. I knew he wanted to ring for beer, but was resisting because he'd already downed two in front of his guests and they weren't drinking. I hoped he could hold out for another few minutes. David wasn't doing as well. "Madam, earlier you stated that you had some thoughts but preferred to hear me first. You have heard me."

That brought a smile, a real one that showed white teeth. "I wouldn't have left without saying my piece," she replied. "Dave will tell you that I'm far from reticent in giving my views. Mr. Wolfe, there's no question in my mind that my mother-in-law killed herself. And I know the reason." She looked at Wolfe as if waiting for him to react, but he refused the bait.

When Carolyn saw she was going this one alone, she licked her lips and leaned forward, as if sharing a secret. "Harriet knew that Ian MacLaren had outflanked her and probably had the shares necessary to control the *Gazette*. She hated MacLaren, which is hardly a revelation. So she did the single thing that she felt would turn both the shareholders and the general public against him. She made the ultimate statement by destroying herself."

"That ultimate statement of which you speak surely would have included a written corollary," Wolfe scolded. "She would have listed specifics about Mr. MacLaren's excesses, perhaps, or something of the consequences that would result from his accession to the helm of the *Gazette*. To my knowledge, no such missive exists."

"I don't know about that—all I know is that I'm convinced Harriet killed herself to call attention to what she saw as a tragic event. She was capable of intense passions. And two of those passions were her love for the *Gazette* and her hatred for MacLaren. Isn't that right,

Dave?" Her husband nodded mechanically, apparently unimpressed by her blinding logic.

"Mr. Wolfe, I realize both Donna and Dave were related, at least in a sense, to Harriet, and I wasn't," Carolyn continued. "Despite that, I think I knew her better than they did, maybe because in so many ways we were similar. I won't claim we were terribly close, but I know what drove her. And I'll say it again: she killed herself."

Wolfe had been studying Carolyn during her oration. When she finished, his eyes moved to David and then to Donna. He made a production out of drawing in air and letting it out. "I have nothing more to ask any of you. Thank you for coming," he said, reaching under his desk to ring for beer.

"Mr. Wolfe, before we leave, I have a question." It was Donna, who stood and rested one arm on the back of her chair. "Are you still convinced Harriet was murdered?"

He eyed her sharply. "Madam, nothing has been said here to change my mind."

With that, he picked up his book and opened it while his visitors were still in the room. I made a mental note to remind him later that Miss Manners would probably call that a flagrant breach of etiquette, and then followed them to the front hall. When I held the door, Donna and David marched out without a word, just about the way they had come in, but Carolyn favored me with a fashion-magazine smile.

I returned to the office just as Fritz was rushing two more bottles of beer to the patient. "Well?" I said to Wolfe as he set down his book and poured. "Your reactions?"

"The man actually contends that MacLaren would be a lively addition. He's a witling."

I wasn't sure whether Wolfe meant David Haverhill or Ian MacLaren was a witling, and I didn't ask. He was in a funk, and I knew why: he always avoids work, and when he has to do it on a Sunday, he gets particularly grumpy. To make matters worse, he wasn't even through for the day. Scott Haverhill, alias The Nephew, was due at four o'clock, now a mere twenty minutes away. That meant there was no time for any of life's simple pleasures, such as harassing Fritz about next week's menus or zipping through the Sunday *Times* crossword puzzle.

For a moment, I was tempted to feel sorry for him, but I'm happy to report that the feeling quickly passed. "Work is a tonic," he once told me when I grumbled about some chore. Right now, a little more tonic might be just what he needed.

When the doorbell rang at five minutes after four, I wheeled to face Wolfe. "Maybe we should have a turnstile put in," I said. All I got for my trouble was a scowl. So much for trying to lighten things up.

Through the one-way glass, I sized up our third Haverhill visitor of the day. Scott was considerably better-looking than Cousin David. He was about six-one and had blond hair and a well-arranged face. He could have used a few hours a week at a Nautilus machine, though. He didn't appear as unhappy as David to be at the brownstone, and he beat me to the draw with a firm handshake as I let him in, which threw me off; when I'm on my turf, I like to be the one who offers the paw. I'm never one to be judgmental, but he impressed me as a good deal of a wart.

I introduced him to Wolfe and he at least had the good sense not to try shaking hands, but homed in on the red leather chair, which probably was still warm from Donna. "Carl said you wanted to see me," he said, unbuttoning his herringbone sport coat to display a pink-striped sea island cotton shirt. "I wasn't sure I'd come at first, but then I thought, why not? What's to lose?" He had one of those New England accents, but which one, I couldn't be sure.

"What's to lose indeed, sir?" Wolfe answered. "Will you have a drink?"

He asked for Scotch and water, and I filled the order. "So, you think Harriet was murdered?" he said in a conversational tone. "After reading the piece about you in this morning's *Gazette*, I must say that I still can't figure out why."

"Call it intuition if that pleases you," Wolfe said, turning a hand over. "I gather you're convinced Mrs. Haverhill was a suicide."

"Well, she had been under a hell of a lot of pressure over the MacLaren business, and she seemed pretty tense when I saw her the day she died. But I have to say I'm surprised she pulled the trigger."

"Why?"

"She just wasn't the type," Scott said, taking a sip of his drink. An appreciative look crossed his face. "She seemed too . . . self-possessed, too stiff-necked maybe. I'm not expressing it right, but I'm surprised anything could drive her to that. Especially after the meeting we had."

"Tell me about it," Wolfe said.

"She had asked me to see her in her office at three o'clock last Friday. I knew what it was about, of course. MacLaren had already made me an offer for my *Gazette* shares."

"What did you tell him?"

We were treated to his self-deprecating smile. "I liked the price he offered, and I wasn't going anywhere at the paper. I've been general manager for ten years now; I'm forty-one, and I thought I'd better make a career change if I was ever going to. Also, I didn't know if my stock would ever again be worth what MacLaren was willing to pay." As I looked at him in profile, I thought of Lon's "oily bastard" description.

"You had accepted Mr. MacLaren's offer?" Wolfe asked.

"Not officially." Scott examined a manicured fingernail. "But I had told him that I very likely would."

"What was holding you back?"

Scott smirked, although I'm sure he probably thought it was a boyish grin. "I wanted to talk to Harriet one more time, to see . . . what could be worked out."

"By that, you mean a better position for yourself at the company?"

"You're very direct, Mr. Wolfe." Smirk two. "Yes, I

thought perhaps she might offer me something more. I feel I've earned it."

"So you went to see her Friday—at three?"

"Yes. She'd already talked to my cousins, as I'm sure you know. From what she told me, they both were ready to throw in with MacLaren, if they hadn't actually done so."

"Had you discussed this with them previously?"

Scott shifted in his chair and took another sip of Scotch. "Yeah, we'd talked about it some, at least David and I had. Donna isn't around much, and she'd been away the last few weeks. But—well, as you may already know, David and I don't get along that well. And we don't talk a lot, except of course in meetings and such when business warrants it."

"What is the source of this animus?"

"No one thing, really. We just haven't gotten along for years. Even as kids, we didn't like each other."

"Jealousy exacerbated by competition?"

Scott shrugged virtuously. "That's probably part of the reason. It's no secret that we both would have killed for the chance to run the paper. Er—let me rephrase that. Each of us thought we could run it better than the other. I *know* I would be a better chief executive than David. Harriet knew it too."

"Indeed? Did she tell you as much?"

Scott nodded. "I guess maybe I should get back to my Friday meeting with her; that will explain a lot. What happened was, I went to her office and could see right off that she was upset. She wasn't crying or anything like that—I don't think Harriet ever cried. But her face was white and she was having a little trouble talking. The first thing she said to me when I sat down was, 'Well, I suppose you're going to sell out to that damn pirate too.'

"I told her I'd certainly been thinking hard about it, but that I was glad we were having this chance to talk first. I started to mention my hope that I might still have a future at the paper, when something odd happened."

"Go on," Wolfe prodded.

"She cut me off in mid-sentence, before I could even begin to make my pitch, and said point-blank: 'How would you like to be publisher of the *Gazette*?' I was so stunned I guess I just sat there looking stupid. Here was the job I'd wanted for years, and had almost totally given up on ever having. When I finally recovered, I think I said something like 'I can start tomorrow.'

"She went on to say that Carl Bishop had been talking about retiring for some time, which I had been aware of. She also said—she always was very frank, often brutally so—that she had some reservations about my abilities, but that she was willing to take a chance if it would keep my shares out of MacLaren's paws, thereby denying him control of the paper. The price for my getting the job would be that I would sell my shares to the trust she was setting up, at a price well below MacLaren's offer."

"What were your thoughts about that?" Wolfe laced his hands over his center mound.

"Obviously I'd lose the chance for a big profit, but I'd get something that was worth far more than that to me."

"In the long run, you'd also more than make up for the loss with an increased salary and benefits," Wolfe remarked dryly.

"True," Scott conceded smoothly. "But in all honesty, that didn't enter my mind as I sat there. I was so excited about becoming publisher that nothing else mattered."

"Did Mrs. Haverhill establish a time frame for your accession?"

"Not definitely. She said she'd speak to Carl Bishop later that day to work something out that was agreeable to him. But she did talk in general terms about having me take over sometime around the first of next year."

"Have you told anyone about this conversation?"

"No one—not even my wife. Harriet asked me not to, said that she wanted to announce it herself. I'm sure that's the reason she sent around the memo later that afternoon asking me, and I think the other stock-holders, to meet with her in her office after she'd talked to MacLaren. Did you know about that?"

Wolfe nodded and Scott went on. "I think she was going to use this to blow MacLaren out of the water when he came to see her. I could tell she was really out for his blood."

"When do you plan to tell the other shareholders about Mrs. Haverhill's proposal to you?"

"I want to wait until the memorial services are over and all the confusion dies down. I assume we'll have a stockholders' meeting within a week, and that would include representatives of the Arlen and Demarest interests."

"What if the others don't believe your story?"

"That's occurred to me," Scott said, nodding. "But when we talked, Harriet made a lot of notes on a legal pad. She may have given them to her secretary to transcribe, or maybe they're still in her desk. I haven't asked about that yet. I thought I'd wait a decent interval."

"Even if the notes are found, they may not be legally binding," Wolfe pointed out. I wonder if he wanted to observe that such delicacy seemed out-of-character.

"I'm not sure about legality," Scott said, "but it seems to me her wishes would be *morally* binding."

"Mr. Haverhill"—Wolfe scowled—"with your agreement to stay in the fold, some fifty-two percent of the *Gazette*'s shares would now be out of MacLaren's reach. That being the case, what would have driven your aunt to take her life?"

"I've thought about that," he said, frowning. "All I can figure is that even with a victory over MacLaren, she was so drained by all the maneuvering and infighting of the last week or two that she went off the rails."

"Twaddle," Wolfe said. "Let me pose another possibility. If either Mr. Dean or Mr. Bishop chose to sell his holdings to MacLaren, the scale would tip back to him."

"Unthinkable!" Scott blurted. "That would never happen."

"And I contend it is equally unthinkable that Harriet Haverhill lifted a gun to her head and pulled the trigger," Wolfe said. "It would appear that no justification exists for her suicide. Sir, where were you from six o'clock Friday evening until you learned of her death?"

The question caught Scott off guard. "What difference does that make?" he rasped, slopping his Scotch when he jerked upright.

"Probably none," Wolfe conceded, "but since you're convinced she wasn't murdered, there's no reason for you not to answer."

"I was at my desk all that time. I had a meeting with the head of our purchasing department at five-fifteen which lasted a little more than a half-hour, and I didn't leave the office until David came in with the news about Harriet."

"When was that?"

"About seven-forty-five, I think. A few minutes earlier, I remember being surprised that she was with MacLaren for so long, and I began thinking about calling her to find out what was going on and when she wanted us all in her office. I was starting to get hungry."

"Did anyone see you between the end of your meeting and David Haverhill's arrival in your office?"

"No."

"And is your office on the twelfth floor?"

"Yes, just down the hall from David's. I think he and Donna and Carolyn were in the conference room, though, when they learned about . . . it."

"Mr. Haverhill, did the police talk to you at any time after your aunt's death?"

"Briefly. I told them I was undecided on whether I would sell out or not. Why?"

"I was just curious," Wolfe said casually.

"It seems to me that you're awfully damn curious about a lot of things." Scott was testy. "Well, whatever you say or think, I'm still sure it was suicide. And the police must be satisfied too, or they would've started asking questions before this. Now, if you'll excuse me, I think I'll be going."

Wolfe watched Scott as he got up and tramped out, but said nothing. I followed him to the hall and held the front door open. "Oh, thanks for the drink," he said vaguely, but didn't offer a hand this time, and neither did I.

"Maybe we should stop inviting people over," I told

Wolfe back in the office. "Every time somebody new comes, this mess gets more complicated."

"Stop prattling," he grumbled.

"All right, I'll get serious. What did you think of that business about him being offered the publisher's chair?"

"The man's an ass," he said, ducking my question. "Maybe not as big a one as his cousin, but an ass nonetheless."

"Agreed. What's next?"

He looked at the clock, probably wondering whether he should go to the kitchen and begin assembling some sort of evening feast for himself. "Confound it, I suppose you'll badger me until I do something. I assume they keep records on when people enter and leave the *Gazette* Building?"

I nodded. "Everybody, including employees, has to check in and out at the guard's desk in the lobby. They keep a log, with times."

"Call Mr. Cohen and find out when all of them signed out Friday—Scott, David and Carolyn, Mrs. Palmer, and Messrs. Dean, Bishop, and MacLaren."

"Aren't you afraid this will put us even deeper in debt to the *Gazette*?" I said, raising one eyebrow, which always irritates him because he can't do it.

"Shut up," he huffed, pushing himself upright and walking out the door, then turning down the hall toward the kitchen. That gave him the last word, but it was a hollow victory for my money: whenever he has to resort to "shut up," I know I've gotten the best of him.

FIFTEEN

The Monday *Times* and *Daily News* each had short pieces, well back in the paper, on Wolfe's contention that Harriet Haverhill was murdered. The play they gave the story meant either (1) the editors felt the whole idea was preposterous, or (2) the *Gazette* had scooped them on Wolfe, and consequently they would all but ignore him. Or maybe it was some of both—take your pick.

The MacLaren press was not so reticent. Fritz ran some food-related errands right after breakfast, and I asked him to swing by the out-of-town newspaper stand to pick up any MacLaren papers they had. He came back and skulked into the office grim-faced, with day-old editions of the Scotsman's L.A. and Detroit rags, slapping them down on my desk with a sniff that clearly said he was dumping garbage. The L.A. paper, Sunday version, played Harriet right out on the front, with its banner screaming "N.Y. LADY PRESS BOSS FOUND DEAD." The story, on page three, was only a few paragraphs, just the basic details, and no mention that MacLaren was angling to buy the *Gazette*. The Detroit coverage was about the same, except Harriet didn't rate the page-one headline in the Motor City. That got reserved for a local police scandal: "CITY COPS CAUGHT REACHING INTO COOKIE JAR!"

Getting back to New York, the Haverhill television reporting was hardly award-winning stuff, but for this, I have to jump back to Sunday night. Wolfe and I were in the office at eleven o'clock with the set tuned to the channel that had sent a crew to see us earlier. About halfway through the program, the anchorman, a wavy-haired specimen whose face was about two-thirds pearly whites, switched on his graveside expression and said that "in the wake of the apparent suicide of Harriet Haverhill, chairman of the board of the New York *Gazette*, a shocking charge has been made that she was murdered. For a report, here's Maureen Mason."

The next image was that of a well-scrubbed, earnest-looking young woman waggling a microphone and perched on our stoop. "This is West Thirty-fifth Street," she purred evenly. "It is an unpretentious section of Manhattan, but this particular block has the distinction as the home of Nero Wolfe, the world-famous and reclusive private investigator." At this, a five-year-old head-and-shoulders photo of Wolfe flashed on the screen. "Here is his hideaway," Maureen Mason said, gesturing with an outstretched arm. "He rarely ventures out, preferring to handle cases in his office like a highly specialized doctor. And much of his time is spent tending a legendary orchid collection, worth millions, that he keeps in a lavish greenhouse on the roof. Wolfe has made the disturbing charge that Harriet Haverhill's death on Friday in her penthouse office was not suicide, but premeditated murder, according to this morning's edition of the *Gazette*. However, Wolfe declined to be interviewed by ActioNews, so we can only speculate on the reasons for his startling accusation. Thus far, both the police and the district attorney's office have refused to comment. From West Thirty-fifth Street, this is Maureen Mason for ActioNews."

"Vile," Wolfe rumbled, irascibly gesturing to me to turn the set off.

"You know, I like that word 'lavish' for the plant rooms," I said. "I never thought of them as lavish, but now that I've heard it, I think it has a nice ring."

"Bah."

"It's your own fault," I said. "You would have gotten better coverage if only you'd agreed to see her. Think of it! They would have come in here with their lights and sound gear and all that other elaborate stuff—cables, the whole show. You'd be sitting at your desk, looking stunningly professorial, while the charming Ms. What's-her-name skillfully posed questions that . . ."

I quit talking because I lost my audience. Wolfe got up from his desk in the middle of my monologue and stomped out of the room. I turned to say good night, but he already was beyond earshot; the elevator door had slammed shut and the groaning of the motor told me he was on his way up to his room.

Back to Monday morning. I'd finished breakfast and the papers and was at my desk trying to balance the checkbook when the phone rang. It was Saul.

"Archie, I've dug up a little bit here and there about Audrey MacLaren, but I won't claim it's a great haul. Do you want it now, or should I wait and come when he's in the office?" When Saul says he's "dug up a little bit," it usually means he has a good start on a hardcover biography of the subject.

"Let's try the latter," I said. "He may just have another chore or two in mind for you. Can you make it at eleven?"

He said he could, and I went back to the canceled checks and the pocket calculator until my watch read ten, which meant Carl Bishop should be in his office. I dialed, and a secretary promptly put me through when I gave my name.

"I was calling about Elliot Dean," I said when he came on the line.

"Yes, I had planned to call you this morning," he answered. "I finally got Elliot last night, and as I predicted when I was at your place, he groused for a while, but I finally wore him down. He says Tuesday would be best for him, in the afternoon."

I thanked Bishop for his trouble and kept wrestling with the bank statement and my own figures. They showed a discrepancy of $103.50, with my numbers adding up to the larger balance. Just before eleven, I finally found the error in addition I'd been making and was forced to concede that once again, the Metropolitan Trust Company computers had behaved themselves.

I was putting the bank file away when Wolfe strode in, wished me the usual good morning, and got settled behind his desk. I made another pitch for a home computer, which he ignored, so I said, "Saul will be here any second with some information on the lady you're seeing later today." He compressed his lips, which was one way he showed dissatisfaction at having to begin work so early in the day—and the work involved a woman at that. The doorbell rang even before he could perfect his scowl. I let Saul in, and once in the office, he slid into one of the yellow chairs, declining an offer of coffee.

"I've got some stuff on Audrey MacLaren," he said to Wolfe, laying his flat cap on one knee, "but I'm afraid it's not much."

"You weren't given a lot of time, Saul. Go ahead." As far as Wolfe is concerned, Saul Panzer can do no wrong.

"As I said yesterday, she's English. Age forty-one. And the daughter of an earl, but one who doesn't have that much dough. She and MacLaren met seventeen years ago in England when he had just bought the London paper that he still owns. At that time, she was considered to be one of the most beautiful women in England. Royal parties, her picture in the papers and magazines a lot, that kind of thing. Gossip linked her name to a couple of foreign playboys. She and Mac-Laren were introduced by mutual friends at that fancy racetrack—Ascot—and the courtship was big society news at the time, so I'm told."

Saul turned to me and moved his hand toward his mouth, indicating he'd changed his mind and wanted a cup of coffee after all. When I came back with it from the kitchen, he was still reporting.

". . . and they had an apartment in London plus a castlelike place up in Scotland and another house in Jamaica. There were two children, both sons, who are now thirteen and ten. Apparently the marriage started to go off the track when MacLaren began spending more time in the States—that's when he was beginning to scoop up papers here. Audrey came along on a few occasions, but he usually traveled alone."

Saul paused for coffee, then continued. "Anyway, when he took over that L.A. paper, he began to run with a show-business crowd, and used to go down to Palm Springs for the weekends. That was where he met the woman he's now married to—a flashy so-so former actress named Penny Wells. The talk was that they spent a lot of time together in L.A. and Palm Springs, and she'd occasionally fly to Denver or Toronto with him in his private jet. Eventually, Audrey got wind of what was going on, of course. The story I get is that she put up with it for a couple of years or so, but finally popped her cork and demanded a divorce.

"The case received gallons of ink in the English press, not so much in the U.S. She ended up with a fat settlement, something over a half-million dollars a year. She's very bitter about the whole business, though, and will tell anybody who'd listen what a bastard she thinks MacLaren is.

"As much as she apparently hates the guy, though," Saul added, "he got her to move over here by sweetening the pot for her by another hundred grand or so."

"So his sons would be nearer?"

"Exactly. She lives in Greenwich, has for the last eighteen months. MacLaren even helped her find the place, or rather some of his people did. In return for giving Audrey the extra hundred big ones for incidental expenses or whatever, he stipulated that she and the boys had to live within fifty miles of Manhattan. The story is they haven't spoken a word to each other since the divorce—she absolutely refuses to see him, although he does spend time regularly with the kids.

"He and his new wife live here, in a glitzy triplex over on the East Side. And despite the fact that he doesn't own a New York newspaper—at least not yet—this has been his U.S. headquarters for the last several years.

"As far as what she does with her time," Saul went on, "she's been a regular bee with a slew of charities up in Connecticut. Built quite a name for herself as a fund-raiser, which also has made her pretty popular with her neighbors. She patronizes the right dress designers and hairdressers. She doesn't date all that much, but she always has an escort for social functions both up there and in the city. She comes in occasionally for the opera or a play. I'm sorry, but that's about it," he said, turning his palms up. "I know this isn't much help, and I'm not proud of it. Consider this one on the house—no charge."

"Nonsense." Wolfe waved Saul's comment away. "I didn't expect to learn this much about the woman. Satisfactory."

Wolfe's not one to toss words around recklessly, and for him to use "satisfactory" is roughly the same as most people jumping in the air like the idiots on those television commercials for a certain brand of automobile. Saul, who's known Wolfe almost as long as I have, is aware of this, but that didn't improve his expression. He shook his head and got up to leave, thanking me for the coffee.

"Why the long face?" I asked as I walked him to the front hall. "You got a hell of a lot of information in just twenty-four hours."

"Archie, I've done better, way better," he said, flipping the gray cap onto his head in a smooth movement. "If he tries to pay me, stop him."

I smiled and said good-bye, closing the door, but made a mental note. Saul would get a check if I had to hide it in his apartment during a poker game. And if he refused to cash it, I'd tell him Wolfe would consider such an action a dishonor to him—Wolfe, that is. Saul Panzer is proud, cagey, smart, and tough, but so am I.

"Well, what do you think about our prospective client?" I said to Wolfe when I got resettled at my desk.

The answer I got was a glare. "I said I would see the woman, and I will. That does not, however, make her a prospective client, to use your term. My primary interest in Mrs. MacLaren is as a source of information about her former husband."

"Yes, sir," I said, smiling inside but putting on what I preferred to think of as a blank expression. Once again Wolfe was confronted with the prospect of a woman in the house, and what made it worse, she might be a source of income.

This is a good spot to say something about Nero Wolfe and women. It's not that he dislikes them—quite the opposite. I've watched on more occasions than I can count when attractive specimens were in the office, and around them, he's different. More guarded, to be sure, but also more observant. For instance, unless I've totally lost what Wolfe once called my "intuitive powers of observation," I'm convinced he pays particular attention to the legs of certain females who park themselves in the red leather chair. And the legs he spends the most time watching also happen to be the best-looking ones. Don't tell me that's a coincidence.

Once, when he was grumbling about having to see a female as part of a burglary investigation, I got fed up and complained about his aversion to members of the fairer sex. I remembered his answer and wrote it down later: "The monumental misadventures of my life, and I'm chagrined to say there have been a number, all have centered on women. I'm reconciled to having them on the planet, and sometimes in this very room when necessity dictates. However, I remain intent in minimizing my contact with them. I confess my prejudice."

Okay, so it isn't exactly the Gettysburg Address, but you get the idea loud and clear that Nero Wolfe is not about to convert the brownstone into a coed dormitory. I was thinking about his words on the subject that Monday afternoon at three sharp when the doorbell rang.

I can't say whether the British newspapers would still call her one of the most beautiful women in England, but as I sized her up through the one-way glass, I was willing to volunteer as a judge, just to see who could possibly finish ahead of her. We're talking world-class looks here. So she's forty-one according to Saul's research, but unless she'd sent a stand-in, I was prepared to admit that the fountain of youth had been found.

"You would be Audrey MacLaren," I said, swinging the door open and standing aside to let her enter.

"And you would be the fabled Archie Goodwin," she replied with a smile that lit the hall as she stepped in.

Someday I'll learn. But what the hell, in that moment she had me. I was ready to cancel any future plans with anyone—Lily Rowan included. For the record, the woman I had just given my heart to was wearing an emerald-green rough silk number that advertised her curves without overselling them. The skin: spectacular. The hair: about the color of an Irish setter, and if she and her hairdresser shared a secret, I didn't want to know. The eyes were blue as the heavens, and they held mine as I gestured toward the office. And yes, the legs were likely to get the attention of her host.

"This is Nero Wolfe," I babbled unnecessarily, steering her to the red leather chair. I then turned to him and introduced Audrey.

"Madam," he said, putting his book aside and dipping his head a quarter-inch.

"Mr. Wolfe," she responded in a voice angels would have coveted, "I know you don't shake hands, which is a good policy. One never knows how much they might become contaminated."

Wolfe's eyes opened wide. She had brought him up short, and I swallowed a "Bravo!" as I eased into the chair at my desk. But he recovered quickly.

"The handshake has been used so indiscriminately by so many for so long that it has become hopelessly trivialized, a meaningless gesture," he instructed her. "I prefer to use words as a means of expressing thoughts and feelings."

"I completely agree," she said, turning on the smile and crossing her legs in a motion that was not lost on either of us. "Etiquette so often absurdly dictates that we cling to many outmoded and obsolete traditions."

"Etiquette does not dictate to me," he growled. "Madam, we both know that the reason for your visit was not to discuss tribal rites."

"No," she said, smiling again. She knew how to do it right, even if it didn't charm Wolfe. "I have a tendency to get sidetracked, I'm afraid, and I apologize. I was heartened when I saw the article in yesterday's *Gazette* about your insistence that Harriet Haverhill's death was murder. As I said on the phone to Mr. Goodwin, I am prepared to hire you to find her killer."

"You also told Mr. Goodwin that you know who that person is."

"I do," she answered evenly, looking at him with her beautiful eyes for a reaction. When she got none, she went on. "There's absolutely no question—Ian is the one."

"Indeed? What proof have you?"

"Oh, I don't have the proof—that's why I've come to you. But I am morally certain that he did it. Or he paid someone to do it. Actually, probably the latter. That would be more like him—using money to sweep aside any obstacle."

Wolfe made a face. "Before we expend any more of each other's time, madam, you need to be made aware of one of the tenets of this office: Mr. Goodwin and I will undertake no assignment that involves any aspect of marital strife, whether it be divorce, separation, or simply animus."

It was Audrey's turn to open her eyes wide. "Oh no," she protested, shaking her head vigorously. "Marital strife, as you call it, is not the issue here. My marriage to Ian MacLaren ended years ago—really long before our divorce became official. What is important is that I probably know him better than anyone else in the world, and I know what he's capable of."

"Come now," Wolfe said, shifting in his chair. "It's apparent that you have no evidence whatever that your former husband had a role in Mrs. Haverhill's death."

Audrey's smile had been replaced by a pout, causing me to hastily reassess my passion for her. "Let me tell you about Ian," she said in a voice just above a whisper as she leaned forward in her chair. "He is obsessed with success, which for him means never standing still. It's always more newspapers, more power, more influence. I don't believe he'll ever be satisfied.

"I'll tell you why I know he killed the poor woman." The intensity in her voice showed in her face. "Once—it was probably four years ago, maybe longer—he was talking to me about his goals. I can recall it perfectly; we were in our flat in London. We had finished dinner, and sat in the study with brandies. He started going over each of the newspapers he had swallowed up, reveling in every purchase. That wasn't unusual, because he liked to relive his victories and I tried to be a good listener, even when I'd heard it all Lord knows how many times.

"Suddenly he started talking about having a New York paper—as you surely know, that has been a longtime goal of his. He stared at the bookcases and said, 'Nothing is going to stop me. And no one. I'd kill first.' Those were his words, Mr. Wolfe, exactly. I've never forgotten that—it was frightening." She looked triumphantly at Wolfe.

"Bravado," he snorted. "He was trying to impress you."

"I don't think so," she said, raising her chin. "By that time in our lives, he wasn't interested in impressing me. That night, I can assure you that I saw the face—and mind—of a murderer. It was terrifying. Not that I ever imagined anything like this would ever happen, mind you."

Wolfe was still scowling. "You and your former husband had an acrimonious parting," he said. "My understanding is that you haven't spoken to each other in years."

"You've been investigating me," she chided softly, with a hint of amusement.

"I make it a point to learn what I can about prospective clients," he replied, reaching for the buzzer under his desk. "Would you like a drink? I'm having beer."

She shook her head and put a hand to the Irish-setter-colored hair. "You obviously don't take me seriously," she said, her face tightening.

Wolfe drew in air and made a production of exhaling. "On the contrary, madam, I take you most seriously," he said. "But consider my perspective: a would-be client comes, seeking the solution of a murder. Her former husband, for whom she holds undeniably rancorous feelings, is a possible suspect. She was not at the scene, and was not even acquainted with the dead individual, so she feels no attachment or loyalty to that unfortunate person. Further, the police blindly insist upon labelling the murder a suicide. What am I to assume her motive is in hiring me?"

"What difference does my motive make?"

"Madam, it makes a great deal of difference whether you seek truth or vengeance. If uncovering the truth is your goal, you presumably will be satisfied with my work as long as I identify the murderer, whoever he is. But if you seek vengeance, you will be contented only if the scent leads me to your former husband."

"In this case, truth and vengeance both point to the same man," she insisted.

"I don't accept that," Wolfe said, shaking his head. "I am not yet prepared to name a murderer, but I have no reason to suspect Ian MacLaren above anyone else."

"Nonsense!" Her eyes flashed with irritation. "The only reason the police aren't calling it murder is because of Ian's power. You can't imagine how deep his tentacles extend—and how many strings he can pull to get his way. He's got them buffaloed—they're afraid of him. Press barons can do almost anything they want. Well, I don't believe he can buffalo you, Mr. Wolfe."

"Don't patronize me," he cautioned. "I summarily reject your outrageous notion. The New York Police Department, whatever its shortcomings, will not be cowed by anyone. And even if they were susceptible to intimidation, it would hardly be at the hands of a press baron, to use your term, who doesn't even own a New York newspaper. He has no power base here."

Audrey swallowed hard but held Wolfe's gaze. "All right," she nodded, "I'm still willing to take a chance to hire you."

He considered her. "Take a chance? You realize, of course, that whether or not I have a client, I will pursue this investigation. Therefore, you would get the same results by saving your money and simply being a spectator."

"I don't want to be a spectator," she said, raising her English voice a notch. "I want to hire you. I know enough about you to realize your fees are high. I am prepared to pay you fifty thousand dollars now, and another fifty thousand when the murderer is named, if that is acceptable. Here's a certified check in your name for the first payment," she said, reaching into her purse, pulling it out, and placing it on the corner of the desk.

"Very well," Wolfe said. "I accept the commission with this proviso: that I receive the second check regardless of whom I name. However, that second payment need not be tendered until the individual is found guilty."

"That sounds most fair," Audrey said, rearranging that breathtaking face into a smile. "Now I have a favor to ask: would it be possible to keep our arrangement confidential? My former husband is a vindictive man. If he were to find out that I was your client, he might very well take it out on the children in some way."

Or take it out on you by cutting down on his alimony payments, I thought as I watched her. How fleeting love is.

"I see no reason to reveal our compact. If a compelling need to do so surfaces, however, I will inform you first of the circumstances."

Audrey realized her audience was over, and she turned to me, smiling and rising. I escorted her to the hall, once again marveling at that face as I saw it in profile. But somehow, the magic had gone, even when she looked earnestly into my eyes and said, "Mr. Archie Goodwin, thank you so much. I do hope we see each other again soon."

As I watched her gracefully glide down our front steps in her Charles Jourdan pumps, I suppose I hoped I'd see her again soon, too. But I could wait.

When I got back to the office, Wolfe was holding the check in both hands. "Is it phony?" I asked.

"Ask our friends at Metropolitan Trust," he muttered, thrusting it in my direction. "And she calls *him* vindictive. Bah."

"Hey, where is it written that you have to like your client?" I asked. His answer was a shrug, which was more than I expected.

SIXTEEN

A few minutes after Audrey MacLaren's exit, Wolfe left the office himself for his vertical journey to the orchids. I studied the check she'd written and pronounced it genuine before putting it in the safe, where it would stay until I walked it to the bank in the morning.

Now that we at last had a client, I needed to get moving before Wolfe lost interest, which for him is an occupational hazard. I dialed a number from memory and Lon answered on the second ring.

"Lord, what now?" he sighed, using his long-suffering tone.

"A grade-B favor, to be charged to our account," I shot back. "Your security people log everyone in and out of the building, don't they? Even employees?"

"Right."

"We—make that Mr. Wolfe—would like to know when on Friday night the following people left the building: Bishop, Dean, MacLaren, and the four Haverhill musketeers."

"So those are your suspects?"

"Ask the man who pays my wages," I said blandly. "You know me—the faithful dog who never questions his master, but just goes out day after day to bring in the newspaper from the bushes or the puddle or wherever the kid threw it."

"Spare me," Lon groaned. "I'll get what you want, if only to shut you up. And please, don't remind me again of all the scoops you've given us." He promised he'd call back before dinner, and I thanked him profusely, while promising not to bring up scoops again.

My next call was to Elliot Dean at his law office. The phone was answered by a woman who sounded like she had marbles in her mouth. She didn't seem overly anxious to connect me with Dean, even after I pointed out that he was expecting the call. I got put on hold, and after ninety-five seconds by my digital watch, marbles-mouth was back. "Mr. Dean will speak to you now," she gabbled.

"Yes?" His mood, I could tell, was not festive.

"Archie Goodwin, from Nero Wolfe's office," I said. "I'm calling to set up that appointment for tomorrow. I believe Mr. Bishop talked to you about it."

I could hear a deep breath, then a cough. "Yes, he did," Dean said hoarsely. Another deep breath. "As you know, tomorrow is the memorial service for Harriet."

"At ten-thirty, isn't it?"

"That's right." A short silence. Dean was obviously hoping I'd let him off the hook for the day, but I didn't say anything. The silence continued for fifteen seconds before he broke it.

"Very well, I could come in the afternoon, I suppose, but I just don't see the need for any of this."

"What about two-thirty?"

More pausing and deep breathing before he finally agreed to come, but only for a short time and only because Bishop had asked him to. "I think all this murder talk is damn silly—worse than silly; it's sensationalizing a very tragic time for a lot of us." There was a catch in his voice, and for a moment I thought he was going to break down, but he stopped himself. I said nothing for fear he'd change his mind and cancel the date. Besides, he seemed determined to have the last word, so I just said we would see him tomorrow.

Seconds after I hung up, the phone rang. "Okay, Archie, here's what you asked for," Lon said. "MacLaren was the first one out of the building Friday, at six-twenty-seven. The others all were still around when Harriet's body was found, so they of course stayed much longer, what with the police and everything. Scott signed out at nine-twenty, Dean at nine-fifty-one, Carl at ten-fourteen, and David and Donna and Carolyn all at ten-fifty-four. And if you have any other chores, please tell me now; I'd like to get out of here at a decent hour for a change."

I said he was perilously close to being owed yet another of Fritz's dinners and told him he should go home, put his feet up, and unwind with a double Scotch. He had a short answer, one word actually, but it's best omitted from these pages.

When Wolfe came down from the plant rooms at six, I was at my desk typing some dictation he'd given me earlier in the day. Because the sound of my typewriter irritates him when he's reading, drinking beer, pouting, or doing anything else in the office, I try to get my work out of the way during his sessions with the orchids. I stopped in mid-letter and swiveled to face him as he rang for beer.

"Mr. Dean was a little grumpy when I talked to him, but he'll be here tomorrow at two-thirty," I reported. "Also, you wanted to know when people left the *Gazette* office on Friday night. Here are the times," I went on, reciting from memory, although I also had them written down in my notebook.

When I finished, I looked up. Wolfe had taken his first sip of beer and was opening his book.

"I hope I'm not keeping you from your reading," I said.

"You're not," he replied, shifting his fundament in his custom-made chair.

"Thank heaven for that," I muttered, turning back to the typewriter and attacking the keys.

I would like to report that major progress was made over the next twenty and one-half hours, but that would be a gross exaggeration. To start with, Wolfe had to suffer through my typing before dinner, and while we consumed Fritz's curried beef roll followed by peach pie à la mode, he got even by lecturing on why Tocqueville's *Democracy in America* was the greatest book ever written by a foreigner about this country. I listened politely, but didn't add anything—I was still hot about his casual attitude in the office.

After dinner I called Lily and caught her on a rare free night, the result being that we went dancing at the Churchill. One of the many satisfying aspects of our relationship is that nobody gets miffed when the other calls with a spontaneous invite. We know each other well enough that neither of us gives a damn what the rule-books say. As with Wolfe, etiquette does not dictate to us.

Anyway, we had our usual fine time, and it was made even nicer because I knew that if I'd stayed home, I would probably have got into a dandy set-to with Wolfe that would have ended with me quitting or getting fired.

Tuesday morning after breakfast, I went up to the plant rooms, where Theodore had the arrangement of rare Cattleyas he and Wolfe had put together to send to Harriet's memorial service. A delivery truck was coming at nine-thirty to take them to the church. I thought briefly about going to the service myself, but quickly vetoed it. I couldn't figure out what there would be to gain. They'd all act solemn and dignified, and no horns would sprout on the murderer, assuming he or she was present. And besides, I'd be viewed by the mourners as a circling vulture, not an enticing prospect. Nuts to the whole idea.

I did, however, deposit Audrey's check, so I guess it's fair to say something got accomplished. After the walk to the bank, I continued east and north, swinging by the out-of-town newspaper stand to get fresh copies of MacLaren's products. Call me a glutton for punishment.

This time they had all three of his dailies from Monday, and I paged them on the stroll home. Each had a six-paragraph article a few pages into the paper on Harriet's death. It was second-day stuff, identically worded, and it mentioned Nero Wolfe's astounding claim that she was murdered. At the end of each story was a box referring to an editorial titled "Murder Mongering."

I stopped at Thirty-sixth Street and Seventh Avenue long enough to read one of the editorials. It was about

Wolfe, of course, and it started by stating that "It is despicable that the tragic death of a noble woman, New York *Gazette* chairman Harriet Haverhill, is being exploited by a publicity-hungry private investigator." It went on to call Wolfe "an unprincipled charlatan" and concluded thus: "Although we do not presume to tell the law-enforcement officials of the great city of New York how to do their jobs, it seems to us that the recent actions of Nero Wolfe may well be grounds for the revocation of his license to practice. We know that his behavior would not be tolerated in this community."

It was ten-forty when I got back to the office. Although all three editorials were identically worded, I opened each paper to that page and placed them on Wolfe's desk blotter on top of the day's mail. I was still sore at him, so when he walked in at eleven I kept my eyes on the books I was balancing.

He settled in behind the desk, but I didn't give him the satisfaction of looking up. I could hear the rustle of newspaper. "A childish redundancy," he grunted.

"What is?" I couldn't keep my head down any longer.

"'Unprincipled charlatan,'" he sneered, tossing the papers aside and attacking the mail. He made a couple of stabs at starting a conversation, but I wasn't having any, and it was more of the same at lunch.

We were back in the office with coffee when the doorbell rang at two-thirty-five. The Elliot Dean I saw through the one-way panel looked older than he had a few days earlier. Maybe because his eyes were red-rimmed. I matched his somber face with my own as I opened the door and gestured him in. He muttered something, wheezed indignantly while I took his raincoat and hung it up on the big old walnut rack, and marched by me into the office, homing in on the red leather chair and nodding to Wolfe as he sat.

"I'm only here because Carl Bishop asked me to come," he announced curtly, smoothing his white hair. "I'll give you fifteen minutes, no more. And I should say before we start that I don't approve of this monstrous murder talk. For that matter, I don't approve of *you*." He took a long, wheezing breath, which turned his face purple.

Wolfe cocked an eye at him. "As Pope wrote, 'Be candid where we can.' I appreciate candor, sir; it allows us to dispense with the trivialities that masquerade as friendship at the outset of a discussion. And given the short time you are allotting Mr. Goodwin and me, an economy of words is doubly essential."

Dean started to reply, but Wolfe held up a hand. "Please, if you'll indulge me, I'll do what I can to honor your desire for brevity. You knew Mrs. Haverhill for many years, and indeed were her confidant, her closest adviser. Are you utterly convinced that she took her own life?"

"Of course," Dean bristled. "What other explanation is there?"

"I've obviously been wondering that myself. In the days before her death, would you have guessed her to be a candidate for self-destruction?"

Dean shifted in his chair and began to wheeze again. "She was under a lot of pressure, with *that man* making his move to take over and all."

"But was it a pressure intense enough to fuel a suicide?"

"Lord, I don't know!" Dean wailed, spreading his long arms, palms up. "I wouldn't have thought so, knowing Harriet, but I guess it must have been." He stared at the floor in front of Wolfe's desk, shaking his head. For a minute I thought he was going to cry.

"Very well." Wolfe nodded. "I understand you spoke to Mrs. Haverhill last Friday morning. I'm interested in the essence of that conversation."

"See here," Dean spluttered, "I was in with Harriet almost every day. That was not unusual."

"I'm not suggesting it was," Wolfe said quietly. "But she may have said something—perhaps it seemed insignificant to you at the time—that might provide insight into what happened just a few hours later. For instance, what about her mood? You of all people would be sensitive to even subtle changes in her behavior."

Dean made a noise somewhere between a wheeze and a groan. "I *said* she was under a lot of pressure. Of course it showed, and it wasn't subtle. Harriet was a strong, strong woman, but that bastard MacLaren had gotten to her. She was tenser than I can ever remember."

"Did she ask you to come to see her?"

"Yes. As you are aware, I have an office in the *Gazette* Building, as well as my firm's offices downtown. Lately I'd been spending the greater amount of my time at the newspaper, to be nearer Harriet, because of . . . this takeover business." His little mustache quivered.

"Did she discuss the takeover with you?"

Dean nodded. "She'd just seen Donna, and from their conversation, it was obvious she was going to sell her shares. 'That's one of them gone,' Harriet told me, and she smacked her fist on her desk as she said it."

"Did she talk to you about the other two, David and Scott?"

The purple was easing out of Dean's cheeks. "She was going to see David later that morning, and she held out almost no hope there. For that matter, neither did I, although I didn't bother telling her what I thought. She was depressed enough as it was."

"You knew her stepson would sell out?"

"Of course," Dean said irritably. "David is a drunken opportunist who doesn't give a damn about anything or anyone but himself. He knew he'd never have the chance to run the paper, thank God for that, so he was delighted with the opportunity to make a financial killing. It was obvious to anybody who knew him."

"That leaves the nephew. What did Mrs. Haverhill say about him?"

"Harriet thought she might be able to hold on to him."

"By offering him the job of publisher?"

"What! Where did you hear that?" Dean croaked. "Absolute nonsense. She may have liked Scott better than David, but make him publisher—never!" He dismissed the idea with a wave of his hand. "He didn't have the brains or toughness, and she knew it."

Wolfe raised his shoulders a quarter-inch and let them drop. "It was just speculation. I thought perhaps that was the kind of enticement necessary to keep his shares in the fold."

Dean leaned forward in the chair. His face was getting mottled again. We were really putting him through the wringer. "Harriet may have wanted desperately to keep the paper away from MacLaren, but she wasn't *that* desperate. I can assure you that she never would have placed Scott in that position. The man's a liar and a cheat and Harriet knew all too well that he'd destroy the paper in no time if she handed it over to him—"

"Even if it were her only hope of keeping control of the paper away from Mr. MacLaren?"

Dean nodded vigorously. "As she told you when we were here last week, she felt confident of holding Scott on her side by offering him one of the three chairs on that board of trustees she was setting up. When I talked to her Friday, she was still taking that tack."

"Did she have a contingency plan if he balked?"

"She didn't think he would balk," Dean said sharply. "As I told you before, she would *not* have offered him the post of chairman or publisher. Out of the question."

"Did you see Mrs. Haverhill again after that meeting?"

Dean looked at the floor, and his "No" wasn't easy to hear.

"Sir, where were you on Friday between six o'clock and when you learned of Mrs. Haverhill's death?"

"In my office on the twelfth floor."

"Alone?"

"The whole time. I was waiting for Harriet's call. In the afternoon, she had sent a note to all of us—the stockholders, that is—saying she wanted to meet after she had seen MacLaren. And when a call did come . . ." His voice trailed off.

"Who called, and at what time?"

"Carl Bishop. I think at about a quarter to eight."

"Did you know that Mrs. Haverhill kept a gun in her desk drawer?"

"Oh God, yes," Dean said, shaking his head. He looked teary again. "I was the one who got it for her."

"Indeed?"

"That was several years back, I can't remember how many. But an editor had been kidnapped, you might recall it, and I was worried that some lunatic might get the same idea here. I convinced Harriet's chauffeur to carry a pistol for a while, too, although he finally quit toting it. As for Harriet, she hated the idea of having a gun around, and until Friday I'd forgotten all about it."

Wolfe poured beer and glowered at the foam. "Why did she keep it?"

"I don't know," Dean said, his prickly tone returning. "Maybe she'd forgotten that it was there."

"Perhaps," Wolfe said. "Had she revised her will recently?"

"I can't see that that's any business of yours," Dean snorted. "But it'll be public soon enough, so you're not getting any secrets. All of her holdings in the *Gazette* are going into that trust she mentioned when we were here last week."

"What about the rest of her estate?"

"God, you need to know everything, don't you? Virtually all of the rest is being left to a couple of charities that she held dear, plus some relatively small bequests to her secretary and her household help—a maid and a cook here in the city and a gardener at her place out on Long Island."

"Did she leave anything to you?"

"Certainly not! Now, if you don't mind, and even if you do, I'll be leaving. I've given you a lot more than your allotted fifteen minutes. I still don't know what you're trying to prove—or why. You don't even have a client."

"But I do, sir," Wolfe corrected blandly.

"Huh," Dean sniffed, rising and drawing himself up to his full height of maybe five-eight, then turning to go so fast that he nearly stumbled. I followed him to the hall, intending to help him with his coat, but he was too fast, snatching it from the hook on the fly and hustling out the door before I could open it. Some people just won't take any help.

"Charming fellow, isn't he?" I said as I returned to the office.

"Huh," Wolfe answered. I started to ask if he was mimicking Dean, but I checked myself. He was working now—sort of—and I didn't want to risk getting him angry. He might just have a relapse, if only to spite me.

SEVENTEEN

Wolfe was in no mood to talk after Dean left. He retreated behind the covers of his book, and for once, I didn't bother him. Theodore had dumped an unusually large batch of germination records on my desk the night before, so I had plenty to do, entering them on the proper cards in my files. I got so involved with this that I didn't notice when Wolfe waddled out, but I did catch the whirring of the elevator, and it surprised me that my watch read four o'clock. As they say, time flies when you're having fun.

A half-hour later, the phone rang. "Mr. Goodwin, it's Audrey MacLaren." There was a little catch in her voice. "Something crazy just happened—Ian called me and demanded to know why I had hired Mr. Wolfe."

"And you of course denied it?"

"I tried to, but he's always been able to see right through me. I make a terrible liar." That was open to question. "And besides, I seem to have been sighted entering and leaving your house."

"Who by?"

"A television reporter, a woman. She recognized me, I don't know how, and she called Ian for a comment."

I swore, but to myself. "Okay, so your little secret is out. Is that really so bad?"

"I suppose not. But as I told you, Ian can be terribly vindictive. I worry about the children."

"Do you *really* think anything would happen to them?"

"Oh, probably not," she said softly. "I just wish . . . he hadn't found out."

"What did he say when he called?"

"What did he scream, you mean? He informed me at the top of his lungs that I'd regret this. He talked about legal action."

"Mrs. MacLaren, that's all it is, talk," I said, trying to sound comforting. It wasn't the kids she was really worried about, it was the whopping monthly payments he might decide to withhold, and we both knew it. "Have the TV people talked to you?"

"No, but I have an unlisted number."

"That's never stopped them before. I think I'd avoid answering the phone for a while if you're shy about publicity on this thing. If I need to call you, and I probably will, I'll let the phone ring once, then hang up. The second time, I'll ring four times before hanging up. The third time, answer—that'll be me."

"I—all right," she said, but the voice was shaky, which surprised me after seeing her in action in the office.

"Look, are you getting cold feet? Do you want to pull out of this?" I didn't want to ask, but I thought I'd better find out right then what kind of client we'd gotten saddled with.

"No!" Her tone became suddenly crisp. "You're absolutely right, I shouldn't worry about Ian. After all, he's the reason I'm doing this. I can't quit now. He has to be stopped."

"Well said," I told her warmly, and gave a breath of relief. After saying I'd keep in touch, I buzzed the plant rooms.

"Yes?" Wolfe is a master at making his irritation show in a single word, especially when he gets disturbed during his playtime.

"Our client called. Seems her ex found out she hired you. He's mad, she's upset. I soothed her, as only I can do, but you can bet he'll be calling anytime now, probably demanding an audience. Instructions?"

The sigh was for my benefit, to show that he was, to use one of his terms, beleaguered. "Very well," he said. "If he calls, I'll see him tonight at nine, or tomorrow morning at eleven."

"One more item to cheer you," I said. "The house is being watched, by reporters. That's how MacLaren knew that Audrey had been here."

The receiver slammed. He can take only so much bad news in a single conversation. I timed it. Twenty minutes later, MacLaren called.

"I want to see Wolfe—as soon as possible," came the burr.

"I'll see if that can be arranged," I responded in a calm, businesslike tone. I wasn't about to be shoved around by the likes of him. "He's busy at the moment, but I'll certainly try to arrange an appointment. May I tell him what it's about?"

"You know damn well!" he gruffed. "Audrey."

"I'm not sure I understand, but I'll try to get through to Mr. Wolfe. Wait a moment, please," I said, pressing the hold button. I watched the seconds blink on my digital watch until a full minute had passed, then I punched him back on. "How about nine tonight?" I asked. When he allowed grumpily as to how that was acceptable, I added, "Remember, Mr. Wolfe and I are insistent on one point: Boy George stays in the car. If he's even standing at the door with you, you don't get in."

That made twice in a row I got hung up on, but at least this time I'd asked for it, and had a little fun in the process.

When Wolfe came down from the plant rooms at six, I gave him the verbatim on the calls from both Audrey and her ex-husband, including the hold-button razzmatazz, which brought a satisfying twitch to the corner of his mouth. But then he started scowling into his beer, which he always does when he knows he has to see someone after dinner.

"Cheer up," I said. "Maybe he'll try to outbid her for your services." The glower that this brought, aimed at me, would have withered limbs, so I shrugged and walked over to the liquor cabinet, where I treated myself to two fingers of bourbon and added a splash of water.

As long as Wolfe was stuck with an after-dinner

visitor, and one he wasn't fond of, he made sure he was well-fortified. He helped himself to four servings of Fritz's braised pork fillets. For the record, I had three myself, and we evenly divvied up the baked apples in wine, leaving only crumbs and not many of those. As we sat in the office with coffee, I tried to restart our dinner-table conversation, which had been about the validity of I.Q. tests, but he was back in his funk again, and I didn't feel like trying to jolly him out of it. I was relieved when the bell squawked at six minutes to nine; now maybe we'd get some action.

Through the glass, I could see that MacLaren stood alone on the stoop; presumably George was sulking in the Lincoln, which was where he belonged.

"Come in," I said politely, but without a smile or, I hoped, any trace of warmth.

He said something that sounded vaguely like thank you and handed me his topcoat, then stomped into the office. "All right," he snapped even before his fanny hit the cushion of the red leather chair, "what's all this crap about Audrey hiring you to investigate Harriet Haverhill's death?"

Wolfe looked up from his book, blinked, then closed it deliberately, studying the binding. "May I offer you a drink, sir? I'm going to have beer."

"No, you may not." He lovingly dipped each word in acid before releasing it. "I didn't come here to socialize, as I'm sure you're aware. I came to find out why the bloody hell my former wife is doing business with you, although I already know the answer."

"Go on," Wolfe said, holding his gaze on the furious Scotsman.

"She's hired you—don't try to deny it. I confronted her today, and she admitted she's been here."

"Then perhaps she told you of the substance of our conversation."

"No, I couldn't get that out of her, but I didn't have to. It's obvious. She loathes me, has since our divorce— and before. There's only one interest she could possibly have in the Haverhill death: she wants it to look like I killed the woman. She's hired you to hang this thing on me somehow, to contrive to make it look like a murder. You don't like me to begin with, and you already think it's a murder, so the two of you make perfect bed partners in this vile thing. She's going to turn you loose on me. By heaven—"

"Come now, Mr. MacLaren." Wolfe raised a palm, leaning back in his reinforced chair. "Surely you can't believe such twaddle. One of the stipulations I invariably make to clients is that no constraints of any kind be placed upon me. I start without preconceptions, at least as much as is humanly possible, and will under no circumstances agree to produce a culprit to order. If you doubt me, I invite you to speak with Inspector Cramer of Homicide or Mr. Cohen of the *Gazette*. I suggest them not as references—my work speaks for itself—but rather as cynical and impartial observers."

"Hah! So you admit Audrey is your client?"

"I admit nothing. An admission is not called for here, nor is it needed. When I do have a client, however, I consider my relations with that individual to .be confidential and, to a large degree, privileged. Now, let me ask you a question, sir: you claim your former wife was on these premises; on what do you base that claim?"

"What do you mean? She admitted it."

Wolfe drank beer and wiped his lips with his handkerchief. "Let me rephrase the question: What made you first think she was here?"

MacLaren's face broke into a grim smile. "As I told you the first time we met, I have my sources—I wouldn't have gotten where I am today without them. I won't be so mysterious now, though. The media are very interested in you. They're apparently staked out nearby, or at least one is. I got a call from a reporter who saw Audrey arrive and leave."

"And the same individual presumably has now seen you," Wolfe said. "I'm curious, sir, as to whether you have your own representative watching this house."

"I do not," MacLaren answered sharply. "You flatter yourself."

"But you're interested enough in my activities to pay this visit. To say nothing of editorials in your newspapers."

"Oh, you saw that, did you? Good. I thought our writer did an excellent job," he smirked. "Between that and the fact that your place is being watched, now you'll know what it feels like to be under the microscope. I've had to live with that damned spotlight for years—let's see how you like it."

Wolfe considered him without enthusiasm. "An intriguing statement, particularly given its source. I would have thought you of all people, a self-styled pillar of the Fourth Estate, could hardly resent persistent journalists. Especially since papers under your governance have raised this persistence to new levels. Your reporters, sir, think nothing of using lies and deceit to gain entry into the sanctuaries of the suffering, to invade the privacy of anyone deemed newsworthy, from the parents of a kidnapped child to the widow of a murdered neighborhood grocer. All in the name of 'enterprise reporting' and 120-point headlines. That 'damned spotlight,' as you call it, gets turned on indiscriminately, without regard for the feelings of those it illumines."

"A pretty little speech, Mr. Wolfe," MacLaren retorted, still looking smug. "You sound like one of those Fascists who would like nothing better than to impose curbs on the media—small and seemingly innocuous restrictions at first, but ones that would gradually, steadily grow until the term 'free press' became a mockery."

Calling Wolfe a Fascist is roughly equivalent to questioning a Frenchman's virility. He tensed, setting his jaw. "And you, sir," he said coldly, "desire the rights granted by the First Amendment without shouldering that amendment's responsibilities. If you had your way, there would be no libel or privacy laws, no protection for the innocent citizen against the malicious probing of your hirelings.

"I applaud aggressive reporting when its means are

noble and well-intentioned—for instance, the exposure of corruption in government, the defense of the rights of the underprivileged and the underrepresented, and vigilance against excesses of myriad kinds by business and industry. But common decency dictates limits to this aggressiveness, and they include a fundamental respect for the individual's rights of privacy."

MacLaren thumped a fist on the arm of the red leather chair. "And you no doubt would presume to set yourself up as the arbiter of these limits."

"No, sir, despite you and others like you, I remain committed to an unfettered press, but one that will make greater efforts at self-policing. The public will be the ultimate arbiter, through their choices."

"Ah, Mr. Wolfe, they have already chosen," Mac-Laren chortled, his eyes flashing. "As I told you on my earlier visit, my papers sell more copies per day—"

"Enough," Wolfe snarled, holding up a hand. He was good and sore. "I've already heard your commercial. You appear to be riding a crest, but public acceptance is elusive. I could cite numerous cases of once-mighty publications that failed, but you know their names as well as I do."

"I'll take my chances with public acceptance," Mac-Laren said through a tight-lipped grin as he rose. "I've read it pretty well so far. As for you"—he waggled a finger at Wolfe—"watch your step. If you think you're going to weave your web around me, think again. I'll make you wish you never got into this sleazy business of yours."

"You dare to call me sleazy!" Wolfe was boiling, but his words bounced off MacLaren's back as he made for the hall. I followed in his wake, but let him put his own coat on—I've got my standards.

"You shouldn't have said that to Mr. Wolfe," I told him at the door. "He's got a little doll in his desk drawer that looks just like you, and he takes this long needle that . . ."

Like Wolfe, I found myself talking to his back as he

opened the door and stormed out before I had a chance to tell him he'd be feeling all kinds of sharp pains when he tried to get to sleep tonight. I closed and bolted the door and watched through the one-way glass to see him climb into the limo, which screeched away from the curb. Among his other failings, George had a heavy foot.

When I got back to the office, Wolfe was sitting with his eyes squeezed shut, but that didn't mean he was relaxing. The giveaway was that his right index finger traced circles on the chair arm, a sign that he was furious. I cleared my throat as I slipped into my desk chair.

"What?" he demanded, opening his eyes and glaring.

"Oh, nothing," I said nonchalantly. "I was just wondering what we do next, now that you've put the press lord in his place and his papers all set out to crucify you."

"Insufferable." He pronounced it like it was a contagious disease, but that's all he said, so I didn't know if he was referring to me or MacLaren. After a minute of silence, he grimaced, started to ring for beer, and then grimaced again, remembering that Fritz had gone out for the evening. I realized the situation was desperate and went to the kitchen, where I got two bottles of Remmers and a chilled pilsner glass from the refrigerator, put them on a tray, and carried them back to the office.

He nodded as I placed them in front of him; then he poured and watched the foam settle. "Confound it." Another grimace. "This has got to be finished. You know it and so do I."

I smiled as if I understood what he was talking about.

"Archie," he said after breathing deeply. "Call Mr. Cohen in the morning. Learn from him precisely what papers were found in Mrs. Haverhill's office and the rest of her suite. If that office hasn't been combed, other than the cursory search the police claim to have made, do it yourself. Also, she had a secretary. Talk to her. Find out what Mrs. Haverhill said to her on the last day of her life."

Okay, I admit those orders weren't exactly inspired, but at least he was putting on an imitation of somebody at work, so I decided not to harass him anymore that night. Besides, he had opened his book, and it seemed to me that after a bout with Ian MacLaren, he was entitled to a little recreation before he turned in.

EIGHTEEN

Wednesday morning, after I had finished breakfast and the *Times*, I sat in the office waiting for Lon to get to work so I could call him, per Wolfe's orders. I was about to pick up the phone when the doorbell rang. Walking to the hall, I saw a familiar but unexpected face through the one-way panel.

"My goodness, we're up and around early today, aren't we?" I said, swinging open the door.

"You won't be so lippy when you hear what I have to tell you," Inspector Cramer retorted as he barreled by me, making straight for the office and the red leather chair.

"Needless to say, I'm honored by your visit," I told him as I slipped into one of the yellow chairs, "but I'm sure you're not here to see me. And since it's now"—I checked my watch—"nine-twenty-three, you know where His Nibs is."

"You'll do," he snarled. "You can decide how you want to break it to Wolfe." He then unloaded, and I had to keep my jaw from bouncing off my knees.

"This is on the square?" I asked.

"Hell, yes. I admit it doesn't bother me to let the air out of Wolfe's tires, but I had nothing to do with digging this up. Like I told you, it just dropped in my lap."

"Yeah. Well, there's only one thing to do, and you might as well get the satisfaction." I went to my phone and lifted the receiver, buzzing the plant rooms.

"Yes?" The bite was in his voice.

"Me. Inspector Cramer is here. He just told me

something that you'd better hear—and from him. We're coming up."

He snorted but didn't veto it. He knows I wouldn't barge in on his orchid time without a good reason.

"Let's go," I told Cramer. "The elevator." Normally, I use the stairs, but since we had a guest, I did the polite thing by giving him transportation and went along for the ride to be sociable.

I've been up there uncounted times, but I still get dazzled whenever I walk in. The sight of ten thousand plants on benches in their shades of yellows, reds, pinks, browns, whites, and some colors that probably don't even have names is enough to get anybody's attention— even Cramer's. He's been up there before, too, and usually has acted like the orchids don't exist. Today, though, even he seemed impressed, particularly by those old show-offs the Cattleyas, as we moved through the tropical, intermediate, and cool rooms.

I pushed open the door to the potting room, where Wolfe, in the usual yellow smock, was on his oversized stool at the bench doing some repotting. Theodore looked daggers at us—he considers this territory a private preserve—but I glared right back and he retreated out the door. He and I get along just fine as long as no words have to be exchanged.

"Well?" Wolfe directed his scowl at me, then at Cramer, and back at me.

"It's your show," I said to Cramer.

He cleared his throat. "Yesterday afternoon, I got a telephone call from a doctor—his name isn't important. He had struggled with his conscience over whether or not to call, he said. But he finally felt he had to, what with the story in the papers about your claim that Harriet Haverhill was murdered." He cleared his throat again. "This man is a specialist, and he had Mrs. Haverhill as a patient. On the recommendation of her regular doctor, she had gone to see him about five weeks ago. He diagnosed her as having an abdominal malignancy. It was terminal, apparently inoperable, and he told her that she had at most two years, probably a lot less."

Wolfe's eyes went to slits. "Is this flummery?"

"No flummery," Cramer declared. "I went to his office immediately after his call and he showed me her records. He said he was violating that sacred doctor-patient trust by divulging this, but he was convinced that under the circumstances it might help. I gave him my word that none of this would come out. I'm telling you, and Goodwin, in confidence. I thought you should know. And this ought to scotch the murder nonsense permanently."

"Thank you," Wolfe said icily. He went back to his repotting.

"I think we've been dismissed," I said to Cramer.

"Okay, I've given it to you," he told Wolfe with a shrug. "Just remember, this story goes no further." He did a crisp about-face for a guy his size. "I'll let myself out," he said to me over his shoulder, and headed down the stairs with me about half a flight behind. He went out the door without a word, and after I slid the bolt, I went back to my desk in the office. I stared at the phone for thirty seconds, then picked up the receiver and buzzed.

"Now what?"

"Do I go ahead with Lon and the office search?"

"I've said nothing to countermand that" was all I got in answer, unless you include another hang-up.

I called Lon, and when I told him what I wanted, he sighed and started to protest, but stopped himself. "Oh, hell, we said we'd cooperate, and we will. I'll have to mention it to Carl, though."

I said I had no objection and that I'd be over by ten-thirty. In fact, it was ten-twenty-one when I walked into the *Gazette* lobby, thanks to light traffic and a cabbie who loved to see pedestrians scatter. Two minutes later, I rapped on Lon's office door and marched in.

"Archie, do you really expect to find anything there?" he asked, pushing away from his desk.

"Probably not," I answered as we went down the hall to Harriet's suite. "But how can it hurt to look? I'd guess eighty-seven people have been through here since the last time you and I saw it."

"Give or take a few. But because nobody except you and Wolfe think it was a murder, who'd want to mess with the papers in her office?"

"The murderer?"

Lon mouthed a word but didn't say it as he unlocked the double doors. The office looked about the same as when I was first there, except that stacks of papers and manila folders were piled neatly on Harriet's desk and the bookcase ledge.

"Her secretary was cleaning the place out," Lon said. "As you can see, there's still a long way to go."

"Oh, by the way," I cut in, "Mr. Wolfe wants me to talk to the secretary, too."

"Can't deliver on that one—not now. Her name's Ann Barwell, but she's out of town. She's worked for Harriet for, Lord, close to twenty years. After a couple of days of going through Harriet's things, she got so broken up that she had to get away and be alone for a while. Carl and David and Donna all agreed it would do her some good. She went down to Hilton Head to her sister's place. Probably won't be back for a couple of weeks, at least."

"Okay. And Bishop didn't object to my going through the things here?"

"Why should he?"

"No reason, I suppose. Any papers been taken out of here, records of any kind?"

"Not that I'm aware of, but then, I wouldn't necessarily know. Most of what Harriet had in the way of records was kept in other places in the building. She didn't really need to keep much confidential stuff around."

"Well, let's start in," I said. "You going to stay?"

Lon looked a little sheepish. "Carl . . . thought it might be a good idea if I hung around and—"

"And made sure that the private investigator didn't walk out with something valuable?"

"Come on, Archie, that's a cheap shot."

"You're right," I said, throwing up a hand. "I apologize. Besides, I like the company. And if you don't mind, you can help me plow through this stuff."

"Just what do you expect to find?"

"Maybe a note, a memo, something to indicate that Harriet was planning to name Scott publisher."

Lon snorted. "Wolfe really *is* reaching."

"Could be, but I like the work, the pay's adequate, and the hours aren't bad, so when he gets a notion, the odds are heavily in favor of my buying it. I'll start with the stacks on the desk."

For the next two hours, Lon and I combed the office, the lavatory, and the little blue bedroom. We went through piles of monthly profit-and-loss statements and other financial records, circulation reports, a few angry letters from readers that she apparently intended to answer, and memos from various department heads on everything from a new design for the corporate stationery to a proposal for a *Gazette*-sponsored annual charity game between the Giants and the Jets. I opened and shook out every book on the shelves, which is saying a lot, emptied every drawer in both rooms, and otherwise conducted a grade-A search—something I like to think I'm very good at. I could find nothing about Scott anywhere, unless you count a few reports he'd written Harriet about instituting some stricter controls in the editorial department. "These people have no interest in or respect for budgets" was how one of his notes to her ended. How the editors would love it if he ever did get named publisher.

"We've been through everything," Lon said, loosening his tie. "Nothing about Scott to speak of—nothing of *any* kind that's very interesting."

"Except the proposal for the Jets–Giants game."

"Yeah, but it'll probably never happen. Makes too much sense." I nodded, and we turned off the lights and left.

I had planned to walk home, but while I'd been playing private eye, a dandy spring squall burst over Manhattan. After fifteen minutes of arm-waving I finally flagged a cab and walked in the door at four minutes to one. I hung my raincoat in the hall and went into the office, where Wolfe was going through a meristem catalog and making notations on his desk pad.

"Waste of a morning," I said, dropping into my chair.

"Zero about Scott in Harriet's office, unless you count a couple of innocuous memos, and to round it out, her secretary, Ann Barwell, was so depressed that she went south to recuperate and won't be back for at least two weeks."

He looked up, frowned at my wet hair, and went back to the catalog. I knew he was trying to stall till lunch. He is opposed to doing anything vigorous, such as thinking, on an empty stomach. The trouble is, he doesn't much like thinking on a full stomach, either. I began rustling papers.

"Is that necessary?" he snapped.

"Sorry, I was just trying to get a little work done."

"You were *not*," he retorted. "You were goading me. What would you have me do?"

"Let me go and talk to the whole batch. An hour with each one, and I'll give nine-to-five—no, make that seven-to-two—that one of them will crack."

Wolfe flipped a hand. "That wouldn't work, and you know it. As Dorothy Sayers has written, heroics that don't come off are the very essence of burlesque. And what you propose would be a burlesque."

"All right—what about the secretary?"

"Where is it that she's gone?"

"An island off the South Carolina coast. It's a high-class resort area."

"How does one get there?"

I went to the bookshelves and pulled down the big atlas, flipping it open. I found the right map and turned to him.

"It looks like a flight to Atlanta, then a change of planes to Savannah. From there, a rental car to the island, maybe an hour's drive."

He shuddered. For him, a ten-minute trip in a car, even with me behind the wheel, is cause for trauma. The thought of someone voluntarily riding in two airplanes and then driving an automobile all on the same day is unthinkable.

"All right," he said after sucking in a bushel of air. "Get Saul. See if he can make the trip down and back tomorrow. I'll want to talk to him before he leaves."

"And what if he can't just pick up and take off tomorrow?"

"Then have him make it the next day." Wolfe heaved a sigh as though he were talking to a third-grader.

I was both happy and sore. Happy because something was getting done, sore because I would have enjoyed a little jaunt to Georgia and South Carolina myself, even for a day. But I knew Wolfe was irked at the way I'd been pushing him, and this was one of his ways of letting me know it.

I started to dial Saul's number and then stopped abruptly. That could wait until after lunch, I said to myself. That decision made, I went back to rustling the papers on my desk.

NINETEEN

As it turned out, Saul was free, and at three-fifteen he settled into the red leather chair with coffee while Wolfe attacked his second post-lunch beer. On the phone, I had told him only that his presence was requested. I figured Wolfe, being a genius, was capable of spelling out the situation.

"A woman named Ann Barwell was Harriet Haverhill's secretary for nearly twenty years," Wolfe began. "She apparently became depressed in the days following her employer's death and requested time off to collect herself. She now is staying at the home of a relative in . . ." He turned to me, his face asking the question.

"Hilton Head Island," I supplied.

"South Carolina," Saul added. "Top-drawer place, from what I hear."

"I hope you can see it for yourself. And as soon as your schedule permits, I'd like you to visit Miss Barwell there. I need one fact: did Harriet Haverhill reveal to her, either verbally or in writing, that she intended to name her nephew publisher of the *Gazette*? Any further details would of course be a bonus for us."

Saul nodded. "I can leave first thing tomorrow."

"Satisfactory. Archie will give you expense money and the woman's address down there. And you'll need directions."

"Not necessary," Saul said. "Just get me a street number. I assume you want me to be back tomorrow night?"

"That's not imperative," Wolfe replied, grimacing,

"although you should report by telephone." I knew the reason for his negative reaction. He didn't want to insist that Saul do all that traveling in a single day—it was bad enough that he would have to ride in four airplanes and a rental car over a two-day stretch. To Wolfe, four plane rides is more than anyone should be required to take in a lifetime. Saul, who knows Wolfe almost as well as I do, said he would play the return trip by ear, but that he'd definitely check in tomorrow.

And in case you're wondering why Wolfe didn't just pick up the phone and call Ann Barwell rather than spending hundreds of dollars to send an operative to see her, you should know this: he has telephones on his desk, in his bedroom, and in the kitchen, so he clearly accepts them as a necessary tool. But he doesn't much like them, and he uses them in his work only when face-to-face contact is impractical or impossible. He would no more ask questions relative to a case on the telephone than I would chase down a suspect without my Marley in its shoulder holster. "Facial expressions, twitches, hand movements—all those things you like to refer to as body language—are integral to the interrogation process," he once told me. "Remove the opportunity to witness those reactions and you become a sailor without compass, stars, or sextant."

With our meeting ended, I opened the safe and peeled off a grand in used fifties and twenties, handing them to Saul and saying I'd get Ann Barwell's address for him. "Have a wonderful trip," I said at the door, "and be careful how you drive when you get there. You know what they say about those Southern cops."

He smirked, gave me a thumbs-up, and walked out, taking the steps two at a time. I closed the door and watched through the one-way panel as he strode down the sidewalk, thinking how I'd be jealous of his little jaunt south if I didn't know that Lily and I would be spending a week in the Virgin Islands in less than a month.

After Wolfe ascended to the plant rooms, I called Lon, who wasn't wild about letting me have Ann

Barwell's address in South Carolina. I assured him that she wouldn't be harassed or abused, and promised that if she reported any ill-treatment I would hand him all my winnings from the next five poker games. That drew a horselaugh, given my overall record at our Thursday-night sessions. He relented, though, and after putting me on hold for a few seconds came back with the information, which I relayed to Saul. "I'm on the first flight to Atlanta tomorrow," he told me. "You should be hearing from me sometime in the afternoon." I wished him well and repeated my warning about Southern police.

The rest of the day wasn't worth mentioning, other than an argument Wolfe and I had at dinner over whether college athletes should be paid. I said they should, that it would end the sham, while Wolfe held out for tougher policing of regulations. I scored myself the winner, because I don't believe it's possible to ever return big-time college sports to a truly amateur level.

On Thursday morning, I was on edge, mainly because nothing was happening. After he came down from the plant rooms at eleven, Wolfe seemed totally unconcerned about anything as mundane as murder and clients, choosing to divide his time among the London *Times* crossword puzzle, *Webster's Unabridged*, and a fresh book, *Revolution in Science*, by J. Bernard Cohen. I'm sure I was getting on his nerves, and I know he was getting on mine, so at eleven-forty I got up noisily from my desk, stretched, and announced that I was going for a walk, which got no reaction from Wolfe.

The morning was tough to improve on. Yesterday's rain had cleansed the air, proving that in the spring, even Manhattan can smell terrific. I walked east all the way to Lexington, then turned north. By the time I'd hoofed it to Forty-second, my tension had pretty well dissolved, although I kept turning the case over. Had Wolfe overplayed it this time? Outwardly, I was more or less agreeing with his murder theory, but in conversations with myself, the idea was hard to swallow.

As far as my gut feelings about the so-called suspects

went, I wasn't too wild about any of them as people, with the possible exception of Bishop. Lon liked and respected him, and I had to score that fairly high on the plus side, even though I had a little trouble warming to him. But maybe that was because of my feeling that he didn't completely trust me. Dean was a pompous, self-important windbag, but beyond that, he seemed relatively harmless. As for the Haverhills, Donna was easy to look at, but a little driven for my taste. David and Scott both needed a trip back to the factory for more parts. Neither one was fully equipped, in brainpower or in manners, but that hardly qualified either of them as a trigger-puller. And there was Carolyn: tough, cooler than iceberg lettuce, and as unaffected as a TV game-show host. But a killer? My built-in hunch-meter gave her long odds.

That left MacLaren. If I were to pick someone I'd like to hang a murder on, he would lap the field. He seemed like a longshot himself, though; he had nothing to gain. The *Gazette* was as good as his—at least if he scooped up nephew Scott's shares. And what about Scott? Had he really been offered the publisher's throne? If so, would we ever know it? Maybe Saul was learning the answer to that from Ann Barwell right now.

After I'd played the whole mess through a couple more times, I woke up and found myself all the way up at Bloomingdale's with nothing to show for the last hour-plus except perspiration and a bag filled with improbable suspects. I thought about grabbing a glass of milk and a sandwich at a little place I like on East Fifty-eighth before I remembered that oyster pie was on Fritz's lunch menu. My watch read twelve-forty-four, which meant that if I wanted those oysters, I'd have to flag a cab. I stepped to the curb and started waving my hands like a trader on the commodities exchange.

The oyster pie was easily worth the fare, even if you throw in the aggravation of having to listen to the cabbie gripe the whole trip about how messengers on bicycles are the greatest menace on the New York streets. He turned around to talk to me so often that I was ready with my own nomination as the number-one menace on the streets.

Back in the office after lunch, Wolfe settled in with his book while I picked at some paperwork but mainly kept looking at my watch. When the call came, I almost knocked my milk glass over reaching for the phone. "Saul," I said, and Wolfe picked up his instrument while I stayed on.

"How was your trip?" he asked.

"Uneventful. The flights were actually on time, the drive was a snap. I just got finished talking to Ann Barwell. She wasn't exactly tickled to see me, but she let me have a few minutes."

"And?"

"And I got what you wanted. She says Harriet did talk about giving Scott the brass ring."

"Indeed? Details, please."

I like to think I'm at the head of the class when it comes to repeating conversations verbatim, but Saul is no slouch himself, and he gave a word-for-word account while I got it down in shorthand. Wolfe interrupted once or twice, but otherwise just listened.

"Well, that's it," Saul said after he unloaded. "I wish there was more."

"Satisfactory," Wolfe told him for the second time in a week. "Stay the night if you wish."

Saul answered that he might, but that he'd be back in New York no later than noon tomorrow.

"Okay," I said, swiveling to face him after we'd hung up. "What's next, world famous and reclusive detective?"

"Chapter four," he replied, gesturing to his book, which he picked up and hid behind. And there he stayed, pausing only to ring for beer and consume two bottles' worth. At four, he got up without a word and walked out, taking the elevator to the plant rooms.

Part of me has always been convinced that Wolfe keeps thinking about cases when he's up playing with the orchids, but when I asked him about it once, he insisted his four hours on the roof each day represents a total divorce from work. After what happened that afternoon, though, I'm more convinced than ever that part of me has it right.

I was in the office reading the *Gazette* when he came back down at six, got behind his desk, and rang for beer. I mentioned something about a page-one article on a possible new round of nuclear-disarmament talks, and he said he'd read it later. I went back to the paper and in a few minutes commented on another story I thought would interest him, but got no answer. I figured he just wanted to be left alone to read his book, but when I looked up, I realized I was wrong. He was leaning back in his chair with his eyes closed and his hands laced over the locality of his belly button. His lips were pushing out and in, out and in, and when he's doing that, he might as well be on Saturn. It could last five minutes or fifty-five, but when he came out of it, things would start to happen. I settled back and waited, timing him just because I always have.

For the record, this one took a fraction over sixteen minutes, which makes it one of his shorter séances. The lips stopped moving abruptly and he opened his eyes wide. "All of them!" he snapped.

"I beg your pardon?"

"All of them. I want all of them here—tonight."

"Negative," I said. "Start again."

He glared. "Confound it, you were the one who craved action."

"True, but this won't get it. You know very well that these people, most of them anyway, resent you and all the publicity you've brought to Harriet's death."

"Do you have a better suggestion?"

"As a matter of fact, yes. I'm all for getting them here, you know that, but I vote for tomorrow night. If we try to bulldoze them into coming on such a short notice, they'll automatically refuse. Matter of pride. We need a little more time. Let me tell you the approach I'd use."

Wolfe started to put on a pout, but to his credit, he listened as I outlined a strategy. After I finished, he closed his eyes again. "All right," he said after several minutes, "but start calling them tonight."

"And you'll want Cramer, of course?"

"I'll call him tomorrow," he said, picking up his book in one hand and his glass of beer in the other. As I turned to begin making plans, I realized that I didn't have the slightest idea who Wolfe was going to finger. And I was damned if I was going to ask him.

Twenty

As it turned out, my approach worked. Wolfe and I agreed that the best way to pull everybody in was through Carl Bishop. He was still at work at six-thirty Thursday night and picked up his own phone.

"Mr. Bishop, this is Archie Goodwin. Nero Wolfe has asked for a meeting here tomorrow night, at which he plans to divulge information about Mrs. Haverhill's death. He hopes that you will come and bring Mr. Dean, David, Carolyn, and Scott Haverhill, and Donna Palmer as well."

Bishop's answer was a snort. "Look, Goodwin, we've gone along with Wolfe so far, but this is stretching things. If what he has to say is so important, why can't he come out with it right now?"

"Hold the line," I said. I cupped the receiver and swiveled. "He wants to know why you can't unload now."

Wolfe compressed his lips. "I'll talk to him," he grunted.

"Mr. Bishop, good evening. What I have to say is of utmost importance, and I want to relate it to all of you together."

"Enough is enough," Bishop rasped. "I see no reason to come or to ask any of the others to. At the risk of sounding pompous, we're all busy people."

"I appreciate that, and I promise not to prolong the evening unnecessarily. I think you will find it time well spent."

"I'm sorry, I'm not coming," Bishop said firmly. "As

for the others, you're of course free to ask them yourself, but—"

"Mr. Bishop, if all of you are not present here tomorrow night at nine, I will release a statement to the New York *Times* promptly on Saturday morning."

"What kind of statement?"

"No, sir, that won't work. The only way you will find out is to read the Sunday editions of the *Times*. Let me assure you that what I have to tell them is newsworthy."

"You're bluffing!"

"Bluffing? Hardly. Bear in mind that I already have spent in excess of thirty thousand dollars on that *Times* advertisement. Is that the action of a bluffer?"

That stopped him. For about fifteen seconds, although it seemed longer, all I could hear was the sound of deep breathing. "All right," Bishop said with gravelly reluctance, "I'll try, but I can't guarantee that I can get them to show up."

"If they're not all here, there will be no meeting and the statement will go to the *Times*."

Bishop signed off by saying he'd call the others, and he agreed to get back to us no later than ten tomorrow morning. "MacLaren next?" I asked, and Wolfe nodded.

He, too, was still at his office. His lackey Carlton answered the phone and made a feeble stab at finding out what I wanted. "Just say Nero Wolfe needs to discuss an urgent matter with him," I said brusquely. I was put on hold, and while I waited, Wolfe got on the line.

"Hello, Wolfe," MacLaren barked. "What is it now?"

"Mr. MacLaren, at nine o'clock tomorrow night, in my office, I will be discussing the murder of Harriet Haverhill. Her stepchildren, her nephew, David's wife, Mr. Bishop, and Mr. Dean will be in attendance. I invite you to join us."

"I told you before that I won't stand still for some cheap attempt to dump this at my feet," he said, his voice rising with every syllable. "And I warn you, Wolfe, I'll sue if you try it."

"I should think you would want to come to protect

your interests and defend your reputation," Wolfe remarked dryly. "I guarantee that the evening will be eventful, and it may well have a marked impact on the future of the *Gazette*."

MacLaren growled. "What time did you say?"

"Nine o'clock."

"I'm supposed to be at a dinner party."

"You would be well advised to regret that invitation."

"I'll see," MacLaren huffed, hanging up.

"That man's got a real problem with manners, doesn't he?" I said.

Wolfe made a face. "He'll be here."

"Three-to-one you're right. What's next?"

"Call Mrs. MacLaren and invite her."

"If I didn't know better, I'd think you were trying to tweak MacLaren's nose by surprising him with his ex-wife when he walks in. But that's hardly your kind of stunt."

"My client has every right to see how I am earning my fee," he answered—somewhat stiffly, I thought. Before I could come up with a fitting response, he got up and headed to the kitchen to monitor Fritz's progress with dinner. Or else he was just trying to get away from me. Anyway, I tried Audrey MacLaren, using our signal, but a bleary female voice said she was out for the evening, so I left a message.

That concluded the working portion of my day. Normally on Thursdays I forgo dinner at home and head for Saul's and the weekly poker game, but it was canceled because he'd taken Wolfe's offer to spend the night in South Carolina, so after dinner I cleaned my guns and sipped a glass of milk while Wolfe read his book and then watched a Public Television program on the history of the Jewish people.

When I slid out of bed at seven-fifteen on Friday, I was glad there hadn't been a poker game. I'd needed my rest for what was sure to be a long day. At breakfast in the kitchen, I briefly laid out the program for Fritz, which got him all pumped up; he saw the end of a case, which also meant a fresh infusion of money.

I was at my desk a little after nine when the phone rang. It was Audrey. "Mr. Wolfe had asked me to call you," I told her. "He's having several people over tonight to talk about Harriet Haverhill's death, and he knew you'd want to be here."

"Will he name a murderer?" she said breathlessly.

"He hasn't shared that information with me, but it's not a bad guess."

"I suppose Ian will be there?"

I told her he would, along with the people from the *Gazette,* but I insisted I didn't know anything beyond that. She said she would come, and I told her to be here at eight-forty.

Next on the list of chores I'd gotten from Wolfe the night before was to call Lon Cohen. "Got a minute?" I asked when he answered.

"Yeah, but not much more. Shoot."

"There's going to be a get-together here tonight, maybe you've heard."

"Carl told me about it when he came in. He's not hot for the idea, but I gather he's trying to round up the others now."

"Satisfactory. Mr. Wolfe thinks it would be good if you came too, but keep that to yourself. You can sit in the front room while the session's going on."

"Wait a minute," Lon said, alarm creeping into his voice. "Are you trying to tell me something? Like maybe that . . ." He didn't finish the sentence.

"I'm not trying to tell you anything, except that my boss issued the invitation. Attendance isn't compulsory."

"Hell, you know damn well I'll be there."

"But without telling anyone," I stressed. "Come at eight-thirty."

He sounded a little dazed but said to count him in.

I dialed Inspector Cramer's number. The flunky who answered told me he was tied up indefinitely, and I insisted that it was important. He covered the receiver and I could hear muffled voices before a familiar one came on.

"Goodwin? What do *you* want?" Good old Sergeant Purley Stebbins.

"I was trying to reach your boss, at the request of my boss. He wants to invite him—and you—to a party."

"What kind of garbage is this?" Purley isn't one to waste words.

"Mr. Wolfe plans to talk about the murder of Harriet Haverhill. Her relatives are going to be there, along with Carl Bishop, Elliot Dean, and the great Scottish press baron himself."

Purley hissed a word that I wouldn't use in polite company and groaned. "One of those." He obviously was referring to Wolfe's round-up-the-suspects-and-name-the-murderer evenings, several of which he has attended over the years. "I'll pass the word to the Inspector," he said, hanging up. No one seemed to want an extended conversation with me these days. I buzzed Wolfe in the plant rooms.

"Yes?"

"Audrey is a yes," I reported. "Lon's coming too, and understands he has to stay in the front room. I called Cramer and got Purley, who grumbled but said he'd tell him about it. We'll probably be getting a call from him soon. I haven't tried Saul, because there's no way he could have gotten back yet from the Carolinas." Wolfe muttered something that sounded like "Very well" and banged his receiver without giving further instructions, so I went to the kitchen to review some of the details of the evening with Fritz.

The day passed slowly and without noteworthy activity, unless you count Cramer's call, which came at eleven just after Wolfe had gotten settled in the office. I answered and stayed on the line.

"All of them are really going to be at your place tonight?" Cramer croaked.

"That is my understanding, sir. We will begin at nine."

"And you claim you're going to name a murderer?"

"It is not a claim—it is an assurance."

"I don't believe you."

"Mr. Cramer, have I ever failed to make good my promise in circumstances similar to this?"

Cramer used the same word Purley had. Limited vocabularies. "I'll see you tonight!" he said loudly, banging his phone down so hard that Wolfe cringed.

TWENTY-ONE

Wolfe passed the rest of the morning, and the afternoon for that matter, reading, filling out order blanks in two new seed catalogs, and signing correspondence. My favorite letter was one he wrote to the editor of a magazine for orchid growers, criticizing him for the increasing number of typographical errors in his publication. "In your most recent issue," Wolfe wrote, "'paphiopedilum,' 'phalaenopsis,' and—heaven forbid—'oncidium' each got misspelled once and 'odontoglossum' was misspelled twice. Far from acceptable from a periodical that purports to be a leader in its field."

At lunch, he held forth on why a free press was so instrumental in the growth and development of the United States, which is as close as we had come that day to discussing business.

Finally at two-thirty, I couldn't hold it in any longer and Wolfe obviously wasn't about to volunteer a thing. "Look," I said, turning to him, "I admit it—I'm stumped. I don't have any idea what you're cooking up. Don't you think you should share your little secret? After all, I might be more helpful tonight if I know where we're headed."

Wolfe leaned back, his eyes narrowed, and one corner of his mouth twitched. Okay, I thought, enjoy yourself all you want, even gloat, but unload. He did, and when he laid it out, everything seemed obvious. But then, it usually does after it's been spelled out.

When Wolfe went up to the plant rooms, I started preparing the office. I got interrupted by two calls, one

each from newspaper and TV reporters following up on
Wolfe's murder theory and wanting to know if there
were any new developments. I said no, wondering how
they'd react when they saw Saturday's late edition of the
Gazette.

I didn't get around to finishing the office setup until
after dinner, when Fritz gave me a hand. While Wolfe
sat reading, oblivious of us, we rearranged the chairs
and brought in some extras from the dining room,
placing them with the assumption that all the invited
guests would show. Fritz wheeled in the big serving cart,
also from the dining room, and we set up a bar with gin,
vodka, rye, bourbon, Scotch, sherry, and a carafe each of
white and red wine. I had my usual argument with him,
claiming that almost nobody asks for red wine except
during a meal, but he held fast and even made sure a
bottle of rosé was on hand too.

At eight-thirty, the doorbell rang. I got to the hall
and let Lon in, and we went to the office, where he
slipped into the red chair. "You'll want to view the
proceedings through the hole in the painting," Wolfe
told him. Lon nodded, and I knew he was bursting to
ask what exactly he would be watching, but he knew
Wolfe well enough to realize he wasn't going to get an
answer—not yet, anyway.

I should discuss the hole in the painting. On the
right as you walk into the office from the hall is a
colorful picture of a waterfall, with lots of greens and
blues. It was made to Wolfe's specifications years ago,
and there's a hole in it that's almost impossible to spot. In
the hall is a wooden panel with hinges. Swing it open,
and you're looking at the back of the picture. But that's
not all you're looking at: the hole, at eye level for
someone about my height, which is five-eleven, gives
you a view of the entire office, and you also can hear
everything that's said. This was where Lon would watch
the action.

At eight-forty-five, the bell chimed, which meant the
first of our cast had arrived. Wolfe and Lon rose and
headed for the kitchen, where they would wait until
everyone got seated. When I asked Lon if he wanted a

drink, he gave me a "No thanks, not while I'm work-ing—try me later."

Through the front door panel, I saw Audrey Mac-Laren, wearing a designer suit the color of her eyes and a nervous look on that stunning face. "Come in," I said as she stepped across the threshold and cut loose with what she probably thought was a fetching smile. She was right. "Am I the first one here?"

"You are indeed," I said, admiring her suit as I followed her into the office, directing her to the red leather chair, which probably was still warm from Lon.

"Where's Mr. Wolfe?" she asked, the nervous look back in place of the smile.

"He likes to make a grand entry. You won't see him until all the players are in place."

"And the players are . . . ?"

I ran down the guest list for her—including Cramer and Stebbins—and asked if she wanted a drink. I got a shake of the head as the bell sounded again.

The newcomers were Inspector Cramer and Purley Stebbins, both of whom nodded grimly as I swung the door open. They marched into the office, and I in-troduced them to Audrey, who turned in her chair, nodded, and then gave them her back. Cramer and Purley, each clad in a dark blue suit about as stylish as what the Russian muckety-mucks wear, moved to the two chairs in the third row, which were spots they had occupied in similar situations.

The next time the doorbell rang, Fritz was there to help out in case there were coats. It was all four of the Haverhills. David and Carolyn had obviously been arguing out on the stoop and both of the men came in griping. "Goodwin, we're only here because Carl told us Wolfe was threatening to go to the *Times* with some kind of stupid story," Scott announced loudly. "That's the only reason, believe me." David seconded the complaint in a whiny echo, and Donna looked somber but said nothing. Carolyn looked pretty good herself in a red outfit that I guessed was a Galanos. If nothing else, the evening would set a record for the greatest number of good-looking women in the brownstone at one time.

Fritz was in agony. He always suspects women visit merely to attempt to seduce Wolfe.

As I was ushering them into the office, the bell rang again and Fritz got it, letting Bishop and Dean in, neither of whom said a word as they entered the hall. I orchestrated the seating, directing David to the chair next to Audrey in the front row and Carolyn next to him. I left the last chair up front vacant for MacLaren. Next, I motioned Scott and Donna to the two middle seats in the second row. They, like David and Carolyn, looked back at Cramer and Stebbins, but nobody said anything. They also shot a curious glance in Audrey's direction, which was understandable, as nobody else in the room had likely ever seen her before. I started to make introductions, but figured I'd leave that for Wolfe.

I showed Dean to the chair in the second row nearest me and gestured Bishop to the one at the other end of the row. Bishop nodded to the various Haverhills, who all nodded back, but Dean pulled his usual slouching act, arms folded. "Where's Wolfe?" he wheezed. "And who's that waiting for?" He gestured toward the empty chair.

I started to reply, when the bell squawked again. Until I heard it, I honestly wasn't sure we were going to see MacLaren. I went to the door, greeting him with a thin smile that nicely mirrored his own. "I don't plan to stay long," he announced, pushing in past me and yanking off his Burberry, which he threw carelessly onto one of the pegs.

When we entered the office, the hubbub began, and nobody paid any attention to me when I walked behind Wolfe's desk and reached under the drawer to push the buzzer. "What's *he* doing here?" Dean demanded shrilly, then had to stop to catch his breath. "Nobody said anything about him. I don't want to be in the same room with that—"

"Elliot," Bishop said, "take it easy." The man's little mustache kept quivering, but at Bishop's urging, he settled back.

"I've heard about these performances," David piped up. He'd already helped himself to a drink. "I understand they're entertaining, but let me tell you, I'm in no mood to be entertained."

"Nor am I in the mood to entertain," Wolfe said as he stood in the doorway. He walked in, edged along the wall because of all the chairs, and seated himself. "I'm having beer—would anyone like refreshments?" He gestured toward the cart.

"I prefer to remain sober," MacLaren said with a glacial smile, and there were nods and murmurs of agreement. David frowned silently into his bourbon. This group was not about to become chums. "No?" Wolfe asked. "Very well. Archie, have you made introductions?"

"Not of our client," I said.

He placed his palms flat on the desk.

"The woman on my right in the front row is Audrey MacLaren," he said, his eyes moving from face to face. "She is my client."

"And for those of you who haven't figured it out, my former wife," MacLaren said defiantly, turning in his chair to face the others. "She's trying to set me up for—"

"Enough!" Wolfe crackled, as Audrey bristled and prepared to attack. "Sir, if everyone is allowed to blurt as they please, this may take all night. I don't think any of you want that." He then proceeded to name each of the others to our client as MacLaren muttered. If looks could kill, we'd be sitting in a roomful of corpses.

"Just a minute," Scott said as he finished. "I'd like to know why these two are here." He stabbed a finger at Cramer and Stebbins. "I recognize one as the policeman who came to see us after Harriet died." New York's Finest looked at him without affection. If I were Scott Haverhill, I would make myself a mental note never to double-park in this borough.

"Come now, Scott," Bishop said. "Do you really wonder why they're here? Isn't it obvious? Our host is planning to unveil a murderer tonight."

"If I may interject," Wolfe said, "Inspector Cramer and Sergeant Stebbins of Homicide are here at my request. I would only echo Mr. Bishop's words—the reason for their presence should be evident." Fritz came in with beer and Wolfe paused to pour, tucking the first bottle cap in his drawer. "I appreciate—"

"You like to use the word 'flummery,'" Cramer cut in, and everyone turned to stare at him. "Well, there'd better not be any flummery here tonight. If this thing backfires, it's going to be plenty embarrassing for you— I'll personally see to that." He waggled his finger warningly at Wolfe.

"Put your finger away, Mr. Cramer. I have no intent of flummoxing you or anybody else. You will find the proceedings straightforward and easy to follow. Now, to continue, I appreciate that you all have pressing schedules, and I'm grateful that you took the time to be here," he said as his eyes traveled over the faces in front of him.

"Well, we're not grateful for the invitation," Scott snapped, and, encouraged, some of the others joined in. We'd have a full-scale riot on our hands in no time. I sat back to enjoy it, keeping my eyes on all of them, but paying particular attention to our client.

"That's understandable. Nonetheless, you all came, and I vow not to prolong the evening unnecessarily, although one among you may not wish for a swift denouement."

"So you're back to thinking it's a murder." Dean's eyes bulged above the little mustache.

"I never stopped calling it a murder," Wolfe replied blandly. "All of you know I have contended from the start that Harriet Haverhill did not die by her own hand. I found no adherents to my position, with the possible exception of Mr. Goodwin, and you may wish to discount his vote, as he is in my employ." I made a face at him, but his eyes stayed on our guests.

"Why was I convinced Mrs. Haverhill was not a suicide?" he asked, turning a palm over. "As I told some of you earlier, including Inspector Cramer, my conviction was based on one conversation I had with her in this room a little more than a week ago. But that meeting, and the impression it left, were enough to convince me that this woman would not under any circumstances destroy herself. And I maintained this even when I learned a fact which I am not free to divulge, but which might well be seen as sufficient motivation for self-destruction." He shot a look at Cramer, who scowled back at him.

"My dilemma was that no one had sufficient motive to kill her." Again his eyes traveled over the faces, stopping at each one. There was some satisfactory fidgeting when he did so.

"Mr. MacLaren, to all appearances, getting Mrs. Haverhill out of the way would do you no good. You either had the shares necessary for control of the *Gazette* or you didn't. Her death could have no effect on those shares, and her own substantial holding was already committed to a trust, as everyone knew.

"Mr. Haverhill," he said, turning to David, "you were determined to sell your shares to Mr. MacLaren for a tidy sum, and your stepmother had no legal means of preventing this foolish action. The same held true for your cousin." He gestured toward Scott. "As for your sister, she too had made the decision to sell to Mr. MacLaren. And your wife," he said, turning toward Carolyn, "may have wielded considerable influence on the paper through you, but could hardly be seen to gain from the death of its chairman. That brings us to Messrs. Bishop and Dean; they were outspoken in their loyalty to Mrs. Haverhill and her causes. One would be hard put to suspect either of them.

"Manifestly," he continued, "it would seem that no one stood to profit in any way from the death of Harriet Haverhill. It would appear that she had lost her valiant battle to retain control of the *Gazette*. Therefore, why would anyone want to murder her?"

"You're making your own case for her suicide," Cramer growled.

"So it would appear," Wolfe admitted. "But I refused to accept the apparent. The key had to lie in the mathematics of the situation."

"What the hell do mathematics have to do with all of this?" David looked like he was going to have a stroke. He splashed liquor on his tie, and Carolyn's smile faded.

"I'll get to that, sir, if you'll allow me. The mathematics are those involving the percentages of *Gazette* stock owned by each of the shareholders. I confess the answer should have been immediately obvious, given the signs. You have my *mea culpa*.

"But to move on: the shares owned by Arlen Publishing and the Demarest family were committed to Mr. MacLaren. Does anyone challenge that?" He raised his brows and looked around. MacLaren, I blush to disclose, simpered triumphantly. Dean looked like he was about to spit fire.

"No? Then we may assume that these holdings, slightly more than twelve percent of the total shares, settle on the MacLaren side of the ledger. Are we agreed in adding to that figure the blocks held by David Haverhill and Donna Palmer?" Again he surveyed the audience.

"What's the purpose of this exercise?" David whined, fidgeting. "Everything you've said so far is obvious."

"Please indulge me, and the purpose will reveal itself," Wolfe replied. "Do you all concur that David's and Donna's shares may be added to the MacLaren total?" More stirring and muttering, but no opposition.

"Done," he said. "Thus, Mr. MacLaren could count on forty-seven-and-a-fraction percent of the *Gazette* stock."

"Wait—what about Scott's holdings?" Carolyn leaned forward and stroked her neck as she asked the question.

"What indeed about his holdings?" Wolfe asked, turning to Scott. "Perhaps he would like to respond."

All eyes shifted toward Scott, who sat up straight in his chair, shot his cuffs, and flushed slightly.

"Come, come, Mr. Haverhill," Wolfe snapped. "Tell them what you told me in the office on Sunday."

Scott looked at the floor and then at his hands, which were gripping each other in his lap. "I—when I saw Harriet Friday, she . . . she offered me the job as publisher."

He muttered it, but everybody could hear, and then they all tried to get their oar in. Elliot Dean's high-pitched whinny rose above the din. "Hah, so that's why you asked me whether Harriet would offer him the job," he carped shrilly at Wolfe. "I'll say the same thing I did then—garbage! She'd never have made *him* publisher."

That started the hullabaloo all over again, and Wolfe closed his eyes patiently until it died down. "If you're through, we'll go on. Mr. Haverhill, do you care to elaborate?"

Scott looked down, shifted again, and looked up defiantly. "I knew none of them would believe me. But she did offer me the job, and when we talked, she took some notes, several sheets of them. I told you that when I was here before."

"Why didn't *we* know about this?" Cramer was on his feet.

"Because you didn't ask me," Scott said weakly, turning in his chair. "You wanted to know if I was going to sell my shares to MacLaren, and I told you I wasn't sure, which was true. I hadn't definitely said yes. I told Harriet I wanted to think about her offer, although I'm virtually positive I would have accepted. I was *about* to accept."

"You were never offered the job!" Elliot Dean roared. "Was he, Carl?"

"I have no knowledge of it," Bishop responded, shaking his head vigorously. "And I'd think I would, considering that I currently hold the position."

"But, Mr. Bishop," Wolfe said, "wasn't it true that you were contemplating retirement?"

Bishop leveled his dark eyes at Wolfe's big face. "I was—I am. I told Harriet several times that I wanted to step down, but she never discussed a specific replacement with me."

"And it wouldn't have been *him*," Dean said, jerking a thumb at Scott. "Where's his proof that she wanted him to have the job? Where are her notes? This is all garbage!"

"They don't appear to exist," Wolfe said. "None were found on her desk, in any of the drawers, or anywhere in her office or the adjoining bedroom. Unless the police found them before Mr. Goodwin and Mr. Cohen made their search." He looked at Cramer and Stebbins.

"Nope, nothing," Cramer said. "Although my men

only looked on and inside her desk, and they were only looking for a suicide note. I want to know where all this is getting us."

Wolfe opened his center drawer and pulled out a single sheet of white bond that I had given him. "Before I read this, does everyone know who Ann Barwell is?"

"Of course," Bishop rasped impatiently. "She was Harriet's executive secretary. Had been for years."

"Yesterday, an operative in my employ named Saul Panzer visited Miss Barwell in South Carolina, where she has been staying. This is a transcript of a portion of their conversation:

"Panzer: Did Mrs. Haverhill give you any notes or instructions concerning Scott Haverhill on Friday?

"Barwell: No, but she did mention him to me.

"Panzer: In what context?

"Barwell: She said to remind her Monday to ask about a memo she wanted sent to stockholders, and later, to department heads.

"Panzer: Did she say what the memo was about?

"Barwell: Yes, she told me it was about naming Mr. Haverhill publisher.

"Panzer: Which Mr. Haverhill?

"Barwell: Why, Mr. Scott Haverhill."

Wolfe set the paper down and surveyed his audience triumphantly. Again the din started. They were all talking, with "I don't believe it!" and "Impossible!" mixed in as they tried to outshout one another.

"Quiet!" Wolfe spat. It wasn't a bellow, but close, and it did the trick. "Does anyone seriously doubt this woman's word? I understand she had been in Mrs. Haverhill's employ for approximately twenty years."

Nobody said anything, although Scott was wearing what I'd define as a smirk. It was hard to believe Harriet would have turned her paper over to him.

"Wait a minute," Cramer objected. "If that's true, it would have given Harriet Haverhill, let's see . . . more than fifty-two percent."

"Yes," Wolfe agreed, "a controlling interest."

MacLaren looked ill.

"But the suicide . . ." It was Donna, and if she'd

been in a comic strip, she would have had a question mark above her head.

Wolfe inhaled several cubic feet of air and let them out slowly. "Again, Mrs. Palmer, there *was* no suicide. Quite the opposite. Mrs. Haverhill was herself bent on ending the life of someone else." That raised the noise level again, but Wolfe silenced it by bringing his palm down hard enough to rattle the Laeliacattleya in the vase on the desk top.

"The bullet that ended her life"—he paused for effect—"was intended for her killer."

Donna cut in again. "You mean Harriet was going to . . . ?" Her mouth started to form a word, but nothing came out.

"She was," Wolfe stated. "You might find that difficult to believe, and it might well have been, under normal circumstances. I am constrained from divulging specifics," he said, looking levelly at Cramer, "but she knew her own death was imminent. What punishment could the law mete out to her that would override the sentence under which she already lived? And by taking this action, she would rid the world of what she considered an unspeakable vermin."

"I assume we're going to get some kind of explanation of all this gibberish," David said. His hands were shaking. His wife started fussing over him again.

"You will, sir," Wolfe replied. "Getting back to mathematics, I realized that the swing of Scott Haverhill's ten percent of the *Gazette* shares to her side made Mrs. Haverhill the majority holder again. That fact must have been immensely satisfying to her as she awaited the arrival of her nemesis last Friday.

"Mr. MacLaren was on time for his appointment— we and the police have Miss Barwell's word on that."

"And mine too!" MacLaren said. His eyes blazed at Wolfe. A muscle was twitching in his cheek.

"Just so. We also have your word, sir, that the conversation was far from pleasant. What we don't have is an accurate report of that conversation."

"See here—"

"You'll have time to talk." Wolfe scowled. "Let me

reconstruct the dialogue, at least in a general way. You probably spoke first, from a position of strength, claiming to have a majority of the shares, and if what you have said at other times is true, you offered to buy Mrs. Haverhill's stock as well.

"This would of course have been an additional affront to her, but she still had a trump card and she played it, undoubtedly relishing the moment. She crowed about Scott's almost certain defection from your camp.

"But you, sir, were able to overruff, and you did. You informed her of another defection, but one from *her* camp, which shifted the balance back, giving you barely more than fifty percent."

"This is ridiculous," MacLaren shouted, starting to rise, but Purley Stebbins moved up from the back of the room and told him softly but firmly to sit down. MacLaren sat, grabbing his knees.

"Ridiculous? We'll see," Wolfe answered. "After you dropped your bombshell, the conversation deteriorated to little more than a shouting duel, and you left her office. She was in a fury, understandably. She had been betrayed, and she phoned her Judas, asking—probably demanding—his presence in her office.

"Her animosity was so intense that reason deserted her, and the long-forgotten pistol in her desk drawer came to mind. When the turncoat arrived, she confronted him with her knowledge of his defection and took the gun from the drawer or some other place of concealment. However, he moved quickly—after all, his life was on the line. He managed to wrest the gun from her, and one of two things happened: either he shot her intentionally or the weapon discharged during the struggle, firing the fatal shell. Then he—"

"Stop!" The shriek was so piercing that everyone in the room recoiled. "Stop, stop, stop!" Elliot Dean held his hands over his ears and shook his head as if he were having a spasm. "It was an accident!" he screamed. "It went off while we were . . . She was dying anyway . . ."

His words degenerated to sobs as Purley Stebbins moved over next to him, easing Bishop aside. "You have the right to remain silent," Purley began, and Wolfe waited until he had finished his litany. Dean seemed to be in shock, but then, so did everybody else, including Cramer.

"My God," he said hoarsely, "what made him do it?"

Wolfe shrugged. "Why do people ever trespass? Money? Jealousy? Revenge? Passion? In this case, I can only surmise. But from the start, I centered my attention primarily on Mr. Dean and Mr. Bishop. My suspicions of these two were heightened when I learned that Scott Haverhill's shares were likely slipping from Mr. MacLaren's grasp.

"I must be totally candid, however," he continued, turning both palms up. "Scott Haverhill also remained on my list of contenders, and I did not absolutely eliminate him until Mr. Panzer reported his conversation with Miss Barwell.

"As I said earlier, I should have fixed on Mr. Dean long ago. As you all know, he and Harriet Haverhill visited here last week. Several hours later, Mr. MacLaren came to see me, and during our discussion, he mentioned that he was aware Mrs. Haverhill had preceded him. I wondered at the time how he knew, but dismissed the question from my mind, assuming he had people watching this house.

"Then on Monday, his former wife came here in an attempt to enlist my services. The next day, Mr. Dean was a visitor, albeit a reluctant one. At the end of our meeting, I said that we had a client, although I gave no name. He appeared to show little if any interest in my revelation, which was in itself suspicious. Later on Tuesday, Mr. MacLaren called, demanding an appointment. He said he was angered that his former wife had hired me. When I asked what made him think this was the case, he claimed he had been called by a television reporter who had this house under surveillance, and that this reporter had seen her entering and leaving.

"On the surface, a feasible explanation," Wolfe said. "Audrey MacLaren's face might be well enough known that she'd be recognized by a journalist. But there's a rub: the same individual who telephoned Mr. MacLaren would also have called me asking why Mrs. MacLaren had been here—even television journalists are known to practice some semblance of thoroughness. No such call came, however, and no reporter ever called Audrey MacLaren for a comment, either.

"Clearly the 'reporter' was Elliot Dean, who wasted no time in informing Mr. MacLaren that I had a client." Wolfe turned to MacLaren, who was slouching with his hands jammed into his pants pockets. "It didn't take you long to guess who that client might be, particularly given your acrimonious relationship with your former wife. You called her, confronting her with your supposition, and you hit a bull's-eye. She admitted our contract, and then you called me in a state of agitation."

MacLaren tried to say something, but Wolfe cut him off, shifting his attention to Cramer. "Why were MacLaren and Dean in league? Mr. MacLaren would stop at almost nothing to get the *Gazette* and establish a New York beachhead. Some time ago he realized he couldn't to a moral certainty count on Scott Haverhill's stock. He correctly sensed the man's indecision. Without Scott, the MacLaren holdings would fall below forty-eight percent. He desperately needed insurance, and who could provide it? Either Mr. Bishop, with five percent of the shares, or Mr. Dean, with three percent, would serve to catapult him back into a majority position.

"In seeking an ally, he may have tried Mr. Bishop first—you'll have to ask both of them that. In any event, he found sufficient weakness of character, and perhaps need of money, in Mr. Dean. I think you'll find that sometime in the last several weeks, Mr. MacLaren secretly co-opted him with the promise of a substantial monetary reward if he would commit his shares and also become a quisling by reporting on Mrs. Haverhill's activities. The latter part of their compact is why he was so eager to accompany her to this office."

Dean responded with a groan, holding his head in his hands. "She . . . always took me for granted," he choked. "Never admitted . . . she needed me." His voice degenerated into sniffles.

"You miserable little bastard," David croaked,

springing up and making a move toward Dean before Carolyn yanked his sleeve. He awkwardly sat back down.

"You can't prove any of this." MacLaren's burr was strangled. "And even if you could, I did nothing illegal at any time." His hawkish face was gray.

"Possibly true," Wolfe conceded, "although I'm sure Mr. Cramer and his men will want to talk further to you. And whatever you choose to tell them, it's likely that Mr. Dean will no longer be reticent to describe your relationship."

"I'm late for my engagement," MacLaren said calmly. You have to give the man credit: he is cool. He started to get up, but Cramer barked him back into his chair.

"Sir, whether you stay or go is of no consequence to me now," Wolfe said coldly. "As to whether you are guilty of any criminal act, that is for others to decide. But if I may be indulged, I would like to ask if anyone in this room honestly believes Mrs. Haverhill would be dead today were it not for you and your foul machinations?"

The room fell silent except for Dean's sobs, which had grown softer. He still had his face down and his head covered by his hands, though. Purley Stebbins stuck to his side.

"One thing I don't understand." It was Carl Bishop, clearing his throat. "What happened to those notes that Scott says Harriet made? And, for the record, at no time did MacLaren approach me. If he had, I think everyone in this room knows how I would have reacted."

Wolfe fingered his bottle-opener. "Yes, the notes. Mrs. Haverhill surely did make some notes, perhaps extensive ones, as her nephew has indicated. When Mr. Dean was summoned to her office for their fateful meeting, she probably had those pages on her desk, angrily using them to show him that she would have defeated MacLaren had not he, Dean, treacherously shifted his holding. After the fatal struggle, Mr. Dean, despite being badly shaken, had the presence to gather up the notes and take them away. They may be locked up in one of his offices, but more likely he destroyed them.

"In fact, it was his reaction to my suggestion that Mrs. Haverhill might have wanted her nephew to be publisher which convinced me of his guilt. When he was here on Tuesday, he became almost violent each time I mentioned Scott Haverhill's name in conjunction with the publisher's chair. You saw him do it again this evening. He was desperately trying to persuade me—and tonight the rest of you as well—that Harriet would never have agreed to such an arrangement. His intent in so doing was to throw suspicion on Scott as his aunt's killer, should the police begin to doubt that her death was a suicide. He wanted it to appear that this man, consistently foiled in his efforts to reach the top of the corporate pyramid, committed this act out of anger, frustration, and desperation.

"In theory, a passable strategy," Wolfe went on. "In practice, he tried too hard, overplaying his hand. At that, however, he probably thought he had succeeded. He had successfully purloined Mrs. Haverhill's notes on Scott, and several days had passed. He felt secure in the knowledge that no one else was aware of her plans for her nephew. And he likely came here tonight thinking I would either point the finger at Scott or concede that Mrs. Haverhill's death was indeed a suicide. Only when I read Miss Barwell's words aloud tonight did he realize the game was up."

"Elliot said something just now about how Harriet was dying anyway," Donna said softly. "What was he talking about?"

Wolfe looked sharply at Cramer, then swung back to Donna. "Apparently Mrs. Haverhill shared with Mr. Dean—and perhaps no one else—the grim news that she had only recently received: that she was afflicted with a malignancy beyond cure. I, too, knew of this—it is immaterial how I came by it. I am somewhat surprised Mr. Dean did not trumpet his knowledge of the terminal illness after Mrs. Haverhill's death. It would have strengthened the argument that she was a suicide, although my own knowledge of her illness never for a moment moved me from my conviction that she had been murdered."

"I also want to know," Donna said, turning toward MacLaren, "whether *he* knew Elliot killed my stepmother."

Wolfe raised his shoulders and let them drop. "You'll have to ask him yourself, madam, or get the police to do it. My thought is that he did not, because—"

"You're damn right I didn't," MacLaren blurted, his burr more pronounced than ever. His suit no longer seemed to fit so well. "I'm a newspaperman and a businessman, not a criminal, and I don't consort with criminals."

"I'd advise you to stop right there," Wolfe cautioned. "You're getting to sound far too much like Richard Nixon."

"From here on in, I'll do the talking," Cramer said. "Purley, let's get moving. And, Mr. MacLaren, I want to see you in my office at nine tomorrow morning—here's my card."

Stebbins got Dean to his feet and snapped the cuffs on him. At that moment, it finally hit the others that the small man with the white hair and the tiny mustache was a killer. Donna gasped. David staggered up and poured a neat Irish whiskey, while Carolyn, though trying to look composed, gave herself away with a quivering lower lip. Scott just looked dazed. MacLaren's face was twisted into a snarl as he moved toward Audrey, started to say something, and changed his mind, heading for the door. In fact, they all filed woodenly out, except for Audrey and Bishop, both of whom Wolfe asked to stay behind.

I hustled to the front hall and held the door open. I couldn't think of anything to say, so I just nodded to each of them, including Donna, at whom I would have preferred to at least smile. It seemed like a funeral procession, and in a way I suppose it was. The silence was broken only by the coughs and sniffles and wheezes of Elliot Dean while Purley eased him into the back of the unmarked car idling at the curb.

TWENTY-TWO

When I got back to the office, Bishop was standing in front of Wolfe's desk fiddling with his unlit pipe and scratching his head. ". . . and I've known Elliot for probably thirty years," he was saying. "I can't comprehend it. Say, I've got to call the newsroom—can I use your phone? Dammit, I wish I had somebody along."

"You do," Wolfe said, nodding to me. I went out to the hall where Lon was waiting and waved him in. "Where the hell did you come from?" Bishop demanded when he saw him.

"He's been here all the time," Wolfe said, the folds of his cheeks deepening. "I knew you would need someone to help you write and relay the story to the newspaper. As you've heard me say, I want to ensure that our relationship doesn't get out of balance. I invite both of you to use Mr. Goodwin's and my desk and our telephones. I'm going to the kitchen. Archie, please escort Mrs. MacLaren to the front room and see that she has something to eat and drink. We can talk in here later."

As I led Audrey to the front room, she was all questions, some of which I answered and others I told her to save for Wolfe. I took her drink order—she didn't want to eat—and went back to the office to fill it. Bishop, who didn't know yet that Lon had been an eyewitness, was rapidly describing the events of the evening to him, and Lon sat at my typewriter banging out a story for tomorrow's editions while probably adding some of his own firsthand observations. At least I figure he was, the way he was grinning. I got Audrey a rye and water and went back to the front room, where I plopped down next to her on the yellow sofa.

"Will Ian get out of this without any punishment?" she asked me.

"Probably, although I'd be surprised if he lands the *Gazette* now. I gather you're disappointed at the way things turned out?"

"Not really." She shrugged and adjusted an errant strand of coppery hair. "Actually, the whole episode has been good for me. In the last few days, I think I've come to terms with my attitude about Ian. I'll never like him, but I really do pity him. I suppose maybe I have unconsciously pitied him for years. He's got all the money he can ever spend, Lord knows, but I don't think he'll be satisfied. And I don't think he'll ever have the respect he aches for from his peers in the newspaper world."

"Do you think he deserves their respect with the papers he puts out?"

"No, and that ought to please me, but it doesn't. Maybe that means I'm finally growing up," she said, looking at me with a funny, lopsided smile.

"You were there a long time ago," I said. "You just didn't know it."

TWENTY-THREE

Three days later, Monday to be precise, Wolfe was sitting in the office after lunch drinking beer, while I had milk. To bring you up-to-date, he got paid the other half of his fee by Audrey. It had been nearly midnight when Wolfe finally saw her in his office on Friday: Lon and Bishop had taken that long writing and phoning in the stories for Saturday's *Gazette*.

When she did see Wolfe, Audrey insisted on paying him on the spot, with a personal check. "I know you said the second payment wasn't due until someone was convicted," she told him, "but I'm satisfied you got the right person, even if it wasn't the one I thought I wanted."

Saturday's *Gazette* carried Dean's arrest as its banner, scooping all the competition, and Wolfe and I again had our mugs in the paper. For hours after it hit the streets, we were flooded with calls from newshounds wanting quotes and interviews. I fielded all the calls, and the most anybody got was a statement from Wolfe that he was "glad to be of help in clearing up this matter."

I was admiring the new entry in the bankbook when the doorbell rang. Through the glass, I saw Donna Palmer, looking pert and businesslike.

"This is a surprise," I said brightly as I opened the door. "To what do we owe the pleasure?"

"Is Mr. Wolfe in?" she asked, smiling up at me. "I'd like just a minute or two of his time. I apologize for not calling first."

"He is indeed. Follow me," I told her.

"Mrs. Palmer is here to see you," I said as I ushered her in.

"Madam?" Wolfe said, looking up from his book. "Can we get you anything? Coffee, perhaps?"

"No, nothing, thank you. I told Mr. Goodwin I wouldn't stay long. But I felt that I should come and . . . representing the family, tell you how much we appreciate what you did. I'm afraid we gave you a pretty tough time. We'd like to compensate you for all your time and effort," she said, opening her purse.

Wolfe held up a palm. "I've been fairly compensated already, thank you. There is only one way in which you and your family could reward me."

"I think I know what it is," Donna said, with her pretty smile. "Let me tell you what happened over the weekend: I decided to sell my *Gazette* stock to the trust Harriet set up. I felt that even if Ian MacLaren is totally blameless in her death, he's not the kind of person that I want to see running the paper my father built up and loved so much. I suppose I should have realized that long ago. But thanks to you, I saw what a monster he really is. I owe you a great deal for that alone."

Wolfe dipped his head an eighth of an inch, which is one of the ways he says "Satisfactory." Donna stood, thanked him again, and held out a hand. To my surprise, he took it, although he didn't totally lose control by standing.

Postscript: Elliot Dean was found guilty of the unpremeditated murder of Harriet Haverhill; he admitted during the trial that after he wrested the gun from her, he shot her. Her death had been no accident. Because of his age and an advanced case of emphysema, Dean was given a reduced sentence, which he is now serving. Ian MacLaren was questioned by the police and the district attorney's office, as Inspector Cramer later told us,' but no charges were brought against him. However, he abandoned all attempts to buy the *Gazette* and, according to a short piece in the *Times* business pages last week, he's focused his attention on a D.C.

paper. Maybe he and the federal government deserve each other.

As far as I know, Donna Palmer went back to Boston, after selling her shares to the *Gazette* trust now being administered by Carl Bishop, Scott Haverhill, and that banker. Bishop is still publisher, but Lon tells me he's going to gradually phase out over the next fifteen months or so, turning the job over to Scott in stages. As for David, he also sold his holding to the trust, using some of the proceeds to buy a small daily paper out in Ohio. Maybe that's more his speed, although my guess is he'll still spend most of his time in New York—somehow I can't picture Carolyn living anywhere west of the Hudson.

Even though the case was two months ago, vestiges keep popping up. Just yesterday, I got a call from that TV evangelist in Delaware who'd phoned us because of Wolfe's ad in the *Times*. "I was just checking to see if that paper up your way might still be up for sale," he said in his syrupy drawl. I wanted to ask him where he'd been hiding for the last eight weeks, but instead said that the *Gazette* was not now on the market.

"I'm sure sorry to hear that," he said. "I really think I'd like to have a newspaper."

"You're not alone, brother," I told him. "Why don't you try looking in Washington?"

• *A NERO WOLFE MYSTERY* •

Here are special advance preview chapters from
THE BLOODIED IVY, the new Nero Wolfe novel
by Robert Goldsborough, a Bantam hardcover now
available at your local bookseller.

THE
BLOODIED IVY

Robert Goldsborough

NERO WOLFE RETURNS
IN A BANTAM DOUBLE AUDIO
CASSETTE ABRIDGEMENT
OF THE BLOODIED IVY!

ONE

Hale Markham's death had been big news, of course. It was even the subject of a brief conversation I had with Nero Wolfe. We were sitting in the office, he with beer and I with a Scotch-and-water, going through our copies of the *Gazette* before dinner.

"See where this guy up at Prescott U. fell into a ravine on the campus and got himself killed?" I asked, to be chatty. Wolfe only grunted, but I've never been one to let a low-grade grunt stop me. "Wasn't he the one whose book—they mention it here in the story: *Bleeding Hearts Can Kill*—got you so worked up a couple of years back?"

Wolfe lowered his paper, sighed, and glared at a spot on the wall six inches above my head. "The man was a political Neanderthal," he rumbled. "He would have been supremely happy in the court of Louis XIV. And the book to which you refer is a monumental exercise in fatuity." I sensed the subject was closed, so I grunted myself and turned to the sports pages.

I probably wouldn't have thought any more about that scrap of dialogue except now, three weeks later, a small, balding, fiftyish specimen with brown-rimmed glasses and a sportcoat that could have won a blue ribbon in a quilting contest perched on the red leather chair in the office and stubbornly repeated the statement that had persuaded me to see him in the first place.

"Hale Markham was murdered," he said. "I'm unswerving in this conviction."

Let me back up a bit. The man before me had a name: Walter Willis Cortland. He had called the day before, Monday, introducing himself as a political science professor at Prescott University and a colleague of the late Hale Markham's. He then dropped the bombshell that Markham's death had not been a mishap.

I had asked Cortland over the phone if he'd passed his contention along to the local cops. "It's no contention, Mr. Goodwin, it's a fact," he'd snapped, adding that he had indeed visited the town police in Prescott; but they hadn't seemed much interested in what he had to say. I could see why: Based on what little he told me over the phone, Cortland didn't have a scrap of evidence to prove Markham's tumble was murder, nor did he seem inclined, in his zeal for truth, to nominate a culprit. So why, you ask, had I agreed to see him? Good question. I must admit it was at least partly vanity.

When he phoned at ten-twenty that morning and I answered "Nero Wolfe's office, Archie Goodwin speaking," Cortland had cleared his throat twice, paused, and said, "Ah, yes, Mr. Archie Goodwin. You're really the one with whom I wish to converse.

I've read about your employer, Nero Wolfe, and how he devotes four hours every day, nine to eleven before lunch and four to six in the afternoon, to the sumptuous blooms on the roof of your brownstone. That's why I chose this time to call. I also know how difficult it is to galvanize Mr. Wolfe to undertake a case, but that you have a reputation for being a bit more, er . . . open-minded."

"If you're saying I'm easy, forget it," I said. "Somebody has to screen Mr. Wolfe's calls, or who knows what he'd be having to turn down himself—requests to find missing wives, missing parakeets, and even missing gerbils. And believe me when I tell you that Mr. Wolfe hates gerbils."

Cortland let loose with a tinny chuckle that probably was supposed to show he appreciated my wry brand of humor, then cleared his throat, which probably was supposed to show that now he was all business. "Oh, no, no, I didn't mean that you were . . . uh, to use your term, easy," he stumbled, trying valiantly to recover.

"No, I, uh . . ." He seemed to lose his way and cleared his throat several times before his mental processes kicked in again. "It's just that from what I've heard and read, anybody who has any, uh, hope of enticing Nero Wolfe to undertake a case has to approach you first. And that I am most willing to do. Most willing, Mr., er . . . Goodwin. I braced for another throat-clearing interlude, and sure enough, it arrived on schedule. If this was his average conversational speed, the phone company must love the guy.

"It's just that from what I've heard and read, anybody who has any hope of enticing Nero Wolfe to take a case has to approach you first. And that I am most willing to do. Most willing, Mr. Goodwin."

He treated me once again to the sound of him clearing his throat. "I will lay my jeremiad before you and you alone, and trust you to relay it accurately to Mr. Wolfe. You have a reputation, if I am not mistaken, for reporting verbatim conversations of considerable duration."

Okay, so he was working on me. I knew it—after all, he had the subtlety of a jackhammer, but maybe that was part of his charm, if you could use that term on such a guy. And I was curious as to just what "information" he had about the late Hale Markham's death. Also, the word "jeremiad" always gets my attention.

"All right," I told him, "I'll see you tomorrow. What about ten in the morning?" He said that was fine, and I gave him the address of Wolfe's brownstone on West Thirty-fifth Street near the Hudson.

The next day he rang our doorbell at precisely ten by my watch, which was one point in his favor. I've already described his appearance, which didn't surprise me at all when I saw him through the one-way glass in our front door. His looks matched his phone voice, which at least gave him another point for consistency. I let him in, shook a small but moderately firm paw, and ushered him to the red leather chair at the end of Wolfe's desk. So now you're up to speed, and we can go on.

"Okay, Mr. Cortland," I said, seated at my desk and turning to face him, "you've told me twice, on the phone and just now, that your colleague Hale Markham did not accidentally stumble down that ravine. Tell me more." I flipped open my notebook and poised a pen.

Cortland gave a tug at the knot of his blue wool tie and nudged his glasses up on his nose by pushing on one lens with his thumb, which probably explained why the glass was so smeared. "Yes. Well, perhaps I should discourse in commencement about Hale, although I'm sure you know something of him."

When I'd translated that, I nodded. "A little. I know, for instance, that he was a political conservative, to put it mildly, that he once had a newspaper column that ran all over the country, that he had written some books, and that he was more than a tad controversial."

"Succinct though superficial," Cortland said, sounding like a teacher grading his pupil. He studied the ceiling as if seeking divine guidance in choosing his next words—or else trying to reboard his train of thought. "Mr. Goodwin, Hale Markham was one of the few, uh, truly profound political thinkers in contemporary America. And like so many of the brilliant and visioned, he was constantly besieged and challenged, not just from the left, but from specious conservatives as well." He paused for breath, giving me the opportunity to cut in, but because it looked like he was on a roll I let him keep going, lest he lose his way.

"Hale was uncompromising in his philosophy, Mr. Goodwin, which is one of the myriad reasons I admired him and was a follower—a disciple, if you will. And do not discount this as mere idle palaver—I think I'm singularly qualified to speak—after all, I had known him nearly half again a score of years. Hale took a position and didn't back away. He was fiercely combative and outspoken in his convictions."

"Which were?" I asked after figuring out that half again a score is thirty.

Cortland spread his hands, palms up. "How to begin?" he said, rolling his eyes. "Among other things, that the federal government, with its welfare programs and its intrusions into other areas of the society where it has no business, has steadily—if sometimes unwittingly—been attenuating the moral fiber of the nation, and that government's size and scope must be curtailed. He had a detailed plan to reduce the government in stages over a twenty-year period. Its fundamental caveat was— "

"I get the general idea. He must have felt pretty good about Reagan."

"Oh, up to a point." Cortland fiddled some more with his tie and pushed up his glasses again with a thumb, blinking twice. "But he believed, and I concur, that the President has never truly been committed to substantially reducing the federal government's scope. The man is far more form than substance."

That was enough political philosophy to hold me. "Let's get to Markham's death," I suggested. "You say you're positive his fall down that ravine was no accident. Why?"

Cortland folded his arms and looked at the ceiling again. "Mr. Goodwin, for one thing, Hale walked a great deal." He took a deep breath as if trying to think what to say next, and he was quiet for so long that I had to stare hard at him to get his engine started again. "In recent years, walking had been his major form of exercise. Claimed it expurgated his mind. Almost every night, he followed the identical course, which he informed me was almost exactly four miles. He started from his house, just off campus, and the route took him past the Student Union and the Central Quadrangle, then around the library and through an area called the Old Oaks and then—have you ever been up to Prescott, Mr. Goodwin?"

"Once, years ago, for a football game, against Rutgers. Your boys kicked a field goal to win, right at the end. It was quite an upset."

Cortland allowed himself a sliver-thin smile, which was apparently the only kind he had, then nodded absently. "Yes . . . now that you mention it, I think I remember. Probably the only time we ever beat them. We had a . . . Rhodes Scholar in the backfield. Extraordinary chap. Name escapes me. Lives in Sri Lanka now, can't recall why." He shook his head and blinked. "Where was I? Oh, yes. Anyway, you should recall how hilly the terrain for our campus is, which isn't surprising, given that we're so close to the Hudson. Innumerable times, Prescott has been cited as the most picturesque university in the nation. There are several ravines cutting through it, and the biggest one is named Caldwell's Gash—I believe after one of the first settlers to the area. It's maybe one hundred fifty feet deep, with fairly steep sides, and the Old Oaks, a grove of trees that looks to me like it's getting perilously decrepit, is along one side of the Gash. Hale's walk always took him through the Oaks and fairly close to the edge of the Gash."

"Is there a fence?"

"A fence?" Another long pause as Cortland reexamined the ceiling. "Yes, yes, there had been—there was . . . years ago. But at some point, it must have fallen apart, and never got replaced. The paved, uh, bicycle path through the Oaks is quite a distance from the edge—maybe thirty feet—and there are warning signs posted. On his postprandial strolls, though, Hale sometimes left the path—I know, I've walked with him many a time—and took a course somewhat closer to the edge."

"So who's to say your friend didn't get a little too close just this once and go over the cliff?"

"Not Hale Markham." Cortland shook his small head vigorously, sending his glasses halfway down his nose. "This was a dedicated walker. He even wore hiking boots, for instance. And he was very surefooted—his age, which happened to be seventy-three, shouldn't deceive you. During his younger days, he'd done quite a bit of serious mountain climbing, both out west and, er, in the Alps. No, sir, Hale would not under any circumstances have slipped over the edge of the Gash."

"Was the ground wet or muddy at the time?"

"It had not rained for days."

"What about suicide?"

He bristled. "Unconceivable! Hale reveled in life too much. His health was good, remarkably good for his age. No note of any kind was discovered. I should know—I checked through his papers at home. I'm the executor of his estate."

"What about an autopsy?"

"No autopsy. The doctor who examined the body said Hale died of a broken neck, a tragic consequence of the fall. He estimated the time of death to have been between ten and midnight. And the medical examiner set it down as accidental death. But there really wasn't any kind of an investigation to speak of. Most distressing."

"All right," I said, "let's assume for purposes of

discussion that there is a murderer. Care to nominate any candidates?"

Cortland squirmed in the red leather chair, and twice he started to say somethng, but checked himself. He looked like he was having gas pains.

I gave him what I think of as my earnest smile. "Look, even though you're not a client—not yet, anyway—I'm treating this conversation as confidential. Now, if you have *evidence* of a murder—that's different. Then, as a law-abiding, God-fearing, licensed private investigator, I'd have to report it to the police. But my guess is you don't have evidence. Am I right?"

He nodded, but still looked like something he ate didn't sit well with him. Then he did more squirming. The guy was getting on my nerves.

"Mr. Cortland, I appreciate your not wanting to come right out and call someone a murderer without evidence, but if I can get Mr. Wolfe to see you—and I won't guarantee it—he's going to press pretty hard. You can hold out on me, but he'll demand at the very least some suppositions. Do you have any?"

Cortland made a few more twitchy movements, crossed his legs, and got more fingerprints on his lenses. "There were a number of people at Prescott who . . . weren't exactly fond of Hale," he said, avoiding my eyes. "I'd, uh, chalk a lot of it up to jealousy."

"Let's get specific. But first, was Markham married?"

"He had been, but his wife died, almost ten years ago."

"Any children?"

"None. He was devoted to Lois—that was his wife. She was one of a kind, Mr. Goodwin. I'm a bachelor, always have been, but if I'd ever been fortunate enough to meet a woman like Lois Markham, my life would have taken a Byronic richness that . . . no matter, it's in the past. As far as children are concerned, Hale told me once that it was a major disappointment to both him and Lois that they never had a family."

"What about relatives?"

"He had one brother, who has been deceased for years. His only living relative is a niece, unmarried, in California. He left her about fifty thousand dollars, plus his house. I've been trying to get her to venture here to go through Hale's effects—we can't begin to contemplate selling the place until it is cleaned out, which will be an extensive chore. Hale lived there for more than thirty years."

"Has the niece said anything about when she might come east?"

"I've talked to her on the phone several times, and she keeps procrastinating," Cortland whined. "When I spoke to her last week, she promised that she'd arrive here before Thanksgiving. We'll see."

"Okay, you mentioned jealousy earlier. Who envied Markham?"

He lifted his shoulders and let them drop. "Oh, any number of people. For one, Keith Potter." He eyed me as if expecting a reaction.

"Well, of course," I said. "Why didn't I think of him myself? Okay—I give up. Who's Keith Potter?"

Cortland looked at me as if I'd just jumped out of a spaceship nude. "Keith Potter is none other than the beloved president of Prescott." He touched his forehead with a flourish that was probably supposed to be a dazzling gesture of sarcasm.

"Why was Potter jealous of Markham?"

I got another one of those long-suffering-teacher-working-with-a-dense-student looks. "Partly because Hale was better known than Potter. In fact, Hale was arguably the most celebrated person in the university's history. And we've had *three* Nobel prize laureates through the years."

I nodded to show I was impressed. "So the president of the school resented its superstar teacher. Is that so unusual? I don't know much about the academic world, but one place or another I've gathered the impression that most colleges have a teacher or two who are often better known than the people who run the place."

"Unusual? I suppose not. But Potter—excuse me, *Doctor* Potter—is an empire builder. His not-so-secret goal is to sanctify his name by increasing the endowment to Prescott, thereby allowing him to erect more new buildings on the campus. The edifice complex, you know?" Cortland chuckled, crossed his arms over his stomach, and simpered.

"I don't mean to sound like a broken record, but that's not so unusual either, is it? Or such a bad thing for the university?"

"Maybe not," Cortland conceded, twitching. "If it's accompanied by a genuine respect for scholarship and research, uh, things that all schools aspiring to greatness should stress. But Potter desires, in effect, to upraise a monument to himself. That goal easily eclipses any desire on his part to improve the facilities purely for academic reasons."

I was itching to ask if the ends didn't justify the means, but Wolfe would be coming down from the plant rooms soon, so I pushed on. "How did Potter's obsession with buildings affect his relationship with Markham?"

Cortland sniffed. "Ah, yes, I was about to get to that, wasn't I? Potter had fastened onto Leander Bach and was working to get a bequest out of him—a considerable one. I assume you know who Bach is?" I could tell by his tone that I'd shaken his faith in my grasp of current events.

"The eccentric multimillionaire?"

"That's one way of describing the man. I prefer to think of him as left-leaning to the point of irrationality. And that was the rub: The talk all over campus was that Bach wouldn't give a cent of his millions to the school as long as Hale was on the faculty. He had the gall to call Hale a Neanderthal."

I stifled a smile, then shot a glance at my watch. "Mr. Wolfe will be down soon," I said. "And I—"

"Yes, I've been monitoring the time, as well," Cortland cut in. "And we've still got six minutes. Mr. Goodwin, as you can appreciate, my stipend as a university professor hardly qualifies me as a plutocrat. However, I've had the good fortune to inherit a substantial amount from my family. Because of that, I can comfortably afford Mr. Wolfe's fees, which I'm well aware are thought by some to border on extortionate. And I can assure you that this check," he said, reaching into the breast pocket of his crazy-quilt sportcoat, "has the pecuniary financial condition, feel free to call Cyrus Griffin, president of the First Citizens Bank of Prescott. I'll supply you with the number."

"Not necessary," I said, holding up a hand and studying the check, drawn on Mr. Griffin's bank and made out to Nero Wolfe in the amount of twenty-five thousand dollars.

"That's just a good-faith retainer," Cortland said. "To show Mr. Wolfe—and you—that I'm earnest. I will be happy to match that amount on the completion of Mr. Wolfe's investigation, regardless, of its eventuation."

I tapped the check with a finger. Our bank balance could use this kind of nourishment—we hadn't pulled in a big fee in almost three months, and I was beginning to worry, even if the big panjandrum wasn't. But then, he almost never deigned to look at the checkbook. Such concerns were beneath him. Even if Wolfe refused to take Cortland on as a client, though, it would be instructive to see his reaction to somebody else who tosses around four-syllable, ten-dollar words like he does.

Maybe I could talk somebody into making a syndicated TV show out of their conversations and call it "The Battle of the Dictionary Dinosaurs." All right, so I was getting carried away, but what the hell, it *would* be fun to see these guys go at it. Besides, I'd pay admission to watch Wolfe's reaction to Cortland's mid-sentence ramblings.

"Okay, I'll hang onto this for now," I said to the little professor. "It may help me get Mr. Wolfe to see you, but I can't guarantee anything. I'll have to ask you to wait in the front room while we talk. If things go badly—and I always refuse to predict how he'll react—you may not get to see him, at least not today. But I'll try."

"I'm more than willing to remain here and plead my case with him directly." Cortland squared his narrow shoulders.

"Trust me. This is the best way to handle the situation. Now let's get you settled." I opened the soundproofed door and escorted the professor into the front room, then went down the hall to the kitchen to let Fritz know we had a guest so that he would monitor the situation. It simply wouldn't do to have people wandering through the brownstone.

That done, I returned to the office, where I just had time to get settled at my desk when the rumble of the elevator told me Wolfe was on his way down from the roof.

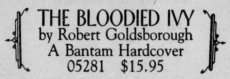